© 2019 Robert C. Holmes. All rights reserved.

ISBN: 978-1-7942-9387-8

S.O.S.

To my wife and inspiration Deborah and my son Charlie who is the bright, shining future.

N.J.J.U.

Contents

Prologue

1. Family

2. The Wild Hunt

3. Poison

4. Brotherly Love

5. Christmas Greetings

6. Message in a Bottle

7. Heard It on the Airwaves

8. Committed

9. Angel

10. Thunder in Spring

11. Reality Check

12. Yul Brynner

13. The Sound of Silence

Epilogue

S.O.S.

Robert C. Holmes

S.O.S.

Prologue

Extract from *Rockopedia International,* the internationally recognised authority regarding rock music:

Hanoi Jane: The band came to prominence in the mid-eighties playing a blues edged heavy rock. Claiming to be influenced by the likes of the *Rolling Stones, Kiss* and *Motorhead,* the band scored two number one albums in the British charts. *Addictions* made the number one spot in 1985 and *Dish of the Day* emulated its predecessor in 1987. They disappeared from the music scene, only for some members to resurface as part of a British "outlaw" motorcycle club, the S.O.S.

Nikki Michelle (Lead vocals, rhythm guitar), Jimi The Weasel (Lead guitar), Vince Sinclair (Bass guitar) John Green (Drums).

S.O.S.

Family

The red needle was nearing eighty on the speedometer and Prez's arms were beginning to ache. The wind resistance against his chest was immense as his black Harley (named *Landwaster* after the raven banner of Viking King Harald Hardrada) thundered towards the sharp bend in the motorway. Normally one would question the sanity of eighteen-inch apehanger handlebars with four-inch risers but Prez wasn't in to the practicalities of it, he wanted to *look* the business. His eyes were watering now as the bend approached, at least there were no vehicles to his left, as he glanced into his iron cross mirrors. There was a feeder lane to his left and it had always been a bone of contention as to who should give way on this stretch, since the motorway only comprised two lanes here and often with vehicles to your right, it was impossible to change lanes to allow traffic to "feed" in from the left. *Too late at these bloody speeds anyway* he thought. The vibration of the sixteen hundred cc engine was nothing compared to the roar of the beast. Another quick glance to the left, no vehicles feeding in, then a sharp bank to the right to negotiate the corner. Then like a cork out of a bottle, bike and rider shot onto the straight and thundered on down the motorway.

Prez was late and he didn't like that. Sometimes it was unavoidable, like today, but he still didn't like it. His crew wouldn't appreciate his tardiness either, although they would be the first to admit that Prez was usually the first at the Unkindness. *If we'd been crows it would have been termed a murder but imagine the heat our meetings being called murders would have brought, just as well we're ravens*! He mused as he approached the Elton turn off he kicked it down to fourth and exited the motorway. Elton was one of those strange dormitory style towns that are quite soulless places. Existing to service the nearby areas of Chester, Widnes, Runcorn and various other places, with no actual identity of its own. Cheap property, though. Which is why the club owned two terraced townhouses which they had knocked into one there. Prices were cheap as there was a major heavy industrial complex close by resulting in any washing being put out to dry getting covered in black specks. *Pollution at its best!* Grinned Prez. Fortunately, hanging washing out wasn't up there in the list of priorities for the club, so it wasn't taken into consideration when it chose the area for the clubhouse. The main considerations were access to roads, affordability and anonymity....to a point.

As Prez passed the Wheelwrights pub (another good reason for the clubhouse venue) he could see the gleaming array of motorcycles parked in the pull-in outside the clubhouse. It was nine PM and he was half an hour late. *Damn 53, an accident every time you used it!* Prez had vowed to find alternative routes to the cursed motorway, but there just weren't any. He pulled up alongside the 'bikes and backed his own machine into line with the others and killed the engine. *Looks like it's a good turnout tonight, mustn't be anything on T.V.* he thought to himself as he trudged up the steps to the front door of the property, giving a cursory wave to the CCTV camera perched above it. Like the ground floor windows, the door was reinforced metal where it had once been glass *Can't be too careful these days.* He sighed grimly. Without having to knock or fish his keys out of his leather jeans, the door swung open, Bear welcoming him in, "What bloody time do you call this?" the huge man grinned. He stood around six foot six, wore a number one buzz cut and was built like a bear. That wasn't why he was given the moniker, though. That was because he'd dressed up in a dancing bear costume when working with the Sealed Knot, an English Civil war re-enactment society, or that's how the story went.......

"I know, bloody M53 as usual, and yeah, I know, set out earlier next time!" Prez playfully punched Bear on his upper arm and strode past the bar and pool table on the ground floor to the stairs where the Unkindness would be held. Bear as Sergeant at Arms dutifully followed him up to the room that was used for official business.

"Gentlemen, the prodigal has returned!" Bear called out as he and Prez walked in, to be greeted by ironic cheers and laughter. The room was adorned with photographs and banners of the club, identical to the patches on the backs of the members. The club initials S.O.S. emblazoned in red on a black top rocker with England likewise represented on the bottom rocker. The central motif being three black ravens on a red background whose legs formed a triskelion that met in a central hub. There was more than an air of medieval great hall about the place, what with the wall hangings akin to medieval tapestries. To add to the effect the wall lights were faux candles and the central lights were hung from a chain in the ceiling which was attached to a faux wood "wheel" from which more faux candles "burned". Beneath them the room was dominated by a large table with five chairs at each side and one at its head, which was reserved for the President, or Prez as he was known. Vince couldn't remember the last time anyone in the club had called him anything but "Prez", to his face, anyway! He slipped off his patch and leather jacket and placed the jacket on the back of the chair whilst putting his patch back on. Taking his place at the head of the table, he slammed his palm down to call for order, "Gentlemen, I call this Unkindness to order, apologies for being late!" grins and guffaws rumbled around the table as club members acknowledged the irony that their always on time Prez was, for once, late.

Prez surveyed the group. On his right was Bear the Sergeant at Arms and the club enforcer. Anyone gets out of line or badmouths the club Bear was the man to sort it out. Hugely loyal and physically menacing. You'd *have to be a complete lunatic to wind that guy up. Or packing a firearm!* Mused Prez. On his left was the Vice President BS, round glasses perched on his nose. *Apart from DJ, BS is the closest thing to a blood brother I've got. We're all brothers in the S.O.S. but you always have your favourites!* BS had been with Prez since the beginning, in fact back in the days before the club when they were performing as *Hanoi Jane*. Another one six foot plus, BS still retained the physique of the swimmer he had been in his youth, the wide shoulders and powerful arms. BS had proved his loyalty time and again, suffering serious physical injury for the club in its early years. A heavy beating had left him with plates in his skull and a party piece of being able to "tune in" to radio stations using his metallic implants and a microphone. Next to BS was Oz, the Treasurer and voice of reason, *until he mounts a motorbike, when he's a whirling dervish of mad intent and "don't give a damn" attitude!* smaller of stature than BS or Bear and carrying the suggestion of a beer gut, he still retained his dark hair as opposed to the grey of Prez the baldness of BS and the greying buzz cut of Bear. Faceman was seated beside Oz. Bearing the craggy features of a fifty something Clint Eastwood, he was another standing over six feet tall, again he had been there since the start of it all. Finally, there was Boalie, a short rotund cannonball of a man. Shorter again than Oz, but boasting the paunch of the dedicated drinker, like BS his pate was hairless. *To call him a drinker would be like calling the sun hot. Rather an understatement! The only reason he rides a trike is because it's the only thing that keeps him upright!*

"Okay Gents, it'll be a brief Unkindness tonight, as I'm tired and you're all probably dying to get back to the bar!"

"Amen to that brother! I've left a gold watch at the bar and it's calling me!" grinned Boalie to a cackle from the assembled bikers.

"You'll be pleased to know that I got the go ahead to arrange another Wild Hunt Run to Aviemore." The group thumped the table in unison. "So all that needs to be done is for our erstwhile treasurer to liaise with the Councils Treasury Committee to ensure that our licence is still intact and that we can still collect donations from the public as we do every year." Prez glanced at Oz,

"Way ahead of the game Prez, it's all set up. All we have to do is roll in and roll out!" Oz grinned like a cat who had got the cream. His organisational skills were invaluable and his job working with the local council enabled him to contact and liaise with other councils in a way that would have proven difficult to an outsider.

"I knew there was something I liked about you!" Prez growled.

"How are things looking on the finance front Mr Treasurer?"

Oz looked sheepish and shifted uncomfortably in his chair. He was never a man for confrontation and delivering bad news to anyone, especially an authority figure was distasteful to him. Even if this authority figure was a lifelong friend, "Well, there's some anomalies Boss....................." the room filled with the uncomfortable sound of silence, punctuated only by the sounds of creaking leather as brothers shifted uncomfortably in their chairs to glance at each other.

"Say it like it is Oz, we're all adults here." Things had certainly become heavy with gravitas and the devil may care attitude that had permeated the Unkindness moments earlier had evaporated like mist at the touch of the morning sun. Oz could feel his mouth was dry and wished he had brought his pint up from the bar below, knowing full well that this was impossible, since alcohol was banned from the Unkindness. He bit his lip before producing a sheaf of papers which had hitherto gone unnoticed by the assembly.

"I've been going through the books of a couple of the Chapters and there are some glaring discrepancies."

"Okay, lay it out mate, which ones, how much?" *This is the part of being King which is tough, deciding what to do when the shit hits the fan.* Thought Prez. Oz took a deep breath and waded in.

"Okay we're looking at London and New York. The numbers just don't add up. Both Chapters are losing money like it's going out of fashion. I won't bore the Unkindness with the figures, but they're substantial. We've not had dues from either for six months and the time I've given them as a period of grace has now come to an end. Both Chapters are telling me they've been losing members and that like us, recruitment has dried up over the last few years. However, both of 'em have got big holes in their accounts that I can't seem to justify. New York 'specially, there's big chunks of cash disappearing and what's on the balance sheets that I can access just doesn't justify the amounts going out. T'be honest guys, I've been on the verge of bringing this shit up for the last few Unkindness's, but I guess I've been hoping that the guys in the

States and the Smoke are suddenly going to turn it around. Or at least come up with a feasible explanation as to what the fuck is going on."

"Hey, Oz, you've done good brother, you gave them an opportunity to sort things out, no one is going to castigate you for that son." *No way that there's going to be a shooting of a messenger on my watch. Oz did the right thing, he's pitched it about right, given them enough opportunity........or rope.* Prez smoothed his moustache, a sure sign that some tough decisions were in the offing.

"Okay, so we've given them the opportunity to right some wrongs, and deal with business. Seems like they can't sort it without Mother Chapter intervention." Prez looked around the table, ensuring he made eye contact with each and every patch holder,

"Looks like we've got some tough decisions to make brothers. I propose that we wait until the Wild Hunt Run to talk to Jimi regarding London."

"Seconded." BS murmured sombrely.

"All those in favour?" Prez looked around the table as each member raised their hands and declared their agreement with the customary "Aye".

"That's unanimous then." Prez sighed as he knew the next call was going to be far more difficult. DJ was President of the New York Chapter. *This is going to be tough. How do you hang a guy cut to dry that you've known since you were a teenager? A bloke who you've lived the life with, full on? A guy who owned a motorbike before anyone else in the bloody club? He's been there since day one. I remember giving him career advice in the Wheelwright's pub when he was deciding to leave a safe job as a retail assistant and strike out as a D.J. A decision which went hugely well for him, which resulted in him touring the World from Norway to Hong Kong and finally ending in New York with his own radio show. Not to mention numerous "voice overs" in advertisements. The Yanks love a plummy English accent! All that time DJ would come back and visit, usually at Christmas, as his Mum still lived in Lower Heswall, a half an hour walk from Sinclair Towers! His visits were part of the calendar, where we'd go drinking at the Jug and Bottle in Heswall and he'd regale me with tales of how he'd gone scuba diving, been taken hostage in China by the corrupt militia and of course the women, always the women. A veritable "Rakes Progress" gone global! We'd done night clubs as teenagers and concerts, ABC at the Deeside Leisure centre for Christ's sake. Played squash at the (then) newly built squash club in Heswall. Breaking in when it went private by putting my then girlfriend Sue in through the changing room open window so that she could open the door from the inside! The time when leaving the Victoria Hotel, that we saw some Frenchmen (the accents were a giveaway) urinating in the car park and we taught them that we don't do that in this country, in no uncertain terms. Or the time that one particularly icy Christmas as we'd wended our way home from said Victoria Hotel, up the steep road towards Pensby which had become an ice sheet, DJ had laid on his stomach in the middle of the rocd pretending to swim up it………………………………..*

"What about New York Prez?" BS had been looking at Prez for what to him at least seemed an eternity, whilst his President had been deep in thought. Wallowing in days of yore. BS's question broke the spell,

"Ideas boys?" Prez asked.

There was again, an uneasy shifting in seats. The assemb y knew the importance of DJ to the club, but more so the importance of DJ as a brother to their president. A bond that was indeed stronger than blood. This was going to have to be handled with great diplomacy.

"I could go over there and bounce the fuckers head against a wall………………."

All heads turned in amazement to Bear. The big man rarely spoke at an Unkindness and when he did they listened. However, his taciturn attitude, whilst appreciated when required, was hardly the tactful response that the Club was looking for at this precise moment in time.

Not a bad idea, I'd go myself if I didn't hate flying! But we don't want bloodshed with DJ, we need to find out what the problem is. Thought Prez.

Oz looked up and broke the silence which was threatening to engulf them all in a sea of negativity,

S.O.S.

"Why don't we wait 'til after the Wild Hunt? Get that out of the way and then DJ will probably be back a couple of weeks later for his usual Yule visitation? What do you think?"

Oz's suggestion was greeted with murmurs of approval, possibly because it broke the silence rather than anything else. Prez looked at BS who nodded agreement then scanned the rest of the assembled throng.

"Sounds good to me Prez, nice one Oz!" Faceman spoke in his usual laconic style. His likeness to Clint Eastwood having transformed his speech patterns in to an attempted imitation of the actor. It was delivered in the kind of patronising way that an adult congratulates a child whom they didn't think was capable of the feat they've just achieved. Faceman always thought he was a cut above the rest of the crew and especially Oz, whom he considered a gopher among the club. *Fortunately, Faceman was in a minority of one with this kind of thinking. Oz is an office holder, Treasurer, which comes not just with responsibility but with power. Indeed, being one of the Unholy Trinity (myself, Oz and BS) meant having the ear of The President, no mean achievement, if I say so myself. Faceman had indulged himself in his spaghetti western fantasy just a little too much and his poorly concealed attitude of derision towards Oz merely illustrated why he was not deemed fit to be an office bearer.* Prez smiled inwardly, although he ensured that just enough of his sardonic smile came to the surface of his outward expression, allowing the assembly to realise that he knew exactly what the score was. And to ensure that Faceman knew exactly what the score was too! Before Prez could reply BS spoke up,

"Yeah, nice one Oz. One step at a time. Let's deal with Jimi The Weasel and London and then we'll let DJ have his say when he jets over from the Big Apple. Jeez that guy's got some lifestyle. You ever been tempted to nip over the pond and checkout the NY scene Prez?"

"And trust some other fucker to do the flying? Not a bloody chance matey!" Prez replied in mock horror. His reply was greeted with laughter from the others, including Faceman, who always realised when it was best to go with the flow. On more than one occasion his brash arrogance had caused problems for the club. And on each occasion, it had been Prez who had extricated everyone, especially Faceman from the mess. With just a look Prez could remind Faceman, without saying a word. It was with just such a look that he now responded to Faceman's crack at Oz. *Parity restored*. Prez inwardly chuckled to himself.

"Let's vote this shit. All in favour?"

A resounding "aye" exploded as one, rather than the usual individual "round the table" vote. It was an expression of relief as much as anything else as the assembled bikers realised they had put the ball back in their presidents' corner and that it would be something he would have to deal with when DJ returned before Christmas. It would still be a club decision as to the final judgement, but it would be down to Prez to illicit the information, using his friendship with DJ as a way in. The Unkindness was merely relieved that a decision had been made to do *something* on the issue.

"Okay boys, I'm aware it's late, courtesy of yours truly, so without any further ado, any other business?" Prez surveyed the gathering.

"Yeah, I've got a request Prez." It was the drawl of Faceman, the tones not quite as assured as usual.

"Err, I'm going to have to ask to drop out of the Wild Hunt this year. I'll pay my fine of course, but I just can't make it boys."

"What's the problem Face?" asked BS

"I've, got to be somewhere…………" again the silence engulfed the room, but this time it was not with an atmosphere of apprehension, rather one of uncertainty, that permeated proceedings.

"Something more important than the bloody annual run to keep us in the good books of the general population, Mr Fenian?" Boalie growled across the table in his strong scouse accent, barely hiding the note of disquiet in his voice. Even his usual jocular delivery of the term "fenian" which he used when addressing Faceman because of his Catholic background, was edged with malice, as one may expect from a confirmed Orangeman.

"No worries, Boalie, we're not going to hang draw and quarter patches 'cause they can't attend runs." Prez held his palms out in a gesture of supplication.

"Why the fuck not?" Bear added to the debate, staring at Faceman the same way a predator would stare at his prey. Faceman felt a cold trickle of sweat run down his back and sensed the blood rushing to his face. Nevertheless, he stayed calm and fronted them down,

"It's to do with work, I've got to go to this golf tournament..............."

"In October?" growled Bear,

"No, in Spain." Faceman again adopted the sarcastic smirk which had on many occasions caused problems. Prez decided to jump in.

"Okay, well it can't be helped. If Face has got other priorities which he can't circumnavigate, so be it. As long as he pays his fine for none attendance, it's not a problem."

"I'll pay double boys." Faceman grinned mirthlessly.

"That won't be required, just the normal fee will do." Prez spoke icily. He didn't like brothers flashing their wealth at others who were not in such a comfortable financial position. He looked around the table,

"Any other business boys?"

"Yeah, I'd like to raise an issue Boss." Oz raised his hands and continued when Prez nodded indicating he had the floor,

"There's a problem in a road near my home. A family's arrived there from Huyton and I'm reliably informed they're peddling drugs. We all know Huyton is rife with drugs, if you want drugs in Liverpool, it's Drugs R Us central. I've got irrefutable evidence, which has been gathered by the immediate neighbours of these scumbags. Car numbers, taxi numbers, deliveries made. Hell, the father's son has even had gangs of teenagers smoking dope on the front drive."

"What have the neighbours done about it mate?" BS queried.

"Well they got up an intimate campaign group and sent letters to the boys in blue in both Wallasey and Birkenhead, citing all the relevant details. They did it anonymously, as obviously, if this family has connections with some of the Huyton scum, then they don't want their kids picked on or a nice Molotov Cocktail through their window in the middle of the night.

"Let me guess," Prez interjected," Fuck all has happened?"

"Right on the money. Big shot daddy of the clan has had gardening work done on the rented property, doesn't drive, as he boasts he's banned and pays cash for everything, including the same taxi that he uses to go God knows where several time a day. Oh, and he frequents the bookies. Not bad for a guy who doesn't have any visible form of income, hey lads?" Oz sighed.

"I think this calls for some serious retribution boys" Bear growled, licking his lips in lupine fashion. Prez nodded,

"I concur my friend. Who do the people turn to when Plod doesn't want to know? This is our home and we're not going to let some scum bags from over the water pollute it. Could be that Plod has resettled them from Huyton to Wirral for turning evidence. Could be that they're protected but are still carrying out their scummy business. Or it could be that Plod just doesn't give a shit."" Prez rubbed his chin and then addressed the Unkindness,

"How about we send them a little message? A message in a bottle?" the assembled patches laughed in unison and banged the table in agreement.

"All those in favour of a warning?" Prez swept the table as the members voted as one in the affirmative.

"That's unanimous then boys. Bear, can you get transportation which we can use?"

"Done Prez, just name the night. I can organise the whole deal, I just need a volunteer." Bear looked questioningly around the table. Prez's eyes lit up,

"Face, tell you what, we'll forget the fine over the Wild Hunt Run if you ride shotgun with Bear on this one." The gaze of the Unkindness was now turned on Faceman who was clearly feeling uncomfortable about the whole thing.

"Sure, err depends when it'll be going down boys-"

"When would it suit?" Prez cut in. Faceman could, for the second time that evening, feel the cold trickle of sweat roll down his neck. There was no getting out of this and he knew it. Going out on a black op with Bear was not going to help him with his objective of slowly extricating himself from the club. This was the very last thing he needed. He was between a rock and a hard place.

"How about Monday, next week? Err, no, Tuesday." Faceman's voice betrayed his uncomfortable state of mind with the whole scenario. Prez looked across to Bear raising his eyebrows. Bear smiled back,

"No problemo. I'll be in touch with the details Face. Just make sure you've got something dark to wear and a pair of trainers we can get rid of." Bear was in his element. A covert operation against drug dealers combined with making life Hell for a member he considered one of the least committed to the club. He was grinning and that meant he was happy. Prez smiled inwardly. *This is just the sort of commitment that Face needed to show. Brothers are doubting his loyalty to the club and a little warning to interlopers from the Club will go a long way to cementing our place in the community too. It's a win-win. Give Bear something to do other than banging heads together for not paying fines or stepping out of line!*

A knock at the door interrupted proceedings,

"Yeah, come in, what is it?" Prez called out and the door swung open. Johnny H, one of the hang arounds poked his head around the door his face holding a glum expression," Sorry Prez, it's the police in Heswall on the 'phone for you." *Christ, the last thing I need right now, more hassle from the Old Bill.* Prez thought. The rest of the crew shifted uneasily and exchanged glances.

"Sorry guys, you're going to have to excuse me for a sec while I go and find out what Plod want now. We'll resume in a moment." Prez stood from the table and followed Johnny to the telephone which hung on the wall downstairs in the pool room. "Hello, this is Mr Sinclair, what's the problem officer?" *first rule of dealing with Plod, be polite and cool.........*

"Mr Sinclair, this is Desk Sergeant Taylor. Sorry to disturb you but we've got a lady claiming to be your mother here at the station, she seems a little distraught and we'd like it if you could come and pick her up and take her home."

"No problem, is Mum hurt? Why is she with you guys?" Prez was concerned, he could think of no reason why his mother would visit the police station, which was a considerable walk from her home, given that she didn't drive.

S.O.S.

"We'll explain it all when you get here. No reason to worry, she's safe and well."

Same old, same old, never get a straight answer from Plod, just the usual politically correct speak, thought Prez, "Okay Officer, I'll be there in about thirty minutes." *I'll have to go home and pick up the car and then pick her up.* Prez lived in Pensby, a few miles away from Heswall and his car was garaged there.

As Prez rolled *Landwaster* on to the drive and parked it by the front door it opened in front of him. Although it was only nine thirty in the evening Nessa was wearing her dressing gown. Even in that she looked stunning, tousled hair falling passed her shoulders. They'd met years ago at a discotheque in Chester. An unlikely start to what became an enduring romance. Vanessa was a strong character and exactly the sort of person that Prez needed in life. Always the kind of guy up for a challenge! She looked at least twenty years younger than she was, alabaster skin and flowing titian strawberry blonde hair falling well below her shoulders. *Never surprised if people think I'm out with my daughter*. Prez was fond of thinking. He could never have got through life without her. Not that it was all a bowl of cherries. Being married to a strong-willed redhead was fraught with clashes of opinion, but neither of them would have it any other way. They agreed on the fundamentals of life, and that would suffice, it would have to!

"What are you doing home this early? I thought you had a Club Unkindness tonight?" her eyebrows arched in surprise, concern in her voice,

"I've just had a bath and was going to have an early one."

"Police called."

"Oh no, not trouble with them again?"

No trouble with them, apart from the fact they think we're the junior branch of drug dealers anonymous. Plod watches too many episodes of "Sons of Anarchy" and reads too many Sunday tabloids. This is England, not the USA. Prostitution, gunrunning and drug smuggling are all pretty much tied up with the existing criminal fraternity and we're not looking to gate-crash that party. Unfortunately, just riding around with a patch on your back is enough to upset Plod. I guess they realised they're in the wrong gang after all. Too late boys! Do anything in England that looks too much like fun and they'll nick you for something!

"Nah, it's a weird one, Mum's at the cop shop, don't know why, so I've got to pick her up."

Nessa's concerned heightened and she took a step back in to the house," Is she okay? I'll come with you."

Prez shrugged, *no point in having Nessa get dressed and giving the coppers a treat down at the station. Anyway, what could she do that I couldn't? No, best thing to let me sort out, whatever it was.*

"No Babe, no need for that, I'll get the car out and go and get her. I'll keep you posted." *Best thing I ever did, marry that woman.* Vince stepped inside the hall, slipping off his leathers and handing Nessa his motorcycle helmet, "Just pass me the car keys and I'll go and see what's happening.

Nessa hurried in to the living room with his gear and returned with the car keys,

"See you later Babe."

They embraced and Prez breathed in the scent of her fragrant wet hair, *Gorgeous!*

The police station was a grim place. To be fair, externally it was a nice-looking building though, dating back to the eighteen hundreds. Inside however, it was dark and foreboding. The faint aroma of bleach attempting to mask out other, more nefarious nasal bouquets. That along with the dusty atmosphere of a morgue, caused no doubt by the reams of paper that were undoubtedly languishing throughout the place, awaiting to be transcribed in to the twenty first century. Prez approached the glass screen separating the desk sergeant from the great unwashed,

"Hi officer, I'm Mr Sinclair, you called about my Mum and I've come to pick her up. What's the problem, is she okay?"

The Sergeant, looked to be around forty (seventeen years Prez's junior) and personified the stereotype of the overweight disenchanted desk bound policeman. Too many doughnuts and too little action. He was busy doing something important to a piece of paper with a ball point pen. Prez waited patiently......seething! After what seemed several lifetimes the officer lifted his head to reveal craggy features and rheumy eyes.

"Nothing to worry about Mr Sinclair. We've got your Mother in the waiting area. She didn't want a cup of tea. She's okay, but I need to ask you a few questions."

"No worries, what do you need?"

The sergeant lowered his voice and moved closer to the glass,

"Has your Mother any history of mental illness?" normally Vince would have made an off the cuff sarcastic remark at this point but something in the sergeant's tone and demeanour alluded to this being a serious question. *What the Hell sort of question is that?* The officer noted the flicker of disbelief in Prez's eyes and didn't wait for a reply,

"It's just that she's been coming out with some strange things. We get a lot of this from the local oldies amongst the population." Heswall was an ageing dormitory town, *A bit like an elephant's graveyard* thought Prez.

"Well, not to my knowledge, what exactly has she been saying? Are you sure it's my Mum, have you got the right person?"

The sergeant looked at the sheaf of papers in front of him, "Edna Sinclair, of Sandham Grove, Heswall?" he looked up at Prez who nodded glumly,

"Yeah, that's her."

A door opened down the corridor and Prez could hear his mother speaking in an agitated tone. She walked into reception with a WPC beside her. She was a short woman, immaculately turned out in her tweed suit and coat, grey hair permed, make up applied sparingly. Her glasses were thicker now with the onset of old age. She spotted Prez,

"Vincent, take me home, I've wasted hours here in this place. If they didn't want to see me, why did they tell me to come here? I've never been so insulted."

The desk sergeant looked at Prez and shrugged, turning to file his papers and the WPC melted in to the background. Prez opened the door and ushered his mother through,

"What's this all about Mum, why did they want to see you?"

Edna walked up to the car in silence and only started talking once they were underway.

"You know Vincent, they asked me to attend the police Station because they wanted to ask me some questions."

"Questions about what Mum?"

"About a string of murders of children."

Prez looked over at his mother who was looking straight ahead.

"Murder? What on earth are you talking about?"

"I'll tell you over a cuppa." Edna seemed at once tense and then relaxed. *Murder? Thank God we're at the house now and she can explain all this. Plod wasn't exactly forthcoming.*

Prez sat in the seat he always used in his mother's lounge. He made sure he visited every Sunday at the very least. He'd moved to Pensby to be closer to his mother after his father died at the age of sixty-two with emphysema, not helped by losing a lung through contracting TB in World War Two. Nor by the fact he had been a chain smoker and had stubbornly refused to give it up, despite being fully aware of the consequences.

Growing up in the Sinclair household had been one strange affair. Like most people, you always think that your family is "normal" and obviously it's the yardstick that you judge everything else by, until you develop enough experience of the world at large to make informed judgements. When you're a child it is only your peers, your school and your parents which fill your head with ideas. Plus, the less tangible things such as television (a whole three channels when I was a nipper) and of course literature. Naturally literature was controlled by parents to a degree as was television. Some of my parent's values I still hold true today. Opposite sex marriage, opening doors for others, giving up my seat on public transport for others, being generally polite and pleasant, all things which can take a maximum of effort on occasion, but it's such things which separate us from the scumbags. Honesty and loyalty and accountability for one's actions, although as I discovered in my teenage years, apparently this didn't stop my parents opening my mail. "Do as I say not as I do" sprang to mind. When I finally passed the eleven plus examination and started grammar school, all the family holidays stopped. No more going to Cornwall or Wales or Ireland or Scotland. I don't know what shifted in the dynamic but it all stopped. My Dad was taken in to hospital on a couple of occasion due to his illness and he spent a lot of time off work. I was never really sure how much of this was depression. At the time no one would have even put this in to the equation as men didn't get depressed in the seventies, especially not professional middle-class men. Looking back, there was always something missing between my mother and father. He was the archetypal cockney, yes, a REAL one, born within the sound of Bow Bells. He went in to the print trade, as did all the men in the Sinclair family. It was just the way it was. I had been expecting to carry on the family tradition, but by the late seventies the trades unions dominating the industry had forced it to its knees and as a result most of the work was dispatched abroad. Spain if I remember correctly. The money was good, and it had enabled my parents to live in an upper middle-class area, Heswall on the Wirral. Neighbours were doctors, lawyers and business people in the main. I'm sure that my Dad felt uncomfortable in these surroundings and this didn't help his melancholy. Perhaps he did it all for Mum, I guess so. He drew pleasure from his car (he once brought down matriarchal wrath by foolishly buying a second-hand Austin Van Den Plas. A huge beast with a Rolls Royce Engine. It drank petrol and was sold within months) and his infernal smoking and his miniature railway set. He had always had a model railway, often passed off as mine, but it was always my Dad's baby, I was just an excuse for him to continue to add to it. He never really hid his working-class roots and it's thanks to him that I have a working vernacular that includes a fair understanding of that most mystical of all indigenous languages Cockney Rhyming Slang and for that I will always be indebted to him. When I see advertisements for that joke of a soap opera "EastEnders" on the state television channel, I always chuckle at how the diverse ethnic clientellegel within the "Queen Vic" pub. I can tell you my Dad would indignantly exclaim that just didn't happen, no way, at least not in his day. Just another Establishment lie. That programme has about as much in common with reality in the East End as "Starsky and Hutch" had with American policing! Not that either of my parents were easy to get along with. I can only ever remember once crying in front of my Dad when I'd become a teenager. Vanessa and a friend of hers had come with me to the Donnington Rock Festival. I had driven us there and it was a cracking summers day, absolutely boiling. We'd set off relatively early and got a good parking spec. At the conclusion of the event we trudged back to the car park to find that some idiot had let my Capri's rear tyre down with a matchstick. Nice! Try as I might, I couldn't get the wheel nuts off. When the car was last serviced they'd replaced the tyre and must have used a machine to screw the wheel nuts on. No way was I going to get them off with the standard gear supplied with the car. There were plenty of well-equipped Police vans nearby, so I suggested to the girls that they play the "damsel in distress" card with Plod. Far more likely that the dashing boys in blue would rescue two attractive young girls in high boots, tight jeans and tee shirts wearing leather jackets, than a long-haired ring encrusted moustachioed yob! Helpful as ever, Plod was having none of it, so I trudged back to the concert site to use the 'phone there to call the RAC. Unfortunately, Plod was ensuring that the thousands of revellers were being allowed off the site. This meant them stopping anyone coming into the site! So, it ended up that by the time the RAC could change our tyre, I'd been awake for over twenty-four hours. Most of that time sweating under a boiling sun whilst rocking out to the bands on the bill. Not good.

    Looking back, I realise that driving home with no sleep and ensuring the girls were warm by closing the windows was a mistake. So was driving faster in an attempt to get home before I fell asleep. Once I saw an old man beside the road and realised I was just seeing things. I was exhausted and should have pulled over. Instead I drove faster in an attempt to get us all home. The next thing I knew, Nessa was screaming as the car mounted the curb. I slammed on the brakes, awoken from my slumber. The car hit a sandstone wall and the rebounded in to the inside of a crash barrier, then back in to the wall, then the crash barrier, then the wall until it finally came to a stop. I checked that the girls were alright *before stepping out to survey the damage. It was first light, and no one was about. Just as well, if anyone had been on the footpath, I would have killed them. We had come to rest at a bend in the road and on a bridge. The wall was actually the wall of the bridge and the crash barrier was there because of the sharp bend. We had been incredibly lucky. The car was a complete write off. Composed as ever, Nessa took some photographs of the wreck. I walked in to the road and flagged down the first car to come over the hill, yes, Plod! Naturally the first thing they did was give me a breath test. You could see the disappointment etched in their faces as I passed! They helpfully gave me a number for a local garage and left us there.*

It was Sunday and Sunday meant lunch with Mum and Dad. They were worried sick as we were late (no mobile 'phones back then!). We turned up in a van and got a barrage to questions from both Mum and Dad when we walked through the door. Shock, sleep deprivation, everything hit me like a tsunami and with my dad shouting at me for my stupidity I broke down and cried. For the first time as an adult I cried, and we hugged. It would be the first and last time I would hug my dad as an adult, something to this day which makes me very sad.

Edna came in to the room with two steaming cups of tea. Her perennial solution to all of life's problems.

"There you are, drink that up." She said placing the tea on the table beside Prez's chair. Prez leant forward as his mother perched herself on the sofa, looking anxious.

"Okay Mum, why were you at the police station?

Edna looked agitated and twiddled her fingers. She was a woman who had been a powerful matriarch within the family unit and she was not used to self-doubt. Now, she looked like a lost and frightened schoolgirl.

"Vincent, I told you next door were spying on me," Prez nodded thinking, *I thought we'd put that to bed weeks ago. Mum had 'phoned Nessa to say that the neighbours, an Asian family who were renting the adjoined property were spying on Mum. We just thought they were peering over the fence, perhaps we didn't take her seriously enough?*

"Well, things have got worse. They've been to the police and the police have accused me of murdering children." Edna's eyes were wide like saucers, between words she was chewing her bottom lip, obviously highly agitated.

"How do you know all this Mum?"

"What do you mean? Don't you believe me?" Edna was now acting in a way that Prez had never seen before, overtly aggressive. He held out the palms of his hands in supplication,

"I mean how do you know that they've told the police this nonsense?"

"Listen!" Edna hissed," Listen, I can hear them talking about me, listen!" she spat the words out and pointed to the wall which separated the two lounges. Prez cocked his head and could hear the drone of a television.

"It's just the television Mum."

"Bloody listen to them!" Edna shouted. Prez was taken aback. *In all my years I can only remember being shouted out by Mum once, that's pretty good going and I have NEVER heard her swear. She is acting completely out of character and I don't recognise her at all.*

Prez stood up and placed his ear to the wall. Sure, enough the news was playing, he recognised the theme music played between news items.

"It's just the news on TV Mum."

Edna stood up, her eyes narrowed as she looked at her son,

"If you bloody listened properly you would hear them!" she stormed off in to the kitchen.

"Look, Mum, do you want me to stay the night?" Prez called after her, there was no reply. He followed her in to the kitchen to find her washing up.

S.O.S.

"Mum, do you want me to stay over?"

"No, no, you go home. Don't worry about me, I'll be fine." Edna's composure had returned, and it was as though the incident had never occurred.

"I'll come and see you in the morning then? Give me a ring if you need me."

Edna followed Prez to the front door and waved him off. Prez was confused and worried but having a full-blown argument with his mother was hardly going to help. *Maybe Nessa can shed some light on this with her feminine intuition.* He thought, at least he hoped so.

Prez finished his story as he slumped in his chair sloshing his port around in its glass. Nessa sat hunched over her coffee on the edge of the sofa, eyes wide and uncomprehending. She was in a state of shock after hearing Prez tell her of the evenings strange unfolding.

"What do you think it is? I've never heard your Mum swear, or shout, I'm worried." Nessa's brows furrowed, and she looked questioningly at her husband. Before Prez could answer the 'phone rang.

"I'll go." Nessa padded from the front room into the hall and picked up the 'phone. Prez gulped down his port and awaited her return. Nessa walked in to the room slowly, looking concerned.

"Who was it?" Prez asked.

"Your Mum, she says that the police are parked outside, and she's worried they've come to take her back to the station."

"Bloody hell, I'll get round there. I'll go on *Landwaster*, it'll be quicker."

"No." Nessa said firmly," I'll come with you." She forced a smile at her husband, "Moral support!"

"Okay, we'll take the car then." Prez nodded.

When they arrived, there were no parked cars in the road. Prez rang the doorbell and Edna answered, letting them both in. Again, she looked anxious.

"Come on in you pair. Lovely to see you Vanessa, you needn't have come"

Nessa smiled back, she had always been treated as a daughter by Edna and she in turn had treated Edna as her mother, her own mother having passed away a number of years ago.

"I was worried about you. Vince told me what's been going on."

"Has he?" Edna glared at Prez,

"I'm not sure he believes me." She said angrily. Prez shrugged,

"I'm here Mum, of course I believe you. Now, where's the police?"

Edna peered out of the window, peeking out from the closed curtains. It was after eleven O'clock and had been dark for hours.

"They've gone. They were parked over the road, I saw them! Perhaps they went when they knew I called you Vincent?"

"How would they know you called Vince Mum?" asked Nessa,

"They've got the 'phone bugged you know. They've been following me for weeks." Edna was wide eyed now and still peering out of the window.

"Following you for weeks?" Prez could not keep the tone of incredulity from his voice. Something immediately picked up on by his mother who stormed through the lounge in to the kitchen.

"I know you think I'm going funny Vincent, but I know what I know." She fumed.

Nessa frowned at Prez and followed Edna in to the kitchen to help her make the inevitable cup of tea. Prez lifted his eyebrows and sat down in his usual spot beside the window. He pulled the curtain back to observe the road, as he had suspected, it was clear of any parked vehicles, as it always was. On a secluded upmarket housing estate like Sandham Grove, any new or suspicious goings on stood out like a sore thumb. Certainly, strange unknown cars parked in the street was not something that would go unnoticed by anyone.

This is crazy. Mum never shouts, she never swears, so what's going on? Maybe I should speak to Plod in the morning, they were hardly forthcoming when I was at the station. Maybe Nessa will get some info from her while they're making a brew? Prez was finding it difficult to comprehend what was happening. Were the police somehow using his mother to get to the club? It didn't seem very likely, but since the massive publicity bike clubs had received through recent television programmes, perhaps the police had swallowed the fictions and jumped to conclusions. The local police had never liked the S.O.S., suspecting them of various crimes, yet never charging anyone.

Jealous bastards, that's what they are. They wish they had the balls to be who we are, but they have to hide behind a uniform. There are more criminals in the Big Blue Gang than there have ever been in the S.O.S. Does that make them a criminal organisation? Of course not, yet if one of us steps out of line the whole club is the new bloody mafia! If it's not Plod trying to have a go at us, then what's happening? Maybe the neighbours need a chat, maybe they've got something nefarious going down?

Nessa and Prez dutifully downed their tea and made small talk for an hour before Prez suggested that Nessa had a busy day tomorrow and that they should head off home. Edna was pleased to have seen them and waved good bye, just as she did every time the pair visited.

Prez pushed the front door open and stood aside as Nessa walked in. Before he had shut the door the 'phone rang. Nessa turned from the living room and picked it up, looking at Prez in disbelief as the voice on the other end spoke.

"Okay Mum, we'll be there in ten minutes. Don't worry, bye"

"What's up now?" Prez asked.

"The police are outside her house now, come on, let's get them!" Nessa pushed past Prez and shot out of the front door to the car. Prez sped after her, firing up the vehicle and they raced off to Edna's. They made it in under ten minutes thanks to some two wheeled cornering and hair-raising driving from Prez. For once Nessa couldn't care less about the recklessness, they were on a mission. As Prez drove down Sandham Grove the cars lights illuminating the road ahead, it was just as they had left it previously. All quiet, no parked vehicles. As they pulled up the drive they saw the curtains fall back as Edna replaced them from looking out. Nessa was the first to the door and Edna had it open before she got there.

"Oh Vanessa, thank heavens you're here. They've been parked over there, they're, watching me!" Edna was gabbling in an emotional state. Nessa put her arm around her and they walked in to the lounge. Prez looked up and down the road before coming inside. He could see nothing untoward. It was late, but he decided to knock on the door of the neighbours who had always been friendly to his mother, the Dorys. Edna had always spoken highly of Mr Dory and his wife. Dory had built his property himself and had always seemed amenable to Prez. Prez's breathe plumed out as he stood outside the Dorys, waiting for them to come to the door. He hadn't even noticed how cold and autumnal it had become for September. Too many things to worry about.

The porch light came on and the front door opened. Mr Dory stood there in his dressing gown looking perplexed.

"Hi Mr Dory. Sorry for disturbing you. Could I-"

Dory cut in before Prez could finish his sentence,

"Do you know what time it is Vincent? We're trying to get some sleep. It might be alright for people like you, but we need our sleep!"

Prez was taken aback. However, he wasn't as keen on Mr Dory as his mother was. *Yeah, just because you live in a big house and have got money doesn't cut any ice with me. I know that you go and sign on at the jobcentre, telling them you're available for work, and you were doing that the whole time you were building your house. Lying bastard. Claiming benefits when, a, you didn't need them and b, under false pretences, since you weren't available for work. So much for your veneer of respectability. Mum respects you, but I don't have to. Nevertheless.........*

"Like I said, sorry for the intrusion. I'd just like to ask you a couple of questions." Prez continued with the smile straight from the Bob Monkhouse school of sincerity firmly plastered on his face.

"What questions, do you know-" this time Prez interjected, glancing at his watch as he did so,

"What time it is? Yes, Minnie's hand is on Mickey's thigh, which means it's time for bed!" Prez grinned and before Dory could make any further "harrumphs" he ploughed on,

"Mum reckons the police have been parking over the road outside her house. Have you noticed anyone suspicious?"

Dory rolled his eyes,

"I don't know what your mother saw, but nothing has happened here. The only suspicious people are you and your gang on those damned bikes. She must be ashamed of you. Now, if you'll excuse me, I'm letting the cold air in." Dory slammed the door in Prez's face. *Thank you, Mr neighbourhood watch. God knows how Mum thinks you're one of the good guys, you prat.*

Prez walked in to the lounge to find Nessa and Edna sat on the sofa drinking the prerequisite cup of tea.

"So where are the police Mum?" Prez asked. Edna turned to him looking scared in a way Prez had never seen,

"They were there Vincent." Her voice wavered, like a child who was convinced they had seen something but couldn't convince the adults around her.

"It's okay Mum." Nessa soothed the conversation," I'll stay over tonight. Vince can bring me some things over and I'll sleep in the spare room, okay?"

"Yeah, and if anything else happens Nessa can give me a call." Prez added. Rheumy eyed and emotional in a way that Prez had never seen her before, Edna thanked them both profusely. Edna had always guarded her feelings and was not a very tactile person, so both Prez and Nessa were surprised when she gave Nessa a hug.

"I'll go and make up the bed." Edna said as she scuttled up the stairs. Prez looked at Nessa,

"I'll get you your PJs and some stuff for the morning. You good with this?" Nessa smiled back,

"'Course, she's my Mum too Vince." The pair embraced and Prez walked out to the car. It had been some day.

As Prez drove home after taking Nessa's essentials for an overnight stay, it struck him that the decisions that had been made earlier in the evening regarding Faceman and Oz's drug dealer issue would not be so easily rectified now.

I'll have to revamp the timetable. This thing with Mum may be more serious than I thought and the last thing I want is for Nessa to have to deal

with all this stuff when the club is on the Wild Hunt up to Aviemore. Without me being here to help, I don't want Plod sniffing around if we've taken action against the drug pushers. If it works out that Faceman can't comply to our new timetable, I'll have to get him to show his commitment another way. Thinking about it though, it may just be his time to leave. Nobody thought the club would have lasted this long and when we started it all those years ago, nobody said it was forever. Hell, if he wants to leave we'll have a heart to heart and I'll put it to the guys at an Unkindness that he goes in Good Standing. He can be a slimy bastard and he thinks he's far cooler than he is. At the end of the day though, apart from treating Oz like the proverbial piece of shit, he's served the club well. If it's his time, we'll let him go without any hassle. At least that's how I'll pitch it at the Unkindness. The only thing that may weigh against him is his high-handed attitude with Oz. The other brothers may not take kindly to his attitude. I can only let them have their say and let them hear my view. Only time will tell. I reckon we'll scotch the Message in a Bottle until after the Wild Hunt, logistics being the way they are. I'll contact Bear and tell him to put the transport on hold, he'll be pleased................not!

Robert C. Holmes

The Wild Hunt

The assembled ranks of gleaming chrome sparkled in the autumnal air. A palpable aura of excitement and anticipation permeated even the coolest facade that was employed by the marshalled bikers queuing for hot dogs, bacon sandwiches and drinks from the overwhelmed vendors.

This is what it's all about, this is why I still run this bloody club. Thought Prez as he munched on his cheeseburger.

"You know what? I feel like bloody Henry the Fifth, or was it Henry the Fourth, or Richard the Third? Christ, whoever the geezer was who walked amongst his troops before the battle.........you know the one in that Shakespeare play......."

"Yeah, I know what you mean. Can't remember the play myself now you mention it." Oz replied between mouthfuls of bacon sandwich.

"Can't wait to get started now" Prez glanced at his watch" Give 'em another twenty minutes and we'll have to get shifting. Bloody motorways will be the usual nightmare I s'pose. I notice the coppers haven't turned up."

Oz wiped his mouth with the back of his hand and raised his eyebrows," Well, they know all about it Boss. I mean it's an annual event, isn't it? I've been in touch with 'em and they've had all the details, route etc, in writing. I reckon they think we're all old codgers now and not worth bothering with!" he smirked.

"Well, they might be right. Simply from a health and bloody safety point of view, you'd have thought the buggers'd be here though. Imagine if there's an accident on their patch, that'd go down like a cup of cold sick."

"Bollocks mate, it'd all be the fault of those nasty dirty smelly bikers!" BS slapped his hand on Prez's shoulder, making him start, he hadn't heard his VP walk up behind him

"Watch it you twat! Nearly choked on my burger!" Prez grinned finishing the aforementioned article and wiping his mouth with a tissue.

"That could've been the first incident, with no Plod to witness it! Biker President murdered by VP, choked on cheeseburger so VP could advance in the ranks! Case comes up next Thursday!"

Prez and Oz chuckled at the thought, "You seriously would kill for this bloody job? You'd be more bloody stupid than I thought!" Prez laughed as BS shrugged his shoulders.

"I'm going to find Bear so that he can tell 'em all that we're motorvatin' in fifteen. Anyone who hasn't had their food by then will just have to wait until the first stop. BS, you know the stops, yeah?" *I bloody hope so, if it was down to me to remember all that stuff, we wouldn't leave the retail park car park.* Prez mused to himself.

"Kemosabe, I am World famous Indian scout and can track anything." BS replied with his best Hollywood Red Indian accent. *Bloody Tonto, that's all I need.* Prez thought as he walked off to find Bear. It wasn't difficult as the big man towered over most of the assembled throng. A naturally powerful man who didn't need to work out and train as Prez did. *It's just genetics I suppose, that guy could deadlift a car without thinking twice.* Prez thought.

"Bear, you ready to rock?" he called across the car park.

"Yup." Bear replied, giving a thumbs up. He was talking to a cluster of hangers on. The run always attracted a number of these folk. They were friends of the club, who were welcome to join in to swell the ranks. They didn't make the full commitment to the club as members, for whatever reason, but unlike some motorcycle clubs the S.O.S. never looked down upon these bikers. They gave their support and on runs like this they would add to the spectacle, which in turn would generate more money for the charities that the run was in aid of. In turn this bought the club good will, at a time when there was precious little of that going around to anyone.

"Give 'em a shout in fifteen bro and then we'll saddle up and leave Dodge, okay?"

S.O.S.

"Yup." Bear nodded and walked to his bike with the swagger of a confident big man. *What's going on in the wider World? Doesn't know, doesn't care.* Prez smiled to himself as he watched the big man stroll to his customised motorcycle. The red machine almost dwarfed by its rider. Bear was not a Harley rider, which unlike some clubs was not a prerequisite of membership, although they drew the line at rice burners.

I'd better go for a leak before we leave, this getting old, it's crap. Prez walked to the DIY store that dominated the retail park, nodding and shaking hands with club members and hangers on alike. Even a few members of the public wished him well as he entered the building. As he approached the toilets Oz emerged,

"Great minds, eh Boss?" Oz grinned.

"Bloody old man's bladder more like."

Everything was in place Prez swung his leg over his machine and glanced to his left at the parked bikes stretching from one end of the car park to the other.

"How many d'you reckon?" he called to BS who was mounted on his machine next to Prez,

"Dunno, haven't done a count, a hundred, maybe more. Good turnout. Probably lose a few at the first stop though." *True, but we'll pick some up on the way. Not everyone wanted to ride all the way to Scotland in a day, some will just take part in a couple of legs of the journey and then meander back home. The feeling of riding in a huge group of bikers wasn't to be missed, especially not in poor old Blighty.* Prez smiled to himself and then took a look at his watch. Time to fire them up. He flicked his "run" switch, waited for the light to show on his speedometer and pressed the start button. *Landwaster* fired like a Panzer tank, resonating around the car park. Suddenly it was like the crashing of Thor's Hammer Mjolnir around the whole retail park as the hundred or so bikes joined Prez's machine in the unholy chorus of homage to the internal combustion engine.

"LET'S DO THIS" Prez shouted and BS nodded. Prez led the way out of the car park on to the dual carriage way, *Landwaster* burbling beneath him, eager to change up the gears. Once on to the dual carriageway it was a short trip to a roundabout, then back on themselves and on to the motorway. As Prez swung his machine on to the slip road to the motorway and glanced behind to check the oncoming traffic he felt the weight of the world lift, just a little. He twisted the throttle releasing the huge amount of torque that *Landwaster* was holding back and joined the flow of traffic. He checked his Iron Cross mirrors and watched as the column snaked along behind him. Some being held back because of oncoming traffic. *Which is exactly why I thought the bloody coppers would at least be here to see us off. Oh well, let's hope it's all incident free. They've probably got their work cut out rescuing cats from trees, now that the fire brigade don't do it!* Another twist of the throttle and some swift gear changes and the beast was unleashed onto its natural black ribbon habitat, doing what it did best, purring.

It's a crazy thing riding a motorcycle. On one level you transcend everyday living, you become a single entity with the machine that you are riding. You're on the edge, inches away from black tarmac, contact with which would mean certain injury or even death. All part of the thrill, the challenge, the "Live to ride, ride to live" mantra so enthused about by biker publications and the cinema, yet probably experienced by very few, in reality. It is this near-death experience which bonds the brotherhood of bikers together. The tiny surface areas of the two tyres of a machine in touch with the road, with huge amounts of torque and power, being the only contact between you and the physical world, your whole life is channelled through those points of contact, one oil slick, one slip..........................then there are the assassins all around you in their steel boxes, listening to rap music, classical music, arguing with their wives, husbands, girlfriends, kids, talking on the 'phone, in fact doing everything within their limited powers NOT to concentrate on driving the lethal steel dodgem in which they are encased. A slight brush with another vehicle may only result in a scrape to the paintwork, perhaps a dint in the bodywork, maybe the other half won't notice, or you can blame it on a shopping trolley in an ASDA car park. Meanwhile any such impact could be enough to send one of the Brothers ploughing off the road into oblivion. The mantra "Sorry mate, I didn't see you" echoing into the ether, played as a "Get out of jail free card" when the case comes before magistrates more interested in stocks and shares than the fate of an undesirable riding a motorcycle. Just another statistic used by the same stockbroker belt brigade to have the victims of the collisions' choice of transport banned from the road. Presumably on the premise that they are too easy to kill. Not that you would suppose that would worry the kind of folk who employ beaters on the moors to flush out their unprotected prey, prior to a volley of lead shot ending said prey's existence. "Shot Sir"! Then there's the other level, where whilst you're riding, the concentration levels peak, so that as part of the machine you are riding by instinct and as such are able to train your mind to address problems which in your normal day during the waking hours, solutions had eluded you. When everyday life (if there is such a thing) has thrown up more questions than answers and the reaction of most folk is to either reach for alcohol or compartmentalise the issues away and turn to the Great God, media. Gaming, reality television, sport, social media, all helpful extensions of people's other selves, or in most cases, invented selves, where one can be whomever you wish and terrorise whomever you wish. If ever the term "troll" was misused, it is within the social media! A way to escape your trials and tribulations and literally reinvent yourself. Terrorised by the boss? Take it out on an innocent abroad on social media. Going nowhere in life? Support a successful football team and ride their coat tails to glory and achievement, even though said teams' players wouldn't give you the steam from their urine! Whilst you finance their multimillion-pound lifestyles, using the ridiculous concept of "loyalty" as an excuse to shell out for ridiculously highly priced tickets, to line the pockets of foreign agents and players who know allegiance only to mammon. Who knows where they will be next season? Riding that chromed machine throws all such nonsense into sharp focus. You don't need the crutches that the media programmes you in to thinking you do! You are a free-thinking entity, with the power to strive for what is good and right. You are empowered to move beyond what the advertising executives and media chiefs are constantly bombarding you with. The mainstream media, constantly insulting your intelligence and marginalising anyone with an idea that may challenge their version of the status quo. If an idea cannot be bought, it must be marginalised and ridiculed. Who was it who said, "What we do not understand, we must destroy"? Let's face it they were spot on! Depressingly, nothing has changed! Clarity of thought and purpose suddenly arrives as both rider and machine weave past vehicles and obstructions, clarity of vision of what is possible arrives. Ideas that would be scoffed at by the very individual thinking them, sat at home in an armchair, are suddenly attainable goals and innovative alternatives. Perhaps it is the same as the near-death experiences suffered in wars that brings about this enlightenment. Look at the way technology leapt forward in World War Two. It started with biplanes and ended with V2 rockets, the very forerunners of the Saturn V, which put man on the moon! All within five years. Yet since then innovation has returned to its crawling nature, with a scrap thrown to the masses every now and then. The internet, what a way to set folk free! A toy which is merely harnessing the dark personalities of folk and indulging their worst fantasies, in a way which was not achievable before. On the motorcycle, you are truly free, whilst hugely vulnerable to the stupidity of others. The reward is that aforementioned clarity of mind, unavailable anywhere else, in my limited experience, although I am sure that there are other ways of achieving this state of mind, I personally have yet to encounter it.

Another motorcycle pulled in to Prez's field of vision. BS was gently gesticulating to indicate that the column should take the next exit to the motorway services. Prez gave him a thumbs up and started slowing *Landwaster* down.

Prez gazed in to the murky depths of his coffee encased in its Styrofoam cup. *It doesn't even taste as good as it looks, and it looks bloody awful.*

BS looked across the plastic table, cradling his own beverage, "Third of the way there Prez, we're making good time this year."

"Any of 'em turned back yet?"

"Yeah some are going back from here, but hell, if they've got work to go to tomorrow, more power to 'em for giving us a good send off."

"Sure, you're right....as usual!" Prez smirked. He was always surprised how many turned out just to be associated with the club. It enhanced the club's standing in the community. A community which was always under the metaphorical lash of "the establishment" which has all the power of money and media at its disposal.

S.O.S.

"Anyway, have all the chapters joined us yet?" BS looked thoughtful before replying,

"I'm not sure, I'll check it out with Oz when we get there. I haven't seen London anywhere, but knowing Weasel, he's probably on cloud nine somewhere!"

"As long as his chapter pay their dues, keep their noses clean and keep the faith, he can be where he likes..........as long as it's here!" Prez laughed and BS joined in, cackling like the very Ravens depicted on their patches would.

It was dark now as the bedraggled posse of bikes pulled in to the final stop before Aviemore. Each and every biker soaked and freezing, this was the character-building adversity which cemented the bond that linked brothers of the road. Riders struggled as they backed their heavy machines in to parking bays. Prez surveyed the scene with grim satisfaction as bikes slowly rolled past him looking for spaces to park. He grimaced slightly as he stretched his right leg, always a cause of aches and pains. A sudden thump on his shoulder startled him momentarily, but he knew whom it would be and turned to deliver a playful punch at the shoulder of his Vice President BS.

"Nearly there brother." BS grinned through the darkness, which was permeated with pools of light from the many headlamps still streaming in to the parking lot attached to the service station. There were few other vehicles, since Scotland in November was not the first choice for your average family holiday. *All the more reason for holding the Wild Hunt in November. Besides, it validates our madness!* Prez thought grimly to himself.

"Yeah. Are you sure they haven't moved Aviemore? I'm bloody sure we're usually there by now?" Prez looked mock questioningly at him.

"Nah, they've just made it get darker quicker this year!" BS smirked as he and Prez removed their helmets and trudged towards the main service station building. A strange place this, a circular building, surrounded by pine forest. Menacing if you were alone in the dark but with rumbling engines, bright headlamps and the guffaws of the bikers the place seemed friendly enough.

Prez sat facing the entrance sipping his hot chocolate, wishing his leather jeans were as water proof as they looked,

"You ever had a trip up here that didn't entail you getting bloody soaked through?" he raised his eyebrows at BS who had his hands wrapped around his cup of coffee attempting to bring life back into frozen digits.

"I like getting soaked. Let's me know I'm alive. 'Sides it's great to get in to dry gear at the hotel."

"Yeah, just so we can get pissed and not care anyway!" piped up Oz who plonked himself beside the two of them, hot drink in one hand, Kit Kat in the other.

"I reckon we're about an hour away now. We all whole?" *Last thing we need is the bad publicity of someone taking a tumble....* Prez thought to himself.

"I spoke to Bear a minute ago and he reckons there's been no probs on that front Boss." Oz somehow managed to speak between mouthfuls of biscuit, "Don't know why they ever made these things in two fingers when everybody always wants the four fingered ones."

"Christ we're not going to have a Joan Collins joke from 1979 here are we?" BS rolled his eyes to the ceiling. Fortunately, Oz was, for once, too preoccupied opening another two fingered biscuit, to reply.

"Gotta be honest, I had a bit of a wobble at that bend a couple of miles back. Thought I saw a fox about to run out and in this bloody weather, you alter you're line in to a bend and you put your fate in the lap of the bloody gods. Brought it back in though." Prez sighed.

"Yeah, I saw that Prez, thought you were going to clean me out!" BS drained the last of his drink.

"You know I wouldn't go anywhere without you Bro!" Prez grimaced.

"We ready to get these last few miles done?" he looked at Oz and BS as he gently eased himself up from the table,

"Shite, you're going to be popular Boss, some of 'em are still coming in!" Oz protested.

"Well it doesn't matter, it's not as if it's daylight and the massed throngs are going to be there with garlands of flowers to welcome us in the pissing rain, is it?"

BS looked quizzically at the two bikers as he also rose from the table,

"And you'd *want* flowers Prez?"

"Yeah, when I'm dead!" the three cackled to each other and headed for the door clutching their riding apparel, bikers entering standing aside to let their senior officers through.

As they walked back to their bikes Prez surveyed the scene. It was like some medieval army had just rolled in to town. *Now all I've got to do is find the camp followers...........Mind you, anyone camp in this outfit would be risking their life!* He chuckled to himself. A large figure loomed up towards them as they mounted their bikes.

"Prez, no accidents that I know of. I've been riding at the back of the column since the last stop and if it's good with you, I'll do the same until we reach our hotel. Just keeps 'em in line and up to speed." Bear was all business, single minded and efficient, as ever.

"Good work Bear. Yeah good thinking, you having a drink to warm up?" Prez replied.

"What do I need to warm up for? I'm only going in there for a piss and to get those fuckers back out on the road." BS and Prez exchanged glances,

"Give 'em a few Bear. It's been a long run and- "

"They can get plenty of rest when we reach base Prez. Start getting comfortable now and they'll be dug in like an Alabama tick!" Bear interjected. Prez pulled on his helmet and shrugged at the big man. *Makes sense.*

"Okay, but give 'em ten minutes, so they can all perform their ablutions, okay?" Bear frowned and then grinned,

"There's plenty of room out here…………" he cast his arm in a sweeping motion encompassing the wide forest surrounding them.

"Ten minutes." Prez smiled and the big man nodded acquiescence.

"See you there Bear!" Called BS as he fired up his machine, Bear gave a thumbs up as he strode purposefully towards the amenities. BS looked over to Prez,

"Ready?"

Prez scanned the car park and could see that whilst some were still dismounting, and some were clustered in groups discussing the journey, there were others who were waiting for him and BS to lead them out. Eager to get to warmth, alcohol, partying and bed, not necessarily in that order. *Ready as I'll ever be. This has been one hell of a ride this year. Can't see my back putting up with it next year. Still, that's for another day. Don't let 'em see weakness.* Prez nodded to BS and fired up *Landwaster* then headed noisily to the exit, bikes falling in to line behind, the huge engines reverberating like surf crashing against a cliff. Prez entered the slip road and with a quick glance to check for oncoming headlights he twisted the throttled and *Landwaster* burst in to life as he punched through the gears. *Aviemore, brace yourself!* Prez chuckled to himself.

It was sleeting in the headlamps now as Prez banked in to a sharp right-hand curve. His back was beyond aching now and his right knee was cramping up so that the pain he had been experiencing had mercifully faded away. The middle finger of his right hand was, however, throbbing fit to burst. Not continually, just when braking was required. *Don't know if it's the onset of arthritis or what, but the joints at the knuckle and the end of the bloody thing are killing me and stiffening up. I'd noticed a few months earlier that closing my hand into a fist agitated that finger and as a consequence I stopped wearing my silver skull ring on it. Didn't seem to make a jot of bloody difference though. Another endearing sign of the encroachment of Old Father Time.* No opportunity for his mind to drift in to any state of higher consciousness now, as he was grimly guiding his metal leviathan through some truly horrendous conditions. The thin front wheel aquaplaning over the sodden tarmac, whilst the fat rear tyre squirmed its way onwards, driving beast and rider forward. Prez's riding position meant that he was sitting in a puddle of rain for hours on end, which inevitably resulted in a soaked posterior. *Not exactly the heroic "Easy Rider" biker presented to the masses by the Hollywood lie factory. There again, northern Scotland is hardly California!*

Finally, the lights of the main street of Aviemore hove in to view. It was a well-lit area, with rows of hotels either side of the main road. There were rows of motorcycles in many of the car parks as locals and those from other areas had already arrived to join the party. This was a fund raiser, so all were welcome, although the S.O.S. had their own hotel to themselves as usual. Admittance to club members and guests only. There was rarely any trouble. *Who in their right mind would come to the middle of nowhere, in weather like this to have a bloody punch up? More fun to sit at home and stick needles in your bloody eyes I'd have thought.* Prez ruminated as he rolled *Landwaster* in to a parking bay at the hotel booked for the S.O.S. BS backed his own machine up and dismounted alongside Prez, to be joined by Oz as the three removed helmets and grinned at each other. Bathing in the grim satisfaction that only folk as crazy as they would even dream of the undertaking they had just fulfilled, yet here they were again.

"HELLOOO AVIEMORE!" Oz howled into the stratosphere, his face gazing skyward. A number of other howls in the distance took up the same call, but most were content to carry their backpacks in to the hotel to get out of the sleet and freezing cold. If Odin was testing them, he'd picked a stern examination. *Stamina, guile, courage and no little skill, all the greatest of qualities in a man. Trumped perhaps only by loyalty, which was also evident in abundance by way of participation in the event.* Mused Prez as he led the way in to the hotel.

S.O.S.

Poison

Another thunderous hard rock track started up from the juke box. Prez tapped his foot in time to the music as he cradled his glass of JD and coke. *Thank God no buggers put "Born to Be Wild" on yet, I can do without hearing that one. Maybe no one from the media is here, otherwise you could count on 'em putting on what they consider the biker's anthem, dipsticks.* Prez scowled at himself in the mirror behind the assembled bottles at the bar. His plaited hair still long but grey, with none of its vitality of years gone by. *Christ, I haven't got crow's feet, I've got vultures feet, not laughter lines, hysteria lines! Even the bloody mussie's gone grey, just can't rely on anything anymore.* The constant drinking had given him an urge to eat and catching the pretty blonde barmaid's eye, he called over,

"Packet of salted peanuts, and the same again please sweetheart." The young girl smiled back and duly brought both the peanuts and large JD and coke over.

"Thanks love, one for yourself." Prez handed over a twenty-pound note. He opened the peanuts and tipped some in to his outstretched palm. *One of the peanuts decided to make a break for it, instead of following his brothers in to the palm of my hand, it decided to break ranks and go for it! Spinning down on to the floor, only to fall between the loose-fitting floorboards. What will it do there? Food for a rodent or just decrepitude in to nothingness. Should it have stayed with the group and shared certain oblivion within the digestive system or should it be lauded for striking out in a futile gesture against conformity? Did it make a conscious decision (pretty unlikely for a peanut, but hey what do I know?) or was it mere random chance, luck, or was it perhaps preordained, the will of the fates or even, a higher power? Bloody hell, you could go crazy thinking such things, at least that's what my old Mum would say when anyone challenged her regarding thoughts of anything spiritual or paranormal. She told me once she'd visited a spiritualist with her Mum, and there were trumpets flying around, all sorts of weird stuff. Pretty full on for a youngster. No wonder she had compartmentalised it all and had always been firmly none committal about any belief system. Fairly decent analogy for the current standing of the S.O.S. though. None of us getting any younger and with all the responsibilities that middle age brings. Children, Christ, Grandchildren in some cases. Losing parents, caring for parents, divorces, age related illnesses, great stuff. Like a golden thread running through all the trials and tribulations of life there was The Life itself. Brotherhood, freedom. That Raven Triskelion on our backs may be a rag to the walking dead out there, but it's our Holy Grail our raison d'etre, it's our battle flag, belief. It's integrity and without integrity and loyalty what do any of us possess? I guess you only really know Brotherhood when the chips are down. No one in the S.O.S. has ever let me down and the inner circle, the Unholy Trinity, Myself, Oz and BS are living proof that our ideas can and do work outside of the media lie factory. They work on an organic level based on loyalty, honesty and integrity. No place for dirty, grubby dealings to get up a greasy pole or line one's pockets at the expense of others. A great man once said, "There are two kinds of people in this world. Those that will help you out of the gutter and those who put you there in the first place", I'd really like to claim the line myself, but Lemmy Kilmister beat me to it!* Another handful of peanuts and a slug of whiskey failed to throw any further clarity on the matter as BS sidled up to his President with vodka and lime in hand.

"Alright Prez? Tell ya, I'm not as bloody young as I look!" he grinned.

"As young as you look? Christ, I feel like Methuselah. Good job this is only an annual run. Why the hell don't we ride somewhere warm like Spain or Italy, why did we pick bloody Scotland in November?"

BS spread his arms wide, "Ask the bloody idiot in charge..............or was that a rhetorical question and you *were* asking yourself?"

Prez puffed out his cheeks then drained his glass, "Y'know, I can't even remember *why* we picked Scotland. Hey, and I'm pretty sure it was a *club* decision, y'know? Taken at an Unkindness, with a vote and all that."

"Yeah, well, probably proposed by you though!"

"Maybe, but seconded by you no doubt and voted through by at least the Unholy Trinity, I'd wager. So put up and shut up you moaning old git. Nobody thought it was a bad idea twenty odd years ago!"

"My whole point Prez, back then it wasn't." BS grinned "How're the old bones holding up, oh wise one?"

Prez shifted and felt a twinge of pain in his right leg. A woman had opened a car door on to it when he was walking along the pavement over thirty years ago and it had never been right since. Now though it was quite painful. Either because he had been standing at the bar for hours, or because it was his rear brake leg, or more likely, both. Then he felt a pain in his lower back. *Always the lower back on the right side. First went when I was twenty-five and I bent down to pick up a bloody cat!*

"Well, I'm here aren't I? And I wasn't the one who went and sat down with the pussies!"

"True. That's why we follow you, it's such a smart idea to ride hundreds of miles and then stand at a bar for hours. That's what makes you the smart one!" BS grinned.

"Fuck off you twat!" Prez laughed and placed a well-meaning punch on BS's shoulder. "Okay, I'll come and sit down with you girlies."

BS and Prez made their way over to a booth occupied by Oz and a wiry individual with an attempted nineteen seventies Keith Richards/Ronnie Wood hairstyle which was now resembling a balding toilet brush. Said individual immediately stood up and grasped Prez's forearm in greeting.

"Prez, long time no see?"

"Good to see you Wease, how's it hangin' mate?"

Jimi The Weasel hadn't been seen since the last Wild Hunt Run to Scotland last year. He'd been the lead guitarist with Hanoi Jane back in the day and along with roadie Pretty Boy John had taken his money and relocated to the Smoke. He was a good-natured guy, but not so good natured that he didn't ditch his wife and two kids to go and play rock god in the Smoke with his best mate. BS and I were actually Godfathers to Cindy, Weasels daughter who has now blossomed in to a stunning blonde........

"Pretty good, Prez. Can't complain" Weasel sniffed profusely, the signature of the long-term cocaine addict.

"Still sniffing the breakfast of champions then sunshine?" Prez smiled,

"Well it hasn't killed us yet has it bro?" Weasel shot a glance at Pretty Boy John at the next booth for confirmation but the blond haired physical wreck face down on the table in a puddle of saliva didn't reply.

"I think he's trying to tell you somethin' pal." Oz muttered.

"What, what did he say?" Weasel looked at Oz wildly,

"He's trying to tell you to give that shit up!" Oz grimaced.

"Good that you could make it up here anyway. What's the deal down south?" Prez reckoned a shift in gears might get them away from the thorny pharmaceutical issues.

"All good Man, really good. It's good to see you cats again, been a while."

There were a couple of things that didn't sit right with the Mother Chapter regarding the way things were being handled down south. Oz had laid it down at an Unkindness that the books just didn't add up. Each Chapter of the S.O.S. is a pseudo independent organisation for legal reasons. However, when push comes to shove the entity as a whole takes its lead from the Mother Chapter, that means the rulings from our Unkindness, which in the main follows the guidance of the Unholy Trinity. That's why we fly "England" on our colours, not designated area chapters like most clubs. We don't consider England as our territory, we regard ourselves to be "of England", Anglo Saxons, one of the criteria for joining. Does that make the S.O.S. racist? Well is it racist to be a member of the Black Police Officer's Association? Or the Muslim Council of Great Britain, or, or, or? Basic rule of thumb for prospects regarding the issue, is that if they can prove they're of Anglo Saxon, Celtic or Scandinavian descent, they can get a shot at the gig. If they can't, hey, there's bigger and tougher clubs out there, go for it. We've had some bad press about it in the past and doubtless it'll revisit us again in the future, but hey, if we wanted to conform to societies supposed "norms" we wouldn't be in an outlaw bike club (the clue's in the word "outlaw") would we? Y'see, "outlaw" doesn't mean we're criminals. And unlike most bike clubs, it doesn't mean we model ourselves on the Wild West! It means that we are outlaws in the Norse sense, we've been cast out by society, it's they who don't want us, and we are proud to reciprocate. We're proud of who we are and what we are and if you don't like it, we are stoically indifferent to your opinions. Our forefathers built what our Green and Pleasant Land is, and we demand our birthright as individuals to do what we damn well like within its shores. We have our own moral codes and our brotherhood, and we owe mainstream society nothing. Having said all that there are areas where our worlds collide and like it or not compromises have to be made. Mammon, unfortunately is usually the problem. Everything has to be paid for, one way or another.

"Sometime this weekend, we're gonna have to call an Unkindness and bring you guys in for a report of what you're getting up to down there." Prez muttered, putting his arm around Weasel's slim shoulders.

"Yeah, yeah, sure Prez, just say the word. Johnny can give you the gen on the books, no problem man, it's all good bro. Not a problem, we're doin' good, all solvent" Weasel's eyes darted nervously as his words rattled out akin to a machine gun discharging its deadly messengers.

"As long as you don't mean the solvent you sniff mate!" joked BS.

"Ha ha, yeah, right. Who wants a drink?" Weasel sounded like a man who had just been told that it was all a mistake and he hadn't won the National Lottery.

Prez, BS and Oz put their hands up in unison,

"Oz, go to the bar with him, he won't remember what the fuck we drink by the time he gets there." Prez muttered. Oz gave a thumbs up and followed Weasel's weaving path to the bar.

"Shit, Prez. This is the worst I've seen him in a while. I don't mean the abuse, I mean the way he doesn't even look connected." BS murmured, concern lacing each syllable, "As for that wanker," he gestured to Pretty Boy at the next booth, who was asleep and still drooling on to the table, "can't we get rid? He's always been a liability and now his looks are shot, he looks to me like he's going full bore for a home run!"

"Yeah, doesn't look like he cares who he takes with him, either." Prez pursed his lips in thought, "How the hell did they get here?"

"What to this state? Years of doing crap I s'pose." BS shrugged.

"Nah, I mean how did they get *here*, to Aviemore? Did they actually ride up here? That pillock doesn't look like he could throw his leg over anything, let alone ride it."

BS shrugged, "I'll ask around Boss. No point confronting them head on, you'll just get a load of bollocks. Leave it with me. D'you want Bear involved?"

Prez smiled thinly, "Not really, not yet. If we want Bear involved, it had better be a club call. I just want to know what the lie of the land is. I'm not sure we can trust these guys anymore, an' if we can't trust 'em. They're out. That's when Bear does his thing."

As Sergeant at Arms, it would be down to Bear to dish out the club discipline, if it was needed. Not for the squeamish. To be honest, I'd been putting off investigating what London had been up to for years, almost making me complicit, should anything untoward be discovered. It's tough being King. Weasel was always a strange guy, playful as a puppy and eager to please. Good guitarist way back when too. But his judgement wasn't the best and clearly idolising dope fiends such as Keith Richards, it was always going to send him on a destiny run. Having said that, for years London ran pretty well. Obviously, the vitality of youth, the music business contacts, knowing all the "right people" down there worked. For a while..................Now he'd probably used up his cash and goodwill in equal measure. Funny how they tend to do that, run out at the same time. Almost as if people were just hangers on and not true friends at all! That's London and more generally, that's what's now called "celebrity culture". I wouldn't be at all surprised to find Weasel had a book being written by a ghost writer to spill the beans on Hanoi Jane. I can see it now: "Hanoi Jane, the Glory Years", quickly followed by the sequel; "Riding with the S.O.S.

Outlaws!". Looking at the state of Weasel and Pretty Boy, it appeared that if their souls, would fetch the right price, (keeping them in coke) then I reckon that'd be their idea of a good bargain. Mother Chapter takes a dim view of drugs on a number of levels. Firstly, they aren't good for you! If you didn't buy in to that, then there was the loyalty angle. Even decent brothers will turn on the Club if they are dependent on the hard stuff. No one can control it, it controls you. Sure, various celebs and stars will tell you otherwise, but trust me, I've seen good men (and women) fall foul of drugs and it's not a pretty sight. Literally, in most cases. Good looking babes turn in to hags and solid brothers waste away or balloon up, depending upon their poison of choice. Most lose their teeth at around the same time as their loyalty shifts from patch to powder. Not good. Seeing Weasel and Pretty Boy, I resigned myself to the fact that that patch to powder loyalty switch was happening right in front of me. Probably had been happening for months, and I hadn't realised it. I s'pose I should have made it a priority to visit the London chapter more often. Although all the domestic strife with my mum had kinda put a block on many of the duties I should have been performing as President of the Mother Chapter.

"There y'go El Presidentti!" Weasel arrived at the booth with Oz and handed Prez his JD and coke,

"I'm just off t'powder me nose boss." Weasel pointed to the toilets and tapped his nose winking.

"Yeah, knock yourself out bro." Prez sighed as Oz took his seat and Weasel swayed off in the direction of the gents.

"I couldn't get any sense out of him re the way they boogied up here Prez. Bloody hell, I didn't get any sense out of him about anything! Ended up buying the bloody round myself!" Oz rolled his eyes and took a sip of his pint. BS took a look at his watch and leaned across the table,

"Well I'm bloody knackered. I'm having this, then going to bloody bed!"

"Anything lined up?" Prez raised his eyebrows. BS returned the request for information with the middle finger salute.

"I take it that's a no then?" Prez chuckled. BS was a one-woman man, besides they all knew his wife Kelly would make earrings out of his genitalia should he stray.

"I could do with an early one myself Boss." Oz chimed in,

"Well it *is* bloody early, it's three in the morning!" Prez yelled as the juke box started playing some horrendous thrash rubbish. Somewhere in the back of his mind he recalled that there was a ride out to the Bon Scott statue scheduled for the morning. *Christ, that may just have to be moved back until the afternoon...*

It had taken Prez an eternity to get to sleep. When it had eventually arrived, it had been a restless affair. Over tired and inebriated, with his mind racing regarding the following few days and the big decisions that would have to be made were not a recipe for a good night's sleep. A ray of light was squeezing through a chink in the curtains and displaying itself on the bedroom wall. Prez tried breathing in, only to discover that his nasal passages were completely congested, and he had been breathing through his mouth all night. A thin trickle of saliva running through his moustache and attaching his lip to the pillow confirmed the fact.

Bloody catarrh, always been cursed with it, couple that with knackered sinuses and it's a cracking combination. Disgusting. He sat up and felt the queasiness that occurs after a night of alcoholic indulgence grip his stomach, coupled with that strange light headedness. *It's that bloody "never again" scenario, that'll be gone in a couple of hours. If I can just force down something to eat, I'll be as right as rain.* He cocked his head listening for any signs of life in the hotel, but his efforts were greeted by the quiet of the grave. Glancing at his watch on the bedside cabinet he nodded in grim satisfaction. *Ten o' clock. I'll bet none of the buggers'll be up 'til after twelve. Good thing in a way though, since it'll give me more time to get reacquainted with the important things in life, like eating, breathing and drinking. It's an age thing, it never used to be this bloody difficult.* Sliding out of bed he eased his aching bones with a stretch. *Damn back is still painful and my leg is still a bit tetchy to take full weight, as the alcohol is wearing off, it won't get any better. Time for a shower and then to the restaurant, to see who else has made it to the land of the living.* Stretching again, he padded to the en suite to perform his ablutions, the room pitching slightly as he made his way. *That Monkees song was lying when it said that the shaving razor stings.* He thought as the razor glided over the shaving foam around his moustache. He carefully avoided both that and his sideburns, all grey and white, matching his hair. *Still at least I've got hair. Couldn't be bothered dyeing it when it's as long as this..................anyway, who am I trying to impress, I'm fifty-seven, so who cares?* He questioned himself in the mirror. Splashing water on his face to rinse off any excess shaving foam he looked at himself for a minute. *Not bad for my age. Still fairly slim, the core exercises every day help, and the weights, and those long walks of Nessa's!* He looked at his tattooed upper arms, his left featuring a lion underneath which fluttered the Union Flag beneath which was a scroll written in Old Norse meaning "Birthright", a statement of his avowed loyalty to his kin. His right upper arm featured the word Einherjar (Norse for "Champions of Odin"), above a heraldic eagle and below it the word Valholl. A separate tattoo below that was of the Motorhead War Pig. On the inside of his arm opposite the Warpig was the S.O.S. emblem. The final tattoo was on his chest over where the heart was traditionally thought to be. The Odal rune surrounded by a circle of laurel leaves. *It's true what they say about tats, they don't tell a person who you are, they tell a person who you were...................Mind you, every bloody idiot gets 'em nowadays. When these were done you were either in the forces, a sailor or a biker. Tats actually stood for something. You had to get inked in disreputable areas like Birkenhead or the inner cities. Now they get bloody sportswear brands tattooed on 'em, just 'cause their stupid bloody false idol football teams wear a kit made by that company, until next year. David Beckham and "celebrities" have a lot to answer for.*

Showered, shaved and booted and suited in his S.O.S. finery, jeans t-shirt leather jacket, silver rings, bike chain bracelet, Odin amulet and colours, Prez made his way downstairs to the restaurant. He scanned the scene before him. It was a big place, used every year for the Wild Hunt Run. The proprietors were glad of the business in November, as the skiing season was still some way off. *Although it feels bloody cold enough for English softies like us. Alcohol in the system from last night doesn't exactly help you cope with the temperature either. BS was right last night. Maybe we should change the venue next year. Somewhere less challenging in Spain or Portugal! Not that I'll be seeing BS this morning, or anytime until the revellers start the party all over again. He's never had the greatest powers of recovery after an all-nighter, oops, take it all back, there he is!* Prez almost gasped in amazement to see BS nursing a coffee beside Oz at one of the tables. Oz, as could have been predicted, was eating what looked like a full English breakfast. At least it *had* been a full English until he had demolished most of it.

"Prez! Come and join us!" called Oz as he mopped up an egg yolk with fried bread. *Now that is a lesson to us all. An iron constitution, if ever there was one.* Prez marvelled. He returned Oz's request with a thumbs up before collecting his breakfast from the delights laid out before him.

He also chose eggs, bacon and sausage, although it was of miniscule proportions to those that his treasurer had devoured. Plonking himself down beside Oz he looked at BS, who appeared thoroughly hung over and miserable.

"Morning VP, how's it going?" BS replied with a raise of his index figure, whilst staring in to the stygian depths of his coffee.

"That's bloody nice first thing, isn't it? Where's your respect man?" Prez grinned.

"Don't be too hard on him Boss, he's a delicate soul the old VP, that's why you gave him the job!"

"You going to be able to haul ass down to Kirriemuir and the Bon Scott statue son?" Prez enquired. BS lifted his gaze to reveal two reddened eyes peering through heavy lids from a pasty white face.

"Christ, maybe we should just drive a stake through your heart and cut your head off!" Prez quipped,

"Have you not got a mirror in your room then, you fucker?" BS growled "I'll be fine once we get going, I'll outride you, any day."

"No doubt mate, but honestly, if you don't feel up to it, you'll be in good company here, since I can't see many of 'em taking a run out today after last night. Have you seen the bloody weather? I put my denim jeans on, but the leathers'll be going on, it's pissing down out there."

Oz rolled his eyes at Prez," What kind of a bloke wears denim, when he can wear leather anyway?"

"Quite." Prez shrugged. He then proceeded to tuck in to his food, scanning the room to see who had made it to breakfast, that was in actuality more akin to lunchtime. The proprietors knew the score and set menus were scrapped for the club regarding breakfast and lunches. These were not "ordinary" customers. Forcing the bacon down with an effort due to his beverages of the night before Prez could see the usual crew form the Mother Chapter, Boalie sat with Johnny H and Chinner. Sweeping his gaze to take in more of the room he spotted Irish Kev, whom he hadn't seen in years, who had obviously made the trip over from his native land. No mean feat, since his old lady must have given him some stick for it. No sign of anyone from London and as expected, no sign of Weasel or Pretty Boy John. Prez turned back to his immediate entourage.

"Anyone seen Bear about?"

"Yeah" nodded Oz, "He's outside tinkering with his wheels."

"I'm thinking we should have a Mother Chapter Unkindness tonight. What do you guys think? I know we've only got a couple of days here, but I really do think we need to sort out this Weasel thing and decide what to do."

BS tore his gaze from the murky depths of his coffee cup, "Don't you think we should give them the chance to have their say in this?"

"Well, maybe they can do that at the Unkindness?" Prez looked at Oz,

"Yeah, that works Boss. I mean we can hear their side of the story and then we can mull it over whilst they go to the bar."

"Hmmm, Oz, how do you feel about contacting whoever is down in the Smoke, whoever hasn't come on the run and asking them to supply you with the books?" BS looked doubtful,

"You think if they're cooking the books, they'll do that?"

"Well, if they don't want us to see the evidence, then they'll either flatly refuse to furnish us with the information, or they'll make up some cock and bull about not having the authority to hand over the info without the President or VP giving them the green light. In which case, you tell 'em that the President of the Mother Chapter is requesting the information. And that if they *still* can't let us have it, we'll bloody come down there and get it." Prez growled.

"Diplomacy at its finest Prez." Muttered BS.

Oz looked crestfallen, "I was kinda hoping to ride out to Kirriemuir Boss."

"It's okay Prez, I'll make the calls. 'Sides, I could use an excuse not to kill myself out there in the pissing rain." BS growled.

"And here's me thinking it was a ready-made excuse not to fall off your 'bike 'cause you're still pissed! An act of unparalleled generosity to another brother BS!" Prez grinned.

"What, not getting myself killed?" the triumvirate erupted in laughter. BS surprising himself that he could summon such a function, when just breathing had required a Herculean effort moments ago.

"Okay that's sorted then. Put the word out to anyone from the Mother Chapter that there'll be an Unkindness at nine o'clock tonight and it's important that they attend. They can all get shitfaced afterwards, but I'd like a sober table if we're discussing the fate of another chapter and Brother's patches." Prez looked at his two companions with an expression of resignation,

"I hope we're just getting paranoid in our old age and that this is just going to be a case of no case to answer…………………………" his voice tailed off as he stood up.

"Yeah, I wish that was the bloody case." BS murmured as he looked at Prez and Oz. Oz nodded and shrugged.

Prez stood and surveyed the scene, then cupped his hands to his mouth, bellowing out his message,

"Saddle up for Bon Scott you tossers, we leave in twenty minutes! If you're too pissed to ride, don't! All members of my Chapter to attend an Unkindness tonight in the McAlpine suite at nine sharp." There was a collective groan from certain areas of the room which didn't go unnoticed by Prez,

"Don't worry, it'll be short, but probably not sweet, then you can all go back to getting drunk and getting laid. But I need you all ready, willing and able at nine. Now let's go see Bon!" The final sentence was greeted with cheering and the banging of fists on tables as Oz, Prez and BS left the room. *Short and DEFINITELY not sweet.* Prez ruminated to himself.

The small procession of motorcycles filed in to the large car park on the outskirts of the little town of Kirriemuir. The low rumble sounded as though a new storm was heading the town's way to replace the downpour that had soaked the area previously. Thankfully however, the weather had taken a turn for the better. Naturally the riders were still wet from the surface water thrown up along the journey. They'd been spared the indignity of a drenching though, which was more than they had expected following the early morning downpour. Now the sky was a clear blue and the day was becoming sharp and crisp, it was going to be a cold one.

Prez dismounted and removed his helmet as Oz did likewise. Irish Kev was alongside Prez and threw his arms wide after dismounting from his Triumph. "President Vince!" the two men hugged and shook hands,

"How long brother?" Kev queried, his breath cloudy in the old air,

"Still the same nine inches!" Prez replied with no hint of irony,

"Still the same lying limey bastard!" Kev replied as both men hugged again, laughing. Oz joined in with a hug for Kev and the three of them walked over to the Bon Scott statue which was surrounded by a wrought iron fence, with an opening so that the statue was accessible.

"You two wanna make like tourists, whilst I snap the pair of yers?" Kev spoke as he produced his mobile phone.

"David Bailey rides again!" Oz joked as he and Prez stood either side of the statue with their arms folded.

"Jesus, you look like a pair of bookends!" Kev laughed as he took a couple of photographs. Only members of the Mother Chapter who had been there in the early days could get away with such irreverent behaviour to two of the Unholy Trinity in public. It wasn't that the club was controlled by fear, it was just that a healthy respect for the club's elders ensured discipline and continuity within the group.

The three bikers walked up the hill in to the small town as the rest of them took more photographs of the statue.

"Still with Nessa chief?" Kev asked Prez.

"Yep, job for life Brother."

"It's a labour of love!" Oz laughed.

"You?" Prez looked enquiringly at Kev,

"Ah, well, you know I always had a thing for a girl with a Geordie accent..."

"So you ditched the missus then?" asked Oz, eyebrows arched in surprise, he knew Kev's old lady wasn't a Geordie,

"Hell no, I'm still with Herself, it's just that I'm looking for a bird with a Geordie accent tonight and thought you two might know of one.... or two!" The trio laughed and backslapped each other,

"One or two, like you're not boasting there then?" Oz cackled

"Fucking Irish bastard hasn't changed a bit!" Prez chuckled.

"Would you have me any other way brother?" Kev held his arms wide apart,

"Wouldn't *have* you any bloody way mate! Not with the price of bloody antibiotics these days!" Prez sneered playfully.

"Gents, the boozer awaits........." Oz stood at the doorway of a small pub gesticulating that they enter. "After you, me beauties......"

Two hours later and after chewing the fat for a couple of rounds of drinks, time demanded that the members present wound up the proceedings to return to the hotel. Besides, they couldn't imbibe too much. Not a good public relations exercise to get done for drunk driving when you're on a charity run. Besides Prez had called an Unkindness for nine o'clock and he wanted everyone at the table to be sharp and focussed.

"So what do y'think Kev, should we go with the old "Message in a bottle" routine?" Oz raised his eyebrows questioningly as he sank another pint of beer. The group had been discussing how to deal with the drug dealers that were operating from a rented house close to Oz's home. Kev looked at Prez and then back to Oz,

"Can't see the problem brother. Bastards sound like they need movin' on."

"Spot on bro." Prez finished his JD and coke," So we'll be dropping in an early Christmas present for those bastards. C'mon lads, drink up and we'll head back to base. I want to see if there's any more news about Weasel and company."

Kev shook his head disbelievingly as he placed his empty glass on the table,

"Bloody shame though boys, say what you like about 'im, he could make a guitar sing could that lad."

S.O.S.

Prez shook his head as he rose from his chair and picked up his helmet,

"Don't think he could tell you what day it is any more, let alone make anything sing son."

The group trooped out to their bikes in sombre mood, a cluster of other bikers following them out. The skies above glowered as if reflecting the mood of the men in leather. Prez felt a pang of unease in his stomach as he fired up *Landwaster*. *This will not be a good meeting, it's a gut instinct. It's never good when you're deciding the fate of a brother. Internal club matters are always the worst to deal with. There are always friendships that are damaged and the whole infrastructure of the club takes a hit when a brother falls from grace. But hey, there's no way around it. Every challenge overcome strengthens the club and what it stands for. At least, that's supposed to be how it works.* Prez frowned as he led the pack back to the hotel, his thoughts racing. *Problem is, with no new blood in years, members are leaving the club like rats leaving a sinking ship. The last thing we need for morale is for members to be expelled. Now we have a founder, Weasel and his best buddy Pretty Boy getting the push. I just hope that BS got in touch with the London Chapter and sorted out some information we can use. Makes you wonder what happens to us as we get older. Values change I guess. Can't all be as constant as some of us I reckon. Still, members know the score when they sign up and founders like Weasel certainly know there's help available from the Mother Chapter should things go belly up. Whether they choose to ask for help is down to them. We're not bloody psychic and can't tell what's going on in the*

Smoke if no one tells us. Something tells me this is going to be a long evening....................................

Prez glanced in to his mirrors to see the small pack following. The sight was not inspiring. Despite earlier indications the rain was falling again, and the machines were throwing up plumes of water from the road. The riders' pallor as grey as the Scottish sky, their demeanour grim with many hung over. *Christ it looks for all the world like Napoleons retreat from Russia. What a bloody joyous occasion!* Clenching his teeth, he surveyed the road ahead and with a twist his wrist unleashed the sixteen hundred C.C. growling beneath him. *Let's sort this bloody mess out.*

Brotherly Love

Prez surveyed the conference room as he paced the floor. It was well lit, as was to be expected of such a facility. The tables were arranged with one chair at the head and a number of seats down either flank. Mounted on the wall behind the head of the table was the banner of the club. Predominantly red with the black triskelion of ravens at its centre and the letters S.O.S. emblazoned on the black top rocker and the word "England" likewise featured on the bottom rocker. *Nice touch that.* Prez smiled to himself. *BS always has an eye for the dramatic.* The brightness of the room and its functional air was about as far away from the medieval inspiration for the usual setting of an Unkindness that Prez could imagine. Nevertheless, some heads could well roll tonight, at least, in the metaphorical sense. A knock at the door interrupted Prez's observations.

"Yeah, come in."

BS walked in wearing jeans and a t shirt beneath a denim jacket and naturally, his colours. Prez was bedecked in similar fashion, bar the denim jacket. He smiled at his Vice President.

"Good job with the banner mate." He jerked his thumb over his shoulder indicating the club standard.

"Cheers Boss." The smile quickly faded from BS's face as he sat down at the left-hand side of the head of the table, as befitting his rank.

"'Fraid I've only got more crap news though."

"Why am I not surprised?" Prez sighed and took his place at the head of the table, "Go on then," he glanced at his watch, "We've got fifteen minutes before the rest arrive, so you can give it to me straight."

"Well, there doesn't appear to be a London Chapter anymore." There was a deafening silence as BS let the news settle in to his Presidents consciousness. Surprisingly Prez sat calmly, stroking his moustache as he digested the information. *So it begins.*

"And what about the dues they've been paying?" Prez looked at BS questioningly.

"All fake accounting Prez. I've had Oz look at the stuff when he got back from the Bon Scott Run. It's creative accounting but he pulled it apart in minutes, you know what he's like, dog with a bone and all that."

Prez frowned, "I wouldn't've thought those two would be capable of putting together a set of fake accounts, would you?"

"Probably got someone else to do it." BS shrugged. Prez rolled his eyes to the ceiling,

"Christ, they've put us in a bloody position, haven't they? What about the property down there? The garages and clubhouse?"

"Looks like they've flogged the lot Boss." BS puffed out his cheeks.

"Flogged the lot……………………………Bloody hell, what the fuck did they think they were doing?" Prez looked imploringly at BS.

"To be honest Prez, I don't think there was much thinking going on. Drugs, that's the bloody problem. The state they were in the other night, I reckon they'd have sold their mothers for the next hit."

Prez nodded as he stood up to get a beaker of water from the dispenser on the other side of the room. *Bloody drugs and money the two most destructive forces in western society. Strike that, in all societies.*

"You want a drink mate?"

"Yeah, water is about all I do want to drink after last night!" BS grinned in a vain attempt to lighten the atmosphere. Prez plonked himself down at his place at the head of the table and handed BS a beaker of Adam's Ale, lifting his own in salutation.

"Skol brother."

BS lifted his beaker in reply. Prez looked hard at his Vice President,

"So what d'you reckon mate? Out in bad standing? I can't see any other way."

BS sipped his water and shook his head,

"Neither can I Vince, it's a bad one. Lying to the club is one thing, but stealing, that's a whole different ball game."

"There'll be no way they'll be able to pay us back either, stupid bastards." Prez checked his anger. He was annoyed that Weasel hadn't come to the club, to him, they were founders, brothers, the whole idea of brotherhood was support. *Support through trust. Now there was no trust, so the support would be gone. Stupid, stupid, lads. That's what you get for taking drugs as a mistress, she is totally uncaring. Problem is, now these idiots would find that the S.O.S. is totally unforgiving. This is not going to end well. The club is, to a degree, a democracy and there would be voices at the table who do not have the deep ties with Weasel that BS and I have. These brothers will only see that the club has been deceived and cheated and, rightly, they will demand their pound of flesh.*

BS looked across with concern etched upon his face,

"I know what you're thinking, man. We've got to do some damage limitation for these guys."

"Damage? I think we'll be looking at bloody carnage BS. We can't look the other way. If the laws don't apply to everyone, then they're not laws at all. We'd be as corrupt as mainstream society if we pulled a flanker to protect our mates. Just 'cause Weasel is a founder and was once with the band, we can't treat him any differently, can we? What sort of message would that send? If we sanction this lunacy we might as well call the whole thing quits. They knew what we stood for when they signed up. For Christ's sake, Weasel was there when we drew up the bloody constitution. I'm not having this club destroyed by an idiot who doesn't give a shit about anything except where his next fix is coming from."

BS shook his head,

"Yeah, I get it Prez, but we're talking about Weasel here, you know he's always been a flake........................"

"That's not going to wash with the guys is it? Yeah, he's a founder, yeah, he was in *Hanoi Jane*, yeah, maybe without him we wouldn't be around as a club. But you could say that about you, or me. You can't rip off money from people. He's lied to us and he's stolen from us and we're supposed to be his brothers for fuck's sake!"

The air hung like a silent shroud around the two bikers as Prez realised he had raised his voice to just below shouting level. They were between a rock and a hard place and both knew it. Neither wanted their old friend to be harmed, yet they knew that crimes had been committed and that, quite rightly, a price would have to be paid.

A soft tapping came from the door and Prez turned in his chair, glancing at his watch as he did so. *Five to nine, let's get started then.....................................*

"Yeah, come on in."

Oz was first through the door carrying files and paperwork. Behind him came the towering figure of Bear, who placed himself at Prez's right, the position held by Sergeant at Arms. Oz smiled weakly as he took his seat,

"Alright guys? I've brought what paperwork I could pull together, guess BS has filled you in Prez?"

Prez forced a resigned smile back at Oz. *It wasn't Oz's fault, I just wish he wasn't so bloody good at his job!*

"Good work mate. Yeah, BS has filled me in and I'll do the same for the rest of 'em once we're underway."

Prez could sense the feeling of despair from Oz and strode over to him, placing a reassuring hand on the Treasurer's shoulder,

"You did well brother. Nothing of this reflects badly on you bro."

"Cheers Prez." Oz nodded as Prez returned to his chair.

Another knock on the door announced the arrival of the remaining members who would be attending the Unkindness. They took their places at the table grim faced, the rumour mill having already been at work.

Prez surveyed the table. BS, Oz, Boalie on his left and Bear, Greg The Vet, and Dazzler on his right. Prez thumped the table with a closed fist.

"Alright gentlemen. No doubt many of you know why we're here. Normally I'd be letting Oz tell you how much the run has made and how much we've raised for charity. Well, we made over three thousand pounds, so that should make us look like heroes to the Wirral public for at least five minutes." Prez's caustic wit was greeted by murmurs and nods of agreement. "But that's not the issue today, as I'm sure you know. The issue is that our London Chapter no longer exists." Prez let the information sink in. There was no sharp intake of breath, bad news had travelled fast. "It appears, and Oz has the proof," Oz waved the files he had brought in as Prez spoke, "that our assets down south have been sold and that the two culprits are Weasel and Pretty Boy John." There was an uncomfortable silence punctuated by the sound of bikers shifting uncomfortably in their chairs. Some exchanged glances of disbelief, whilst others nodded sagely. "You can have a look at the books, Oz has made notes in red in the margins to explain what's fiction and what isn't. I'll give you time to look at 'em all and then we'll have to come to a decision."

Dazzler, the pocket rocket gym bunny who was one of the less established recruits, only joining a few years ago raised his hand,

"So, if it's as you say, what are our options?" He asked, flexing his biceps as he did so.

"Well, it'll be for this Unkindness to decide whether the pair have a case to answer or not. Then we'll have to bring 'em to a hearing to have their say and present a defence." Prez looked over at Bear who shrugged his massive shoulders,

"They've checked out Prez. Just gone. Looks like they drove here, no one saw them on 'bikes." Bear rumbled. Prez nodded and addressed the assembly again,

"It was my intention to have them here, to defend themselves, but as you've just heard they've split."

"Probably got wind of what was happening" Boalie retorted in his strong scouse accent.

"Probably........." Prez mused. *I just hope one of the softer hearted members who may feel loyalty to these idiots didn't tip them the wink. I know that BS had the chance to tip them off whilst I was on the Bon Scott Run........... Hold up, I'm doing just what I hoped wouldn't happen, I'm letting these scum bags sow mistrust in the ranks. They probably couldn't score anymore dope and scarpered.* Prez put the thought to the back of his mind and turned to Boalie,

"Probably couldn't get hold of anything they fancied in the drug department and high tailed it out of Dodge."

There was a rumble of agreement from the assembled throng. The paperwork had made its way halfway around the table now and Prez could see from the expressions on the faces of those who had studied it that it was not going to be a happy outcome for Weasel and Pretty Boy.

By the time the paperwork reached Bear he passed it straight back to Prez without even looking at it.

"Don't want to take a butchers?" Prez queried.

"Oz has told me what's in it, I trust my brother. I just want these bastards to pay for stealing our money and destroying our club."

Prez nodded,

"I can understand that."

BS raised his hand and Prez acknowledged him.

"I did talk to a couple of ex members from London on the 'phone. Apparently, it all folded six months ago, drug gangs forced the club out, it got too hot for the folks down there. They ended up dealing with a bloody cartel, we're not built to take that sort of heat. That's where the property went, to pay off drug debts. The crew down there thought we'd been kept in the loop. They all handed in their patches and thought it was all above board and sanctioned by us, as Mother Chapter."

Dazzle puffed out his cheeks.

"So, the buggers have fooled everyone then. C'mon Prez what are we going to do?"

Prez looked at BS who had a look of resignation on his face,

"Well, we could have a vote regarding a trial in absentia."

"Seconded!" Bear leapt in before Prez could continue. Prez then looked around the table,

" Okay then, all those in favour of trying Jimi The Weasel and Pretty Boy John in absentia?" *I'm, not sure this is right, but what they did wasn't right either. We can't waste time scouring the country for these junkies, we need to sort this out now.* Prez thought to himself as he looked at the man to his right.

"Aye."

Said Bear, as they knew he would. Next to him sat Greg The Vet, a man of average height and thickening waist, yet he was a decorated hero of Afghanistan. A helpful soul who always wanted to do the right thing. He played the scenario through his head for what seemed like an eternity before looking at Prez and giving his reply,

"Yeah. I can't see any way 'round it."

Next was Dazzler the gym bunny, in his case it was cut and dried,

"Yay."

Prez's gaze crossed the table to Boalie who was equally forthright,

"Yeah, they've scarpered knowing the score boys."

Oz was next, and he was possibly the most thoughtful and sensitive of the assembled throng. He'd had plenty of time to perform his soul searching as the creeping death had approached him round the table.

"You're all right. I just don't think we should excommunicate anyone without giving them a chance to put their case....................."

Prez and the others looked hard at Oz, Prez spoke as president and chair,

"It's a yes or no Treasurer, it's not a debate now, it's yes or no."

Oz fidgeted with his pen and then came to a decision,

"Okay, it's err, yes then. But under protest."

Prez turned to the man on his left, his Vice President BS,

"I'm with Oz, I don't like it, but I don't like what they've done to us, so it's a yes from me."

Prez felt the whole room relax. *Thank Christ for that. So now we don't have to go looking for these traitors, we can just judge them here and now. They forfeited the right to be heard when they slipped away, knowing what was coming.*

"Okay then, that's carried. I would rather these bastards were here to account for their misdeeds, but they're not. You've all seen the paperwork where it is obvious and indisputable that these two have misrepresented the club, sold club properties and lied to club members. They have disgraced themselves and by doing so they have disgraced our club. Does anyone have anything to say in defence of these two club members?"

BS raised his hand,

>"Jimi has always been a strong supporter of the club and he did a good job back in the day setting up London chapter"

Bear butted in,

>"Yeah and now he's destroyed it. The S.O.S. isn't here for personal gain, we're not the bloody Freemasons."

BS continued, his tone betraying the fact that he was losing the argument and knew it,

>"Like I say, he was there from the beginning, he was a founder. I never had much time for Pretty Boy John, but Jimi sponsored him, and we patched him in. We all knew there was an issue with substances with the pair of them."

Oz nodded in agreement,

>"Yeah, maybe we should've done more to help............"

Prez stroked his moustache *Nobody wants to see brothers, especially founders thrown under the bus. But we're a club based on laws and our own morality. To look the other way because a popular founder member has done the wrong thing would be wrong in itself.*

S.O.S.

"We all know what we signed up to. I'd expect the same treatment if I stole from the club. The laws must be sacrosanct or me might as well pack up and throw everything we've built over the last thirty odd years away. I know some of you feel bonds of loyalty to these guys. Especially to Weasel, but if we let either of them dodge a bullet for this, then it'll spread like wildfire that the club can be used for personal gain without any retribution. We've all made personal sacrifices that the ordinary Joe on the street would never do, to keep this club and its ideals alive. To live on the outside, on the periphery if you will, of mainstream society. To build a better way, a way where our people don't backstab and cheat and sell each other out to get to where they want to go. We've made sacrifices to prove we're better people in a world that will suck you dry of your honesty, your integrity and anything else which makes you a good person, just so you can pass go and collect two hundred pounds."

Prez paused for effect then raised the tempo further,

"It's a choice we all made, a choice to be better people, in a better society, where standing for something means sacrifice. Where integrity is the key, where brotherhood isn't just a name but a bond. Stronger than money, stronger than religion, stronger than life itself. We parade our belief, it's sewn on our backs, tattooed on our skin. We advertise ourselves because we believe we're better than the rest, because we believe in a life of honour."

Prez took the tone back down, knowing he could now commit the coup de grace,

"Now is the time for us as brothers to realise our values, no longer a concept, not just a mindlessly insulting two fingers to society. Now we must stand up and punish our own, for their indiscretions, selfishness and above all, betrayal of the cause. Freedom is not given, but won, trust is not given, it's earned and when in mainstream society there's no justice, there's just us."

Prez had concluded using the club motto, "No Justice, Just Us." Silence enveloped the room. Suddenly Bear started smacking the table with the palm of his hand, others took up the applause and for a couple of minutes the whole room filled with the thunder of palm on table, with the odd shout of approval thrown in. Finally, the applause subsided, all eyes were on Prez. He stretched out his arms with upturned palms,

"It's down to you Brothers, anyone else got anything to say?"

The silence was total, not in a suffocating way now, just a barren emptiness where previously there had been uncertainty. Prez looked to Bear,

"Let's vote this. All those who feel that Jimi The Weasel and Pretty Boy John are guilty of stealing from the S.O.S., guilty of lying to the S.O.S. and guilty of besmirching our ideals and reputation, say aye."

Bear raised his hand,

S.O.S.

"Aye."

Greg The Vet followed suit,

"Yay."

Dazzler likewise,

"Aye."

Boalie shook his head,

"Yes, they're bloody idiots."

Oz looked at Prez with rheumy eyes,

"Yep Boss."

And finally, BS, whom along with Prez had played beside Jimi in *Hanoi Jane*, the band that had made the S.O.S. possible, raised his hand,

"I can't believe I'm doing this, but the sad fact is, they've brought this on themselves boys. Aye."

Prez spanned the table his face set in a grim expression,

"We all know there are two ways to do this. Obviously, they're out in Bad Standing, we've just voted that. Now we have to decide whether it's going to be fire or knife." *The two ways to remove the club tattoo. It can either be burned out or cut out. The most humane way is to obliterate it by burning, however, it's a club call.* Prez grimaced as he once again turned to his left to take the vote from the Unkindness,

"Bear?"

"Cut 'em." Bear stared in to the distance as he spoke.

"Burn." Greg The Vet sighed, Dazzler nodding as he stared at the table,

"Yeah, burn them."

"Burnin's too good, cut the bastards." Boalie spat with venom.

All eyes turned to Oz, the conscience of the group, who turned his hands up showing his palms in resignation,

"Christ, it's like the bloody dark ages, is this what we're offering boys?" the silence was deafening,

"Okay, okay, burn them." All eyes turned to BS

"Yeah, they knew the gig when they took it, and when they took our money, burn 'em."

Prez surveyed the table, well aware that he had bucked protocol by going to the table before announcing his own preference,

"Like Oz, I've got reservations, but as BS says, we all know what we signed up to and I've already made one Churchillian speech tonight, so yeah, it's a burn for the two of 'em. Bear, can you arrange it and keep me in the loop?" Prez raised his eyebrows at the big Sergeant at Arms who nodded sombrely.

"We get back home Prez, I'll track 'em down and sort it."

"We'll need officers present, so either BS, Oz, me plus yourself need to be there, you know the drill."

These events are not for the squeamish. Fortunately, they don't happen very often. The last one was years ago, a member called JJ, who brought dishonour upon the club. He also had his tattoo removed via the burning principle, using a domestic iron works. I believe he can use his right arm nowadays, just can't ride a 'bike anymore. Prez thought.

Bear nodded to his President who concluded the Unkindness,

"Any other business boys?" the silence was that of the grave as Prez banged his hand down on the table to denote the close of proceedings.

Christmas Greetings

Vanessa placed the final length of tinsel across the frame of the mirror in the hall and stepped back to admire her handiwork. As she did so the phone rang, her shoulders fell, her expectation being that Edna was ringing again.

"Hello, who's calling?"

"Hi Nessa, it's DJ, can I talk to Vince please." The voice was not quite its usual plummy self, there was something about it that Nessa couldn't quite put her finger on. Something different. She'd always disliked DJ, or Nigel as she had known him for years, pre the S.O.S. She always felt he was a philanderer and drew Vince into his intrigues regarding the fair sex.

"Sure Nigel, just hang on a mo." Nessa put her hand over the receiver and called up the stairs to Vince who was working on the computer in the spare room,

"Vince, it's Nigel"

Tremendous! These bloody accounts were beginning to give me a blinding headache. Besides which, after all that's gone on over the last few months I could do with a bloody good session! Thank God for Nige and our Yuletide libations, don't know where I'd be without him! Prez grinned to himself as he leapt up from his chair and bounded down the stairs. The look Nessa gave him as she handed him the receiver was as frosty as the weather outside. Winter had arrived at last and Prez welcomed it. A time to put *Landwaster* in to hibernation, stock up and indeed, take stock, although he admitted stock taking was the very thing he'd just been cursing himself for doing. The irony was not lost on him.

"Nige, when did you get in matey?"

"Been back a couple of days old chum. Are we good for a few at the Jug and Bottle tonight?"

"Yeah, about seven thirty is good for me, how about you?"

"Let's make it eight, I'll pick you up in Maters car and then we can walk from her place if you're good with that?"

"Excellent mate. You can fill me in on your latest conquests"! Prez chuckled,

"See you in a few then."

Prez replaced the receiver and padded in to the living room where Nessa was scanning her mobile 'phone.

"Guess what kid, I'm out on the town!"

Nessa looked up, her face bordering on disinterest and stern disapproval,

"Well, I'd been expecting it, just don't get too plastered." Her voice as icy as the air outside.

"I'll just have a quick shower and he'll be here for eight."

"What do you want for tea then?"

Prez shrugged, "I'll just have some toast thanks"

"You can't go drinking on toast"

Here it comes, she won't have a row about drinking with Nige, but she'll find another way of making it into an unpleasant confrontational situation. Why do folk have to be like that? It's not as if the pair of us don't deserve some downtime after the pressure we've been under. Nessa goes out on about four different "do's" over Christmas, and I only go out with Nige. I only see him twice a year if that. And he is my oldest mate! Known him since the days of Calday Grange Grammar School. That place was the pits. It was trapped in Tom Browns bloody schooldays. Even in the seventies the prefects wore flowing gowns, any friend of Batman...............I'm certain the film "If" with Malcolm McDowell, was modelled on Calday School, it had to be! Weird thing was that years later it turned out that Weasels mother married the Deputy Head, strange world. Being a teenager in the late seventies meant that you wore a three-

piece suit and went to discos. Nige and I used to frequent Tiffany's in Chester (it's now a load of private apartments!), thought we were quite the thing. Mind you Nige had always thought that about himself. He actually liked the rubbish that pumped out of the speakers, Kool and The Gang, Chic, Michael Jackson, Earth Wind and Fire, Candi Statton, Gloria Gaynor, I hated all that stuff. Occasionally a decent tune would chart, and the DJ might play "I Surrender" by Rainbow, or a personal fave of mine "5705" by City Boy (whatever happened to them?) but that was as rare as hen's teeth. As a rule, it had to be black and it had to be funky, yeah, right. Tiffany's was, a white and relatively affluent crowd..........but on a Thursday night it was the new Studio 54, blacker than Harlem, on the turntable and tougher than the Bronx (in attitude!). Or so we all thought! Until the lights came on and we trudged back to whoever was unlucky enough to be driving the car.

"Well, what do you want for tea?" Nessa's barbed enquiry snapped Prez back to the here and now.

"Christ, I'll have whatever you're having kiddo"

Nessa looked at him thoughtfully a slight pout playing around her lips,

"Well, I *was* going to ask you to go to the chippy.." her voice tailed off. Prez could feel his anger rising, he knew she had had no intention of doing that, it was just another ploy for a row.

"Well, if that's what you want."

Nessa looked at Prez, furrowed brow and narrowed eyes,

"No, I can see you don't want to, it doesn't matter.

"Nessa, c'mon, if that's what you want-"

"No. I'm not hungry now. You go and have your shower and I'll do you some toast." With a toss of her red hair she returned to her mobile 'phone as if dismissing a lackey. Prez was fuming, but was smart enough to know that to continue the conversation would be to escalate the situation to a falling out of possibly biblical proportions. The very last thing he needed before heading out for a night on the drink. He turned on his heel and bounded back up the stairs to have his shower and lay out his clothes for the evening's revelries.

Prez always found himself contemplative whilst in the shower. As the water fell and he shampooed his hair his mind drifted to previous nights out with DJ and he found himself chuckling at some of the laughs they had enjoyed. DJ had been instrumental in setting up the Hong Kong chapter of the S.O.S. the power of his personality being such that the chapter folded when he moved to New York. Prez had always wanted to visit the New York Chapter, but things always seemed to get in the way. He'd always kept in close contact with DJ, either via snail mail in the days before the internet, or later via e mail. He regarded DJ as his oldest and closest confidant, something he knew always riled Nessa.

Give Nessa her due though, she'd agreed that DJ should be our son Eddie's Godfather. That was a bit of a surprise. Not as surprising as DJ turning the idea down though. I guess he was right to be honest, since he was never in the country, how could he vow to look after a nipper should anything untoward happen to Nessa or me? Still, it was a bit of a slap in the face at the time. To be honest it showed the class of BS as a person and as a friend that he happily stepped in to the role as Godfather. Prez thought.

Towelling himself down as he walked in to the bedroom he smiled to himself at the clothing arrayed on the bed. Predictable to put it mildly. Black denim jeans, black t shirt, silver rings and bike chain bracelet and at the foot of the bed were his trusty black cowboy boots. Prez grunted as the towel he was drying himself with caught on his silver amulet of Odin riding Sleipnir hanging round his neck. He'd never worked out what the damned towel actually caught on. Nessa had argued with him on more than one occasion, telling him to stop showering wearing his Motorhead ring, as "it pulled the towels". Prez answered back with the fact that he never wore rings in the shower, so the towels being pulled wasn't that. *One of those really annoying times in life when you sincerely tell someone something, someone who should believe you, because they trust you, and what you're saying is true, yet they just bloody well don't believe you!*

 Showered and dressed Prez took a deep breath as he entered the front room. Nessa was bringing in two plates of toast and handed one to him.

"Thanks Babe." Prez smiled in an attempt to calm the atmosphere.

"I s'pose you'll be in bed most of tomorrow?" was the curt response.

"If you play your cards right!" Prez cackled, still attempting to lift the atmosphere.

"Well, I've 'phoned my sister and we're going to Ikea in the morning, so I'll be gone when you get up."

"Hey, that's a bit unfair. The last few times I've been on the lash, I've been fine the next day. Okay, maybe not up to running a marathon, but certainly lucid and able to walk and talk!" Prez countered.

"I s'pose so. Anyway, eat your toast, he'll be here in fifteen minutes." Nessa had calmed down a smidgen.

"Hey, you know Nige, he'll be here when he's here. Always fashionably late!"

"Oh yes," Nessa looked thoughtfully at Prez, "I know Nige........................"

True to form at eight fifteen there was a knock at the door. Prez bounded from his chair in the living room and let his friend in. He was surprised to note that DJ had grown his hair to shoulder length, which was only shocking because he was a creature of fashion and long hair for men went out with the ark. Indeed, Prez liked to joke that it was the last taboo. He also looked tanned and younger, plus he had a pair of stud earrings, reminding Prez of Lewis Hamilton.

"Hi Nessa, are you alright?" came DJ's familiar plummy upper-class tones as he warmed himself on the radiator.

Nessa beamed at him, "Hi Nige, how was your flight? How's your Mum?"

"She's good, I still can't get over how frail she is every time I come back. She's like the incredible shrinking woman. In good spirits though, thanks. How's young Eddie?"

"Oh, he's at university, didn't Vince tell you?"

"Oh yes, sorry, I've got a head like a sieve lately!" DJ smiled back.

Prez was eager to get him out of the house and in to the pub, so that DJ could relate his latest tales and of course, give an informal update on the New York Chapter of the club. He scooped up his leather jacket and kissed Nessa on the point of the nose,

"See you later babe, don't wait up." Nessa smiled back, with no hint of animosity,

"Have a good time you two, nice to see you Nige."

"You too Nessa, don't worry, I'll look after him!" Prez snorted at that remark.

Two miles later and DJ had parked the car at his mothers' large house in Lower Heswall. It had a tremendous view of the river Dee and Wales across from it. The old saying was that if you could see Wales from there it was going to rain and if you couldn't see Wales, it was raining already. The property was probably worth around a million pounds, maybe more. DJ had a sister, so one day the whole pile would come to the pair of them. As DJ and Prez marched up the hill to the local hostelry, the Jug and Bottle, Prez couldn't help chuckling to himself.

"What's up Vince?" DJ asked as the wind gusted something akin to rain, but colder, in to their faces,

"Just thinking, do you purposefully keep that brown leather jacket at your mums for these nights at the Jug?" For as long as Prez could remember when he and DJ went drinking at Yule, DJ wore the same leather bomber jacket.

"Funnily enough, I do!" Both men laughed at the thought of it and both felt a warm glow as they pushed open the door to the tavern.

"What are you having mate, usual?" asked Prez as he leant on the bar,

"Err, no, I'll have a glass of red please." Answered DJ,

"Hey, I'll join you then! Sick of getting hairs on your chest with spirits?" Prez grinned,

"Yeah, trying to become more refined!" DJ chuckled.

The first couple of hours flowed freely, with both men reminiscing about the past and DJ regaling Prez with his previous exploits, which Prez always enjoyed hearing about. DJ had been through some dark times too. He had confided in Prez regarding a Chinese girl he was going to ask to marry him whilst in Hong Kong, but it hadn't worked out. Indeed, at one point she had threatened suicide. Prez had recommended he give her a wide berth. *Although I never did find out exactly what the problem was between them. It was something intimate, but DJ never got exactly to the point.* Prez thought as he waved another ten-pound note at the barmaid. By now the pair had started purchasing bottles of red wine rather than glasses, saved time and money. It was well after ten o' clock now and as with such events talk was turning to more serious matters, the previous banter serving as a superfluous precursor to more personal and pressing matters.

"So, how's your Mum doing?" DJ asked as he sipped his wine,

"Not good mate. Every night it's 'phone call after 'phone call. I've got a doctor coming out to see her, but it took me over a month to organise that. She thinks that her neighbours are spying on her. Bloody hell, a couple of months ago she went to the coppers in Heswall thinking they were going to use a truth drug on her to find out where she'd buried the bodies of kids that she'd murdered."

"Bloody hell, when did all this start?" DJs eyes were round like saucers. Mrs Sinclair had always been looked up to by both of them as a highly intelligent and articulate woman. Her own brothers had always said that she went to London a Scouser and come back a snob. Meaning that she (unlike them) no longer had a trace of a Liverpudlian accent, whilst they had retained theirs like a badge of honour. Prez's mum had married a Londoner and had done well for herself, despite her husband being injured in World War Two (contracting TB and losing a lung, this would come back to haunt him as a heavy smoker, in later life resulting in an untimely death at sixty-two years of age). He was a professional, a printer as were all his male line (in later years Prez traced this as far back as the seventeen hundreds). It was good money and a respected trade. They relocated to The Wirral two years after Prez was born, it often amused members of the S.O.S. when Prez would come out with the language of the East End in an unguarded moment, talking about the "currant bun" or his "mince pies", a translator was called for on more than one occasion at an Unkindness. Through all his fathers' health issues his mother had supported the family with part time work and towards the end his father had been a shadow of his former self. Quick to anger and without the strength or inclination to tinker with his pride and joy, his car in the garage, he was eaten away with emphysema and became a bitter and unapproachable man, cheated from enjoying life to the full, through having served his country. To exacerbate the family's loss, Prez's mother then had to take the Government to court to win a war widows pension, since they denied her husband had passed away due to injuries sustained in the war. Thankfully the British Legion had helped fund her case and at the end of the day justice was done. Not without leaving a nasty aftertaste with Prez as to what the government thought of those who laid down their lives to serve. Both Prez and DJ had strong matriarchs and were both fiercely proud of their mothers, DJ had been brought up without a father and Prez had never wanted to ask the situation, it wasn't his place.

"When I look back, it could have started months before we realised it." Prez stared in to his wine glass, he would find no answers there. Suddenly the lively intoxicating atmosphere had dissipated, and the heavy burden of responsibility descend upon his shoulders once again,

"You don't even notice this stuff, you know? When you look back you think, why didn't I notice this earlier, but you just don't. As you know, me and Nessa visit Mum every Sunday, it's one of the reasons we moved closer after Dad passed away. Well, she started moaning about the neighbours, some Asian family had moved in next door, renting the place. My Mum had lived in Heswall for over forty years, hardly a hot bed of multiculturalism, so we figured she was just a bit set in her ways. She'd described the old guy of the family standing outside with his strange robes, I s'pose it is a culture shock if you've barely seen these cultures except in documentaries on television. I know it's easy to scoff, but many people of that generation, especially if they don't move around the country, don't see a black face, and certainly don't think of these characters as English. Well, they're not English, are they? That's because

English is classed as an ethnic group in the National Census, as it should be. British maybe, as members of the Empire as was. Point is, to my Mum they were strangers with strange customs, clothes, whatever, and we just thought she was unnerved by them. We just told her to ignore them and get on with her life." Prez shook his head and placed his hand to his moustache, a sure sign that the emotion of the moment was manifesting itself. Not being given to displays of emotion, it was obvious that this was difficult for him. DJ placed a hand on his shoulder, "You okay mate? I know you two, you'd do all you could"

"Yeah, I know, you just feel that if I'd spotted things earlier.........."

"But you only see the signs if you're looking for them Vince, don't bloody torture yourself over this."

Prez poured them both two more glasses from the bottle on the bar and nodded,

"It just went downhill from there. She started 'phoning us to ask me to visit and there were cars parked outside the house that she thought were spying on her, then when I'd get there, there'd be no cars. I'd have a cup of tea and a chat and then return home and the 'phone would go again, and it'd be Mum telling me the cars were back. I'd go back, and yup, no cars. Then we had the scenario with the television, she couldn't remember how to work it. So, I'd go round, write down which channel was which, show her how to use it, then come home. Only for her to ring again asking how to work it. She would be 'phoning, literally every five or ten minutes. Sometimes we had to take the 'phone off the hook. Obviously, by now we knew something was amiss, but it was only when she started saying that both her neighbours and the police were watching her that we twigged. That was it, that was the stone-cold moment that you come out of denial and you realise that there's a problem that you can't deal with yourself. Your family, that has never asked for help from anyone, suddenly implodes and you have to deal with *The system."*

DJ puffed out his cheeks, "Bloody hell, makes my news pale by comparison really."

Prez snapped out of self-pity mode immediately,

"What's the news, you okay?"

"Yeah, I'm just walking from my radio job. Bit of a lack of confidence really, not sure I'm doing the right thing."

"You, lack of confidence? We're talking DJ here, yeah?" Prez spread his arms with upturned palms in mock surprise, "C'mon man, you're the most confident, talented guy I know. You can sell oil to the bloody Arabs. Suave, sophisticated, I know you don't think much of the new James Bond, but if there was ever a role model or an example of art imitating life then you and Jimmy B are right up there! The globetrotting celeb, who's got a licence to scuba! Held by the Chinese militia when visiting foreign chicks, interviewing the stars on radio, voicing commercials in the States, hot and cold running babes, c'mon, how can *you* be having a crisis of confidence?"

DJ started wrapping his long hair round his fingers in a show of nervousness that Prez hadn't seen before, a quirk he was sure he would have noticed over the years. Needless to say, DJ had never had shoulder length hair before, so maybe that was why he had never displayed the trait before. Nevertheless, there was a strange vibe emanating from his body language that Prez couldn't read, something different. *Maybe it's all this shit with Mum, maybe it's all the alcohol, maybe I'm just bloody losing it myself! There's definitely something amiss here...............*Prez thought as he gulped another mouthful of red wine down before reiterating his praise for his friend,

"You've never been backward in coming forward mate, c'mon, you're fishing here, right? You *know* you're talented! You were the one who got you where you are, no one else. Drive, talent and determination. Guys I know would give their eye teeth to be in your position, so what's the problem? Girls?"

"No, it's not women, nothing happening on that front......................." DJ looked down at his glass, his voice trailing off.

"You told me this in your last e mail, all about music and bloody football. When did you get so interested in the Premier League? You know the only reason we do these Christmas, sorry, Yule sessions, is so that you can give me the, err, ins and outs of your latest lady friend!" Prez chuckled at his own clumsy innuendo, a sure sign that the wine was having an effect." What's going on with you man? You haven't got one pregnant, have you?"

"Nah it's nothing mate, a personal thing."

Prez was tempted to push the issue, but decided against it. *If he's having a crisis of confidence, a good bollocking isn't going to help. Maybe it's something medical, maybe he's reached the male menopause and has to take handfuls of Viagra!* Despite himself Prez found himself smiling at the thought of the stud that was DJ eating Viagra like Smarties.

"What's so funny Vince?" DJ surveyed him with rheumy eyes, himself becoming the worse for wear from the volume of alcohol.

"Sod, it, cheer up, what can be so bad? How's the Chapter running?"

DJ poured the remnants from the bottle in to Prez's glass and shook his head,

"There is no Chapter."

Prez looked up sharply,

"What?"

"There is no Chapter, I dissolved it a couple of months back. I would've told you, but I'd rather do it face to face, so I am." DJ looked at the bar as he dropped the bombshell.

"What about the members?"

"There haven't been any members for about eighteen months Vince."

This is crazy, you don't just dissolve an S.O.S. chapter, it's a convoluted process of decision making and selling or transferring of club assets. It's all got to be voted on by the members. What the Hell has been going on in New York? Prez could feel his anger rising, fuelled by the wine.

"They all sort of drifted away, either to other clubs or out of the life altogether." DJ was still avoiding eye contact and shaking his head.

"Christ, what about the dues? You've been filing accounts, Oz has been scrutinising them, how was all that done?"

"Don't worry, it's all above board, I've paid everything off. I was paying the subs and the dues for a while" DJ murmured.

"What, out of your own bloody pocket?" Prez snorted.

"Yeah, Mum helped out."

Prez was incensed now,

"Your Mum! Fuckin' hell, why get her involved? If things were going tits up, the club could've helped! Screw it, I could've helped! Is this why your e mails have been full of trivial bullshit like football, instead of club stuff?" Prez fought to keep a lid on his emotions but was inwardly still reeling. *How could DJ not have trusted the club to help him? Why had he not trusted ME to help him for God's sake. I know his Mum is well off, but we don't run to our Mums when the going gets tough any more. We're there for THEM now. What the bloody hell was he thinking? None of this makes any sense, it's like I'm talking to a different person, not the DJ I know. My Mum, the NY Chapter, the drink, it's all too much.* Prez's head was spinning in a million conflicted directions.

"Last orders please!" came the call from the bar. Prez looked at DJ who had drained his glass,

"You want another?"

DJ shook his head. Prez could feel his anger subside, replaced with utter confusion. Scooping up his glass he drained the remnants within.

"C'mon then, let's get going."

The pair pulled on their leather jackets and walked to the door. Upon opening it they were greeted with something akin to a minor blizzard. The roads and pavements were white, and the wind was combined with a blustery snow. Somehow it lightened the mood,

"Christ, what's been going on for the last few hours?" cried Prez

"Where are the huskies Vince?" railed DJ. Ramming their hands in pockets the pair trudged towards Heswall centre. DJ didn't have to walk half of the way with Prez, as it would have been closer for him to just return to his mothers' house. It was a sort of tradition that he walked half of the way to Prez's home though, and to his credit, he wasn't going to allow a little thing like a snowstorm distract him. Besides, if Prez thought this was a storm, he should see the weather that DJ had to put up with in New York. Probably one of the many reasons why New Yorkers were so uptight. Prez looked across to his friend as they marched through the bleak conditions, just in time to see him perch a red woollen bobble hat on his head at a jaunty angle.

"What the fuck's *that*?" Prez said laughing and getting a mouthful of snow for his pains.

"First thing I could get hold of. It was on the forecast this might be coming." DJ called over.

"Well you look a right twat in it!" Prez laughed, at which DJ shrugged his shoulders. Not far to go now until they reached the point that DJ turned back.

"Christ, it's a good job the welders only have half a job to do with me!" Prez joked. He had required an orchidectomy some years ago to prevent cancer spreading from his right testicle. He had asked DJ, who was in the country at the time to drive him to the Oncology unit at Clatterbridge Hospital, rather than have Nessa take him. He didn't want to show weakness and have her worried for him. As it transpired he showed no weakness or trepidation anyway, although he had been terrified at the thought of surgery.

DJ called over, "You can have one of mine if you like, I don't need either of them!"

Prez looked across laughing, only to see DJ staring at him stony faced. They both stopped walking.

"What are you talking about?" Prez wasn't sure whether he was too drunk to understand a joke or too drunk to understand anything. DJ moved closer,

"I won't be needing them anymore. I'm having transgender surgery."

"What the hell are you on about?" Prez was teetering on the edge of reason now.

"The surgery Mum paid for in Bangkok-"

"I thought that was just a face lift, you being a vain bastard" Prez cut in.

"It was, but it was the start of it. I've met people in New York who I hang with. That's why I never wanted you to come over. That's why the Chapter folded."

"Who are these people you've met? What crap have they been poisoning you with? Who knows you better than me? How can you want to become a woman in your fifties, what the fuck is wrong with you?"

"I've been seeing a shrink for years, I just know it's the right thing Vince. Look, it's a lot to take in, I'll give you a bell before I go back to the States." DJ held his arms open and the pair hugged

"Okay, I'll see you in the week. If people can't handle what you're doing, fuck 'em!" Prez mumbled. The alcohol and shock and stress had all kicked in now, he turned and stumbled back towards home. In shock and mental torture, his mind had closed down any rational processes and all he was left to cling to was his affection for his oldest friend. There was no rhyme or reason to any of this, nothing made sense anymore. His mother descending in to madness, his best friend announcing his decision to become a woman, the club losing chapters and in turmoil, his mind fuelled with alcohol decided to just shut down and tacitly accept what DJ was doing, even though it was obvious to Prez that it was horribly wrong.

Once home Prez quickly discarded his wet clothes and slipped in to the pyjamas that Vanessa had left out for him. He cleaned his teeth and slipped in to bed beside his wife, who stirred,

"You okay? What a horrible night." She murmured sleepily.

"Yeah, you don't know the half of it." The tone in Prez's voice was enough for Nessa to immediately realise something was amiss. Years ago,

S.O.S.

Prez could be driven to anger with too much drink but he had been a changed man since the birth of Eddie, twenty years ago now. Alcohol no longer had the power to drive him to anger. Yet the tone in his voice recalled the days when it could, immediately setting off alarm bells for Nessa. Prez lay on his back staring at the ceiling, Nessa propped on her left arm looking at him through the darkness.

"You're not going to bloody believe this kid." Prez sounded lost, bewildered

"Try me."

Prez related the whole thing to his wife who was as dumbstruck as her husband. She had never liked DJ, but she knew that Prez held him in the highest esteem, both as a person and a friend. Nessa also knew Prez's views transgender. Basically, what people did behind closed doors as consenting adults was nobody's business but their own. However, Prez drew the line at aggressive, militant groups who weaponise gender for their cause and the promotion of such ideology by the establishment. The idea that the liberal establishment sold, that anyone who thought transgender transitioning was wrong was a bigot, made Prez sick to his guts. He felt the whole notion that sex is just a recreational pursuit and gender a social construct (when in fact it is biologically determined by chromosomes), not for the procreation of children angered him immensely. He never expected any of the club to have the same views, but many did. There were no club rules discriminating against such people, they were just never attracted to the life. Prez believed that the establishment, which was riddled with those of strange practices had made it fashionable. Anyone who did not agree with the establishment view was to be labelled and marginalised. Prez stared up at the ceiling as Nessa tried to return to sleep. His mind racing with thought.

Transgender. The latest cause celebre in high society, with celebrity endorsement from upon high. We've got to the stage where five-year-old children in the UK who want to dress up as girls are now considered transgender, by their parents! Does anyone remember tom boys? Were they really women who were frustrated men? Poor George of the Famous Five books by Enid Blyton, she'd be the first pumped full of hormones and re-educated! She obviously should be a man! Just because we have the medical science at our disposal to remove and add hormones and organs, should we be? There's a guy in the US (where else) who is tattooed from head to toe, has had fake long whiskers attached to his face and his teeth filed to points, does that make him a cat? He thinks so! It's maddening. Because we can medically alter people, should we? If the science wasn't there, we'd be calling these people mad! Instead of curing cancers we're giving people a medical wish list as to what they want to be. DJ could never be a friend now, not because I'm a bigot, because I'm not, but one has to put friendship under the microscope and evaluate it. What is it? Well, I offer that it's a mixture of things. It's shared experience, it's agreement on certain basic principles. It's a similar outlook and viewpoint and it's trust. The more invested in these facets the deeper the friendship. I abhor the term "bromance" (another bastardisation of our Anglo-Saxon language to suit the licentious would be modernisers) as there's no need to sexualize everything. Men can be great friends, brothers in The Life, but that does not suggest homosexuality.DJ, Nige, has lost my respect. He lost my trust by destroying the New York Chapter behind my back. He lost my friendship as his values are no longer my values and through his decision to change his life, literally, he cut me from the loop. The media and so called "progressives" (another bastardization, that implies that every "change" is positive) would have you believe that transgender folk are brave and courageous to take the decisions regarding surgery etc. Personally, I find the surgery required to change gender mortifying. Yet there is a craze in the US, some are actually addicted to surgery, some people actually want to be operated upon, again, again and again. Does that make them courageous? Does that make them brave? Should they be admired? So why when someone changes gender, especially as in DJ's case, in his fifties, after years of chasing ladies, does that make him brave? Doesn't it suggest, in all honesty, that there is a mental issue that needs addressing? To want so badly to be something you're not, which can be arranged by the exchange of large amounts of cash, the overriding motivation for encouraging this is clear, the usual culprit, money. If you want something badly enough, if you've got the spending power and if the upper echelons of the establishment give you their blessing, someone's on to a winner. Someone's making a lot of money out of my ex best friend and he's too stupid or more likely, ill, to see it. He's seen a shrink, who knows him better than me? My advice would have cost him nothing! You want to know who the brave people in this situation are? The folk these transgender people leave behind. Their past friends left with the memories of a life before Nigel was Nigella. Of times which can never return and are now buried as if they never happened. Forty years of memories eradicated on the treatment table for a significant amount more than thirteen pieces of silver. What of Nige's Mum? Losing a son and gaining a daughter. If she concedes defeat and embraces him as a her, what is she really thinking? What sort of man would put his elderly mother through such a thing? Not the Nigel I knew.

Eight o'clock in the morning and the telephone rang. Prez, who had slept fitfully rolled from his bed and stumbled down the stairs to answer.

"Hello?"

"Vincent," it was Edna," You need to come quickly, the police are here!" she was agitated, on the verge of panic,

"Are they in the house Mum?"

"You need to come here quickly Vincent!"

"Okay, I'm on my way."

Prez put down the receiver and quickly made his way back to the bedroom and started getting dressed. Vanessa propped herself up on one arm, her red hair tumbling over her shoulders, her eyes half closed,

"Mum?" she queried in a way that meant she knew the answer,

S.O.S.

"Yeah, the police again she reckons."

"I didn't tell you last night, for obvious reasons, but she 'phoned about ten times last night."

"Why, what happened?" Prez sounded concerned as he slipped a t shirt over his head.

"Same as now, the police outside."

Prez sat on the bed pulling his boots on. He looked at Nessa over his shoulder, some of the urgency draining away,

"Sounds like you had a busy night too. Let me guess, you went 'round and no Plod?"

Nessa let out a sigh and slipped out of bed to don a dressing gown,

"'Fraid that's exactly it Vin. I went over there, and nothing was happening."

Prez's shoulders slumped.

"I've made that appointment with her GP, it's the only way that we can get her referred for psychiatric help. It's not until Friday though,-" before Prez could finish his sentence the telephone rang.

"Leave it Vin." Nessa implored as Prez hurried down the stairs.

"Hello?"

"Vincent, are you coming or not?" Edna now sounded angry.

"Mum, I've just got dressed, I'm coming now."

Edna slammed down the receiver.

Nessa padded down the stairs and put her hand on Prez's shoulder.

"D'you want a drink before you go?"

"What and get another half dozen bloody 'phone calls before it's cool enough to drink?" Prez snapped, then immediately wished he hadn't, "Sorry kid, Christ, I'll have all the tea I need in fifteen minutes." He attempted a smile, but no one was convinced of the hilarity of the situation.

As Prez backed the car from the drive Nessa stood in the doorway to wave him off. The telephone started to ring again.

Pulling in to his mother's drive Prez could see, that as usual there were no cars, police or otherwise in the proximity. He sighed to himself. *I hope the bloody Doctor can find something concrete we can address on Friday. Knowing them it'll probably be blood and water tests and "leave it with us for a week". Reading up stuff on the internet, it could be anything from a water infection to other more horrible things, that I don't even want to think about. It was bad enough getting the appointment for Mum without her knowing, the old phrase "stab in the back" springs to mind.*

S.O.S.

You can know that you're doing the right thing on a rational level, but it still feels like betrayal to me. Guess it's the way I'm wired.

Edna opened the front door before Prez reached it. She glanced around furtively as she let him in.

"Where are the police Mum?" Prez had a tired and disbelieving note to his voice that he hadn't intended. What with the revelations from Nigel, the alcohol, the lack of sleep, the internal issues within the S.O.S. he just found it impossible to keep up a front.

Edna turned on him,

"If you don't believe me, why did you bother coming here at all?" she hissed, eyes staring from behind her spectacles. After being initially shocked by this behaviour a couple of months ago Prez found it disturbing that he was now half expecting such a virulent reaction from his mother. Prior to that time, he had never seen her shout since he had been an adult. Not at anyone about anything, how quickly all that had changed. Prez shrugged as they walked to the kitchen for the perfunctory cup of tea,

"I'm just asking where the police are Mum. That's why I'm here isn't it? Because you think they've come for you?" Prez tried to sound as supportive as possible.

"They *were* here, if you'd got here quicker you'd have seen them parked outside, watching me, just like the neighbours next door." Edna's voice rose and fell, from accusatory to the tones of a hurt disbelieved child. One moment all accusations and thunder, the next a pitiful waif looking for protection. These were sides of her personality that Prez had never seen. Edna had always been in control and prided herself on her independence. Now she was a shadow of that woman, crying out for help which never seemed to allay the fears she had. Fears which Prez was now almost certain had nothing to do with reality. That was what scared him the most. Physical illness can be fought, mental illness? He wasn't sure that he was up to fighting that. Not that he didn't have the will to fight, he would have to learn the techniques in how to combat this new most supercilious and covert of illnesses, if indeed it was a mental issue. Time after time Prez and Nessa had discussed what the problem could be, they were running through DADA. Prez was still partially in the denial stage although he was certainly angry too. Nessa had been able to step back, and she offered more than just support. She had seen with more clarity than Prez that the issue was out of their hands and would have to involve the medical profession. Prez didn't like that. Like his mother, he believed in dealing with issues in house, like the Club. Outside the parameters of everyday life, asking for no help from anyone. However, even Prez now conceded that something had to be done. Continually running back and forth to his mother's was resolving nothing. Indeed, it was feeding her fears and helping to make the apparently delusional scenario she was creating ever more real. That was why Prez had visited the doctor's surgery and implored the GP to make an appointment for his mother. The GP had told him that it could be a water infection, backing up Prez's internet research. But the GP had also warned that it could be something much more serious, possibly dementia.

"Sit down and I'll make you a cuppa." Edna spoke in her usual composed way, as if the last few minutes hadn't happened.

"Okay, thanks." Prez took his usual window seat in the front room.

Minutes later Edna brought him his tea and then went upstairs. Prez gazed out of the window.

I remember living on the other side of the road, four bungalows down. Where Mum's house is now, used to be all derelict, right up to the railway line that runs at the back of her garden. Rumour was that the builders of the upper middle-class estate had run out of money and never finished it. Certainly, many years later the land was sold enabling the likes of Mr Dory to build his detached property next door to Mum's current property. Then we moved to a smaller bungalow in Heswall, I was in my twenties then. I never understood why Mum moved back to Sandham Grove after Dad passed away. Maybe for the happy memories. I always had pretty fond memories of the bungalow in Sandham. Great times playing with Action Men as a child, they never let you down! Or the times before going nightclubbing, when I would play air guitar in my bedroom that was illuminated by the streetlight outside. Psyching myself up for a night on the town to the likes of "Bat Out of Hell", yes, I've actually got an original vinyl copy from way back when. Happier times, more innocent times.

Prez was suddenly snapped from his reverie as he heard a loud thump from the floor above him, Edna's bedroom.

"Mum?" Prez stood up and called again, "Mum, are you okay?" Again, there was silence. Prez quickly ran up the stairs and in to the bedroom. He was horrified to find Edna unconscious on the floor, a pool of black vomit at her side. He quickly looked around to see if she had tripped over anything, but it was clear she had collapsed and not fallen. Prez grabbed a pillow from the bed and placed Edna's head on it. She was breathing but still not conscious. Prez checked her airways to ensure she wouldn't choke then hurriedly ran downstairs to the telephone and dialled for an ambulance.

The ambulance pulled away with Nessa riding with Edna. Prez had decided to follow them in the car. Nessa had arrived before the ambulance via taxi, since Prez had 'phoned her the minute after hanging up from the 999 call. Once inside Arrowe Park Hospital's A&E Department Edna was whisked away, still unconscious, whilst Prez and Nessa were left to sit consoling each other in a waiting area. After what seemed an age a doctor finally appeared.

Bloody hell, he only looks about twelve, I thought it was the policeman who started getting younger as you got older! Prez thought.

"What's the news Doc?" he queried.

"It looks like your mother has had a fall." The young doctor replied.

"What about the bruising on top of her head? I don't think she fell, my husband said she didn't fall" implored Nessa, who had had time in the ambulance to notice what looked like bruising on Edna's head. Prez hadn't spotted it in the turmoil to get the ambulance and the shock of the event.

"Just the result of the fall, nothing to worry about."

"What about the vomit Doc?"

"Probably just shock."

Prez inwardly smiled grimly. *I don't think they've got a clue what it is. I know Mum didn't trip or fall. There's more to this than they're letting on.* Prez and Nessa exchanged glances and they both knew they were thinking exactly the same.

"She's stable now, you can go in and see her. We'll be transferring her to a ward later." With that the doctor, who had now gathered a small entourage of even younger nurses around him, swished off to his next emergency in a flurry of green coat. A single ward sister ushered Prez and Nessa to Edna's bed, pulling back the curtain so that they could enter its proximity. Prez had slowly got used to seeing changes in his mothers' appearance over the last few weeks, but nothing prepared him for the sight of her lying unconscious with tubes protruding from her arms and nose. Her hair flattened on to her scalp being thin and white, he could clearly see the bruising Nessa had asked about. To the untrained eye it certainly looked bad. All purple and angry. Nessa held his arm and whispered,

"I've been doing some research on the internet," she waved her mobile phone, which she had been using whilst they had been in the waiting area, "this all looks like a stroke to me. The bleeding on the scalp, the vomit, the whole thing."

Prez looked hard at her, then turned to the sister,

"Has she had a stroke Sister?"

The matron looked quizzical, "Is that what Doctor Rogers said?"

"No but-"

"Then she hasn't had a stroke." The matron butted in sharply, "A fall we think. Not uncommon for this age group. I shouldn't worry, she'll be fine. We've got her sedated, then we'll put her on pain killers and move her in to another ward, away from A&E."

The reassurances did nothing to ease Prez and Nessa's concerns.

S.O.S.

Message In A bottle

Prez rubbed his hands together and blew on them despite wearing gloves, his breath pluming out in the cold night air. No colours tonight, just black jeans a black bomber jacket, black gloves and a black woolly hat. Christmas was pretty much over now and he had enjoyed having Eddie back from University. They both enjoyed talking politics whilst Nessa made herself scarce in the kitchen. She had never been a political beast. Prez gazed down the road and gently stamped his feet as he stood at the bus stop, looking for all the world like he was waiting for a bus.

What a year it's been, Mum falling ill, Jimi being excommunicated from the club and to top it all DJ "coming out". Bloody hell, talk about an "Annus Horriblus"! Still, at least we can do our bit to redress the balance tonight and strike a blow for decent folk. Prez smiled to himself at the very thought he'd just had, *Of course "Decent folk" wouldn't be doing what we're about to do, but they won't mind guys like us doing it for 'em. It's all a bit like the hired gunslingers who ride in to town to clear out the gangsters. All well and good to the townsfolk when you're standing up for them, not so good when you've served your purpose as useful idiots and they then want you to get the hell out of town. It was always thus. There are those who are prepared to get their hands dirty and there are those who aren't. I used to have some sympathy with the police's position regarding vigilantes, that was before we started allowing all sorts of illegal practices to go on, in the name of social cohesion. Female Genital Mutilation for example, sure, there's a law against it but to date, despite thousands of cases being reported there hasn't been one prosecution! Sharia law, where a woman is worth half a man! Perhaps worst of all, halal meat. What's the point in having an animal welfare act when if you are of a certain religious persuasion that act doesn't apply to you? Does the beast being slaughtered feel better knowing a holy man is about to slit its throat? Yeah, I'm sure it does, no need to stun the animal then! Where are the RSPCA on all of this? Silent that's where! Just like the feminists regarding grooming gangs, where are the feminists marching against the grooming gangs? Incidentally, I object to the term "grooming". It normalises the acts of abuse and rape. You groom a dog not a person. It's just crazy. Couple all of that with police cuts and you have a country where people don't feel safe anymore, despite the fact that we're the most "watched" nation on Earth. More CCTV cameras than anywhere else. It makes you wonder how anyone can actually commit a crime and NOT get caught! The drug dealers seem to manage to get away with it though. But not tonight, that's why I'm here.* Prez glanced at his watch, twelve P.M. *Boys should be here any minute.*

Prez looked up to see a large yellow and green vehicle coming down the road. The bus stop was about a hundred yards from a T junction. The target property was situated on the junction, with two sides of the property facing the two roads. Prez was on the main road, the front door of the property was situated on the smaller turn off. Spotting the vehicle Prez started walking towards the junction. A wry smile played about his lips as he realised the vehicle was an ambulance. *Surely, they haven't got their hands on a bloody blood wagon!* He thought to himself. As the ambulance drew closer the headlights flashed and Prez knew then, if he had actually had any doubts that, yes, the boys had actually brought a bona fide ambulance to the proceedings. Spotting that the ambulance was indicating to turn right in to the road Prez crossed the main road so that he would be outside the house being used by the dealers. The lights were off, and it was reasonable to suspect that the occupiers of the rented property had gone to bed. Local residents had had the place under surveillance for months and had sent their findings to the police, who predictably had done nothing. So, they had forwarded their information to Oz, who lived locally, in the hope that by some festive miracle, something could be done.

The ambulance pulled up beside Prez and the back doors burst open. Bear grinned at Prez as he quickly handed him a plastic bin bag,

"You got the envelope?" Prez enquired.

"Yup." Bear replied as he jumped down on to the pavement. Both men scurried to the front door, glancing down the road and spotting that there was no traffic about. Bear swiftly posted the envelope he was carrying though the letter box. Whilst he was doing that, Prez pulled a soaking rag from the bin bag Bear had handed him. Being careful not to get drenched in the petrol that soaked the rags, Prez placed a third of the rag in to the letter box. As he did so Bear laid a box of matches at the foot of the door. As one they both turned and jumped back in to the ambulance. At the shutting of the rear door the vehicle lurched forward, sirens blazing as it shot off down the road.

"How did we do?" Prez called to BS who was at the wheel.

"Like clockwork Prez, no one about, all we have to do is get this baby back to the hospital vehicle maintenance pool and then off to bed!" BS called over his shoulder. Prez looked across to Bear who was looking inordinately pleased with himself,

"Go on then, tell me how the hell you managed to get hold of this thing." Prez waved his arms to encapsulate the ambulance they travelled in.

"Well, Troll reckoned he could release a vehicle that was signed in for some minor repairs and that on a night like tonight, no one would miss it. So why not?"

Bear working at the hospital often came in handy. It was sheer coincidence that he had met Troll there. Troll actually attended the same primary school as me, he'd always been a loner in to bikes. He'd tried to join the club but had found the commitment and our ideals too much. He'd settled

on being a friend of the club. He was always dominated by his father, although the old boy must be around ninety by now! Still, Troll was useful to know. Despite not being a risk taker, he was a good mechanic and often serviced the bikes of club members. Him working at the NHS vehicle maintenance depot and what with Bear working in the hospital itself, the two had struck up a friendship that is, how shall I put it, beneficial to the club. As for his nickname, that came about after one of his marathon moaning sessions when one of the Brothers told him to get back under the bridge and scare goats! His physical appearance, short of stature, premature baldness and a face like a, well, like a troll, also helped!

After about twenty minutes BS killed the blues and twos making it easier for Prez to speak and be heard, "Good work Bear. I can't even smell bloody petrol in here." Bear nodded,

"Cheers Prez. What did you put in the letter?"

"Fuck off back to Huyton you drug dealing scum, or next time we light the rag." Prez grinned.

"Marvellous!" Bear grinned back, not a sight that was seen on a regular basis.

So, there you go, message in a bottle, signed, sealed and delivered. What about the bottle? Well, we decided not to go full bore and lob a Molotov Cocktail at the place, it is Yule after all. Maybe if the scumbags don't get the message, we'll re-evaluate the situation. Time will tell.

After about fifteen minutes BS called out again, "This is you Prez."

Prez stood up unsteadily as the ambulance turned a corner. He made his way to the front of the vehicle and put his hand on the driver's shoulder, "Well done, take it easy on the way back. Good work."

"No worries Boss, have a good one." BS replied as the ambulance slowed to a stop. Prez slapped Bears arm as he passed him on the way to the rear doors which he yanked open,

"Excellent stuff Sarge, pass on my regards to Troll, tell him to drop by the clubhouse and there's a couple of beers in it for him." Bear nodded and gave a thumbs up. Prez jumped from the ambulance and secured the rear doors, watching as it pulled away, half expecting BS to fire up the blues and twos again, just for the hell of it. It was about a twenty-minute walk to home and Prez savoured the cold air that filled his lungs as he walked up the hill. Nobody appeared out for an early morning stroll. Most had drunk and eaten their fill over the days of Christmas Day and Boxing Day and were probably sleeping it off before the next Bacchanalian extravaganza that would be programmed in to their lives by the controlling media, New Year.

It would be easy for some sanctimonious individuals to sit in judgement of what we've just done. Some lawyer would make money out of it and a judge would sit in judgement after being in his or her closeted, protected world, straight from their Ivory Towers to condemn our actions. But what we did tonight wasn't to advance our cause as a club. Nor was it to enhance our personal reputations. It was certainly in no way going to increase anyone's bank balance. In fact, there was a huge risk involved of incarceration should we have been caught. There was even a slight chance of a physical altercation, had we been challenged by the criminals on their home turf. All this had been skilfully avoided. So, does that make us heroes? Well, Hell I guess it does. However, rather like comic book heroes such as Batman, we'll never receive or be able to accept the thanks and gratitude of the local people that we've helped. A few knowing individuals who passed the information to Oz will know the truth and in time, when the furore has passed, perhaps more will come to know of our influence in removing the cancer of drugs from the area. We didn't do it for plaudits. We performed, what I would call, our civic duty. We exist outside mainstream society, but we have a vision of a better society. What sort of hypocrites would we be, if we stood by and let the society we are currently living beside, be dragged down by criminal elements? To allow children to be made slaves to addiction by scum who respect nothing but money? Our children are our future and whilst I would never preach to anyone about the use of drugs, I would point out the type of folk that profit from it and what they do with that money. How it all ends up in the hands of criminals who in turn use it to fund modern day slavery and people trafficking. How one can easily become an addict and as such all your values, your world view and indeed your personal self-worth, become as nothing in the all-pervading search for the next fix. Life, it's all about choices isn't it? But you can only make choices that count if you've got a clear head. That's why you've got a brain in the first place, to make a choice. Naturally some folk will always choose a path of self-destruction, that's their right I suppose. Expecting others to pick up the pieces and nurture them so that they can go on and on relying on others to support them, no matter how foolish, selfish and stupid they may be. That is one of mainstream society's problems. It panders to the weak, it continually "turns the other cheek", it almost rewards the victim and allows them to wallow in their own self-pity, rather than get up and face their demons. "That which does not destroy us makes us stronger" is a maxim I have adhered to all my life, it's a tough phrase to live up to, but it can be done. Especially if you surround yourself with like-minded folk who will not suffer fools gladly. Support is always there in the club, but it is not unconditional. For all that the media portrays us as "outlaws", "sworn to fun loyal to none", "barbarians on wheels" and other clichés, they don't realise that we encapsulate all that was once good in society. The ridiculous way that Christianity has been used since the twentieth century to represent an "all things to all men (and women)" mentality. The cringing attitude where if you're an indigenous citizen of the United Kingdom you must respect everyone else's points of view that comes to settle amongst you. Indeed, not just respect their religions and beliefs, actually alter or destroy your own age-old laws and customs to accommodate these beliefs! Ridiculous. Religion itself makes me laugh. How can you have a religion that truly "tolerates "another religion? By the very definition of a religion, you believe yours is right, so somebody worshipping something else, MUST be wrong! Yet the craven Church of England wants to accept everybody else as having a right to be offended by everything we say! Once again, the cringing craven cowardice that the liberal establishment has instilled in to this great nation is evident. Then we have the "great and the good" pontificating upon what actually are British values nowadays. It's rather like rock'n'roll, if you over analyse it, you're wasting your time. You see these Muppets hark back to when we were great, but then hate everything we ever accomplished that made us great. If we hadn't accomplished these things, then these navel gazers would never be in such a position. They'd be under the lash of a foreign power rather than thinking up new insulting ways to decry our indigenous peoples. Coming up with ridiculous phrases like "We're a nation of immigrants", gosh, I wonder how long it took some genius to come up with that one? I constantly hear talk of Islamophobia (another nice label to compartmentalise folk, just like "racist"), yet I never hear debates about why the Sunnis hate the Shias, or what the Salafists are doing. Islam is large and complex and very, very dangerous. These idiot politicians, whom after every terrorist attack in Europe squawk, "It won't change us, we won't let it!" then all hold hands and march down a street under the gaze of armed soldiers, knowing that the fact that a nation such as France is under a state of emergency for months on end and that in every major European city the police are armed. Which obviously proves it HAS changed us! Yet they persist with the lie that nothing will change us. We are becoming the places that these "migrants" are running from because they bring their mindset with them. Look at Sudan, it had a civil war between north and south. Eventually after years of suffering, drought, war and chaos South Sudan becomes a nation state in its own right. Six months later, guess what? Yep, South Sudan is having a civil war, kids are starving, etc, etc. When will we learn that these people MUST learn for themselves. Put down the weapons and pick up the plough. But they will never learn, they want to take not make. That's why economic migrants want to travel all through Europe to get to our little off shore island. Do they do it because they like the British? Because they like the weather? No, because they want what we have got. Make no mistake, many are prepared to lie and cheat and commit violence to come here. So why, when they achieve their intention of getting here, would they put away those tools that have worked so successfully for them? Do you think they will stop lying and cheating and committing acts of violence, when such tools have served them so well? I have nothing against genuine folk driven from their lands seeking help. I do have a problem with people who do not obey laws that state they can claim asylum at the first nation they arrive at, lying about their age or sexual orientation to gain admittance to Blighty or stowing away in articulated lorries, which could well lose the driver his livelihood, should they be discovered. Last time I looked there aren't many western nations at war, so why do these folk tramp through western Europe to get to us? Do you think our society that is policed by consent will be able to control such people? Look at Sweden, delightful, liberal Sweden, for years the jewel in the crown of the northern European states, now the rape capital of Europe!

Prez snapped from his musings as he realised he was home. Nessa had left the porch light on. Prez felt a warm glow to be back. Now he would settle for a nice cup of tea and perhaps a bacon sandwich to warm himself up.

S.O.S.

Stepping in to the living room Prez was surprised to see his wife sitting on the sofa, Star the cat on her lap. Nessa eyes were dark with smeared eyeliner and it was obvious that she had been crying. Prez quickly sat beside her and put his hand upon hers.

"What's going on Ness?" Nessa turned to him replying in a voice that sounded drained and flat,

"It's Mum Vince. I can't carry on with this. She needs medical help." Prez nodded and attempted to reassure her,

"I know that. C'mon I've got an appointment sorted at the medical centre with Dr Detlaff. That's in a week. Since Mum had her fall they gave me an earlier appointment. Now she's back out of hospital I'm assuming they don't want her back in any time soon!"

Nessa looked at him with hooded eyes,

"I can't take another week of this. She's been on the 'phone literally, every ten minutes. I've been 'round there five times in three hours. She's raving Vince. I've had to disconnect the 'phone to stop the calls. Thank God she hasn't got my mobile number."

Prez put his arm around Nessa's shoulder. An act that somehow increased the volume of Star's purring.

"Okay Babe, In the morning I'll ring the quack and see if I can get the appointment moved forward. I'll tell 'em it's urgent." Nessa nodded in agreement.

"Tell them they'll have another case on their hands if they don't deal with this soon!" Nessa smiled weakly.

"I'll make us a drink." Prez smiled and stood up, walking in to the kitchen.

The appointment with the quack is only the first step. Mum needs to see a G.P. so that he can then make a referral to a psychiatrist. Then Mum will be evaluated to see what is wrong with her and what sort of help is required. None of this is going to be pleasant or easy, for any of us. You would have thought that this could have been arranged whilst she was in hospital recovering from her fall. All they wanted to do was get her home after a couple of days to release the bed! There just didn't seem to be any joined up lines of communication between the arms of the NHS, from local G.P. to the hospital, to even different wards in the hospital, never mind departments. It seemed like organised chaos to me.

Prez returned with a coffee for Nessa and a tea for himself,

"Is Eddie asleep?" he enquired.

"Yeah," Nessa cupped the mug in her hands as Star jumped from her lap and wandered in to the kitchen via the dining room, "He was here for part of it though. He even came with me on the first two visits. Your

Mum is so much easier to deal with when Eddie's there. I can see the effort she's making to be "normal" around him. It's like she knows what is happening to her, but just can't control herself. When Eddie's there she is almost like her old self. When I went back the third time though, she was absolutely uncontrollable. Ranting on about murders, the police, the spies next door. She needs help Vince and she needs it now."

Prez sank down in to his arm chair, releasing a slow sigh as he did so,

"Like I said Ness, I'll 'phone the quack first thing and see if I can get the appointment moved forward. I think you're right about Eddie. She certainly acts differently when he's there with us. It must be awful to think that these things are happening, but you have to remain composed in front of your grandson. What the hell must be going on inside her bloody head?"

Nessa sipped her coffee and attempted to lighten the mood,

"How was your night? I thought you'd be home later."

"No probs with anything. Just a little club business me Bear and BS needed to handle."

Nessa knew better than to ask about the details. She knew that it was club policy not to discuss club business with non-members. It was an insurance policy, so that ignorance really is bliss. If you don't know what is going on you cannot be an accomplice or a witness or a source of information to a third party. Safety first towards loved ones was a priority to the club. Prez stood up, "I'll plug the 'phone back in, I'm sure mum will have gone to bed by now." Nessa nodded in agreement as Prez crossed the living room and out in to the hall to replug the telephone. He jumped back with a start as the machine started ringing as soon as he had reconnected it. *Bloody hell, surely it can't be Mum ringing now!*

"Hello?" Prez answered,

"Vincent, is that you?" Prez recognised the agitated tones of Mr Dory immediately.

"Hello, yes it's me, is that Mr Dory?" Prez enquired not liking the tone the man was using,

"Yes, it's me alright. What's going on with your mother Vincent? She's been 'round to our house saying she can't contact you. What is going on? My wife and I are sick and tired of these interruptions from your mother! What is going on and what are you doing about it?" Dory spat out the final sentence, taking Prez aback.

What a sanctimonious prat. To think that Mum was always the most helpful and pleasant person in that road, always looking after properties when folk went on their foreign holidays and cruises. At one point she went in and fed peoples pets! Now this toe rag is getting some unwanted attention from her because she looks to be losing it and all he can do is give me down the banks!

S.O.S.

"Yeah, sorry about that." Prez's voice was dripping with sarcasm and laced with menace, he wasn't sure how much of his glowering countenance was transmitted through his voice via the 'phone, enough to make Dory think twice hopefully.

"Mum's in a bad place at the moment, which, if you've listened to anything she's had to tell you, you'll have worked out by now. I've got everything under control and we're seeking medical advice. I can only apologise if you're finding the situation stressful." Prez paused for effect, "Being an intelligent man, you must realise how stressful all of this is for my wife and son."

"Well, err, yes." Dory stuttered out a reply before finding his metaphorical feet again and resuming his tirade, although not with the original aplomb, "Yes, it must be difficult. But you must appreciate that she's not our problem and we can't be having her coming 'round to us at all hours with these ridiculous stories regarding the police."

"Like I said, apologies. Trust me I'm doing my best. Goodnight." Prez slammed the receiver down as Nessa poked her head around the door, "Who was that?" she asked,

"Bloody Dory, what a shit of a man he is. Mum always thought the sun shone out of his arse! Does the idiot think I can just turn Mum on and off to suit him?" Prez shook his head and accompanied Nessa back in to the living room. Before they could sit down a voice called from the top of the stairs,

"Dad? Who was that Dad?" Eddie had been woken by the telephone and was at the top of the stairs calling down. Prez and Nessa had tried to protect him from the worst of Edna's outbursts and indeed Edna had managed to control herself with visible effort whenever Eddie had visited her with them. Eddie was no fool, however. Eventually Prez and Nessa had had to explain what they thought was happening with his grandmother. The fact that they thought she was suffering from some sort of mental illness. Whether that be Alzheimer's or something else. Prez went to the bottom of the stairs and looked up. Eddie was tall and slim with brown shoulder length hair, not unlike his father had looked at eighteen. *Only taller!* Prez observed.

"Just that idiot Dory moaning about Grandma going next door with her weird tales mate. Nothing to worry about. I told you I was getting her to see the quack soon, didn't I? You get back to bed, nothing anyone can do until the wheels of the NHS grind 'round."

"Jeez Dad, I thought Mr Dory liked Gran?" Eddie called down, confused,

"You'll find everyone *likes* you when they can use you mate. It's a sorry lesson in life, just make sure you choose your own mates wisely. Dory was always a chancer with a veneer of middle class respectability. Just a tosser, really. Do you want to come down and have a chat?" Prez replied. Eddie shrugged his shoulders,

"Nah, you two will want to talk, I'm going back to bed,' night."

S.O.S.

"'Night mate." Prez gave the thumbs up to Eddie who returned the salutation then turned away to go back to bed.

This has got to be the worst Christmas ever. Prez thought as he sat down to be reunited with his now luke warm beverage.

December the thirty first. Prez was not a huge fan of New Year. *Probably stemming from all those family New Year Eves spent watching Andy bloody Stewart in his kilt on BBC One. I don't hold anything against the guy (well you wouldn't want to with him wearing a kilt, would you?) but watching Mum have her one and only tipple of the year, port and lemon and Dad sat grumpily in his armchair, did nothing to mark the event as an occasion. No one ever came 'round and we never went anywhere. To be honest, the whole false bon homie of the event leaves me cold. However, I understand that the British and indeed, the whole of western society need an event at this time to prepare them for the forthcoming perils of, in our case, the long cold winter. Whilst, as I will continue to remind anyone listening the S.O.S. regard ourselves as "apart" from mainstream society, we still come from that society and we still have to rub along with it. We're not a religious sect, indeed we have differing religions and faiths within our ranks, from pagans to Christians to hardcore Liverpool Football Club fanatics! Some don't disclose their religion and the club is fine with that. All that we ask is that you stand beside your brothers, so if your faith isn't going to impinge on your duty to the club, it's not a problem. If it is, you'll probably never make it past the hang around or prospect stage and your sponsor might be looking to explain himself to Bear!*

Nevertheless, he realised it was a big deal for most folk. For a start in Merrie England it was still a Bank Holiday on the first of January, so plenty of time for recuperation before those members who were still wage slaves would have to return to the grind. BS and Prez were two fortunate members who no longer had to bow to mammon on a regular basis in the form of its own particular demand of worship, paid employment! Both had invested shrewdly with the money made from *Hanoi Jane* and anyway, BS's wife Kelly was a full-time teacher whilst Nessa worked part time, both from choice. Neither of them wished to be "kept women". Indeed, it was the fact that they were both strong and independently minded women that attracted their spouses to them. BS and Prez were still at a loss to see what the girls had ever seen in them. *Hey, rather gives the lie to the dumb biker bitch "property of" stereotype doesn't it?* Prez often amused himself with that thought.

Prez surveyed the clubhouse. Everyone had done a good job with balloons and paper chains, which Prez had insisted upon, as it got a whole group of hardcore bikers working together with coloured gummed paper, just to enhance their "rock'n'roll" credentials. *Anyone who thought being part of the S.O.S. was about downing a bottle of Jack Daniels, riding a chopper at a hundred miles an hour and slapping girls about would soon realise that the S.O.S. was not about machismo.* Prez chuckled to himself.

S.O.S.

To enhance his chuckle to a full-on laugh was not easily done, but Bear managed it as he swung precariously from a stepladder whilst attempting to affix a string of paper chains to a corner of the wall. His tongue sticking out between his teeth, in a mask of concentration. He may well have been considering an answer to a million-pound quiz question. As he managed to complete his task Prez burst in to applause much to the amusement to the assembled throng.

"Excellent work Brother!" he called out. Bear stepped down from the ladder a grim look of satisfaction on his face. Prez glanced at his watch. *Seven thirty. The others will start arriving soon. Not sure how long I'll stay this year. I'm feeling pretty knackered to be honest and I could do with an early one. Might be a good idea for Nessa to let her hair down with Kelly though. Nessa's got her own set of friends that I don't really mix with, but one S.O.S. event I know she enjoys is New Year. Pretty sure it's so she can see the decorations that Bear has put up!* As it was, Nessa would not be arriving until after eight o' clock, as she had family visits to make. She came from a large family and had five sisters and a brother to wish "Happy New Year" to, before she could relax and party with the club. She was close to her sisters, Prez was never sure whether that gave her inner strength or created inner conflict. Either way, he usually kept his distance. Attending the obligatory weddings and funerals, with due respect. Otherwise, he left the Chester based clan pretty much alone whilst respecting his wife's decisions regarding her ties to them and her perceived duties. The main door to the clubhouse banged shut downstairs and Prez could hear the raucous tones of Boalie announcing "Happy New Year" to all and sundry, albeit many hours too early. The little man, short of stature but great of girth bounded in to the room with the elegance of a space hopper, with a ruddy complexion to match, his bald pate gleaming.

"Happy New Year Prez! Happy New Year! Now, I'll have a gold watch if you don't mind young lady!" Boalie addressed one of the girls behind the bar that had been drafted in to help. Prez didn't know them all but he knew Bear would have vetted anyone allowed on to the premises. They were more than likely all girlfriends or wives of members.

"Boalmeister, good to see you. The Mrs not coming?" Prez enquired.

"No, we couldn't get a sitter for the nipper Prez, so it's just me. But never mind lad, I'm drinking for two!" Boalie cackled as he passed his already empty glass back to the girl behind the bar. Bear, who had finished his duties as chief decorator joined Prez and Boalie at the bar, indicating that he wished to be served a neat vodka,

"Good work with the deccies Bear." Enthused Boalie.

"Thanks Bro." Bear winked as he received his libation, "I fuckin' hate New Year." He added flatly.

Bear was always a paradox. Loyal, taciturn, yet intelligent and well read. The sort of, person who chose his words carefully but at the same time

S.O.S.

was quick to act when required. He may be thought of as a miserable bloke, but hey, if I was married to my sister Julie, then I'd be bloody miserable as well. Years ago, we were close, then she ditched her first husband and got pregnant by some idiot. An idiot, incidentally who swung yours truly around by the neck at the Stairways nightclub, before other S.O.S. members waded in to separate us! My Dad passed away after many years of illness after discovering that Julie was living just down the road at a static trailer park near to what is now the S.O.S. clubhouse. Mum and Dad had been worried sick, as they didn't know where she'd gone. He and Mum had lunch with me and Ness and talked about little else. The following morning Mum 'phoned to say he was dead. Rightly or wrongly I held Julie responsible for my Dad's passing at sixty-two, although he'd been ill for years. The fact that my Mum told me his last words were "She'll be the death of me." referring to Julie, may just have coloured my opinion. I didn't speak to Julie for ten long years, even though my Mum brought up Julie's son for long periods, whilst she returned to full time employment. In the end, under pressure from Mum, Nessa and the situation itself with Mum caring for Julie's son, I caved in and we became friends again. We could never recapture how close we had once been, but there was no longer any animosity between us. To be honest I was probably a fool to do what I did, although I was only twenty-five at the time, but hindsight is a wonderful thing, isn't it? Anyway, she moved on with her life, meeting and marrying Bear, who is a good lad.

Armed with a Bacardi and coke, Prez ventured through the house and out on to the patio where a large fire pit burned. BS's wife Kelly was holding a glass of wine staring in to the flames,

"Penny for 'em, Kel?" Prez enquired, sidling up to her.

"Hi Vince. I'm just thinking that's all. Come and sit with me." Kelly motioned to the bench near the fire pit. It was a cold evening but not wet so Prez sat beside her. The flames were painting her long blonde hair red.

"The Viking thing Vince, how'd you ever get in to that?" Kelly had obviously started celebrating early as it was one of those "meaning of life moments", although Prez was aware she was still a sharp as a tack,

"Christ Kel, doesn't *everyone* know that story?" Prez shrugged. Kelly pushed his shoulder with hers playfully,

"Go on, tell me, let me hear it from the horse's mouth!" she giggled.

"Horse? Your old man been bigging me up again?" Prez feigned shock as Kelly spluttered in to her wine glass,

"Okay, okay. Are you sitting comfortably? Then I'll begin. Way back when I was about five or six I went to Barnston Primary school, which unlike now, was then in Barnston. A couple of years later it relocated to Heswall. Anyway, it was a collection of old army style buildings. One day I was playing tick with a guy called Robert, can't for the life of me remember his last name though." Prez rubbed his chin trying to recapture the past, "He was older and taller than me and just as I was passing a doorway he jumped out yelling "Tick", problem was the finger he used to touch me went straight in to the old mince pie." Prez indicated his right eye.

"Ouch!" squirmed Kelly.

"Ouch was bloody right kid! So, after lunch I'm sitting at the back of the class blubbering, wiping all sorts of shit into my eye, what does the teacher do?"

"Enlighten me." Kelly was sitting forward now, a teacher herself she was keen to hear the tale.

"Told me not to be a cry baby! Can you imagine that now? Parents would sue the school and the education authority now!"

"Okay," Kelly pursed her lips thoughtfully, "So where's the Viking connection?"

"Well, I can't remember the time frame but not long after this episode, (where I was incidentally taken to hospital by Mum and Dad as I was screaming in pain when I got home, and the quack said it had missed my sight, another bloody good reason to never believe a quack!) I was allowed to stay up late to wait for my Dad to come home from his shift. Probably wasn't late as we know it, but for my age I guess it was. Anyway, Mum let me watch a film, "The Vikings" where poor old Kirk Douglas loses his eye to a hawk! He then also loses his girl and eventually his life. How cool. That my dear, set me up to explore Norse mythology and all its trapping, ad infinitum!"

"That's pretty cool" Kelly whispered, staring at the fire again.

"Not only that, young lady, I discovered that the TV archaeologist and presenter Neil Oliver got in to it all by watching the very same film!" Prez grinned and downed his drink. "Y'know how desperate I was to fit in and not let my folks down?"

"Tell me." Kelly shook her head.

"Well back in the day we had eye tests at school where you held a card over one eye and read out letters from a board at a prescribed distance away."

"So, you failed, right?" Kelly interjected.

"Nah, I cheated for at least two years, I just slipped the card to one side, so I could see with my left eye! They never cottoned on! Why would they? Who'd be dumb enough to cheat a test like that?"

Kelly put her hand on Prez's knee and looked in to his eyes,

"A sad little boy wanting to please Mummy and Daddy and not wanting to be the odd one out?"

Prez smiled back as they both got to their feet to get more drinks,

S.O.S.

"And that Kel, is why I've tried so hard to fit in ever since!" with that they both entered the house howling with laughter as they pushed their way through the much increased throng to the bar.

BS was at the bar now and stood aside to let his wife and friend through,

"You two at it again?" he winked as Prez replied,

"Don't know what you mean Occifer!"

"Take her, take her, what's yours is mine brother!" BS called, whilst at the same time the pair of them linked arms, beaming.

BS was taking the Michael out of one of the more ridiculous parts of the perceived "Outlaw Biker" code, that women are mere objects. I don't know if it's a transatlantic thing, but I don't know any woman involved in the club who would ever be happy to be called "property of". In fact, I'd go out of my way to have a word with any member who treated a woman so disrespectfully. It's true that women can't be patched members, but that's a club call and no one has ever challenged it. I think Kelly has come close a couple of times but like Nessa, I think she can see that power can be wielded more effectively from behind the scenes. What woman hasn't got power over a man? They just like to let us think we're in charge, right? Which is just the way we like it..........................

Suddenly there was a light punch on Prez's shoulder, making him spill some alcohol. Boalie was back at the bar,

"Prez, sunshine, where's the little woman tonight?" Prez scanned the mass of bodies that was now filling the place to capacity, whilst the music started to blare out.

"She not here yet?" Prez asked BS who was standing next to them with his arm around Kelly,

"Not seen Nessa Boss. Maybe she's upstairs?" BS shrugged.

Upstairs was the room we held Unkindness's in and was strictly off limits, so I'd be surprised if she'd be in there. That left the bathroom and a couple of bedrooms used for visitors, or members who "overdid it".

Prez bounded up the stairs and checked each room, all were empty.

"Any luck?" BS queried as Prez returned.

"No, something's not right mate, can Kel give her a bell-"

"Hey Prez, you're a poet and you don't know it!" roared Boallie as he pointed to an empty glass and shouted to the barmaid, "Another gold watch in that and make it large lovely!"

BS and Prez rolled their eyes and Kelly stepped outside with her mobile 'phone.

Minutes later Kelly was back, and her humour had gone,

"Nessa's not coming Vince, it's something to do with your Mum."

S.O.S.

"Christ, not again. BS can you take over and see this through if I don't come back?"

BS nodded," Sure, no worries. If we don't see you later, err Happy New Year! I'll call you."

Prez pecked Kelly on the cheek and he and BS grasped each other's forearms before Prez turned and left the party behind him. *Drinking and riding is not a good idea, but I don't think I've had too much. Besides, this is an emergency.* Prez thought. Grim faced as he fastened his helmet and fired up *Landwaster*, leaving the serried ranks of motorcycles behind him as he sped in to the night.

Happy New Year.

Robert C. Holmes

Heard It On The Airwaves

Prez and Edna sat in the musty waiting room of Wainwright Clarke and Smith, Edna's solicitors. Prez had organised the meeting after persuading Edna that she should hand over her affairs to him via power of attorney. Since Christmas things had deteriorated and even Edna had accepted that she was having difficulty caring for herself. Often when Vanessa and Prez called to see her, she would just sit at the end of the sofa staring in to space. Sometimes she had lucid moments, other times there was the blank vacant moments and worse there were the paranoid delusional moments. Prez was hoping that they would get through this interview with the lawyer without any of the latter. Away from the waiting area Prez could hear keyboards clicking and telephones ringing as the clerical staff went about their duties. He was wearing his "weddings and funerals suit". He felt uncomfortable in a shirt and tie, reminding him, as it did, of his few years as a civil servant, before he formed Hanoi Jane and could afford to leave that life of crushing conformity. Unfortunately, there were more things to worry about than an uncomfortable collar.

"Won't be long now Mum. You've done the right thing with this. It's just one less thing to worry about isn't it?"

"Yes, you're right Vincent, I'm just glad that you're here to help me, I know you and Vanessa will look after me."

So why do I feel I'm betraying the person that gave birth to me, raised me, cared for me? Why do I feel that I'm taking everything she ever worked for away from her? Prez thought as he nodded at his mother. Edna suddenly tensed,

"That's them, that'll be them." She whispered curtly to Prez whilst looking straight ahead.

"What's them Mum, what are you on about?" Prez raised his eyebrows questioningly.

"She's on the 'phone talking to them now, couldn't you hear it ringing? Can't you hear them talking about me?"

Prez fought the rising panic he felt. Edna had heard the telephones ringing and her delusions were kicking in again.

"It'll just be office work Mum, nothing to do with them". He replied calmly. In his meeting with Dr Detlaff to arrange an appointment for Edna, Detlaff had explained that everyone should go along with the delusions and not try to contradict Edna's views.

"Don't worry son, they'll not stop me from going through with this, that's what they want you know. They want the house, that's what it is." Edna's voice was still a whisper, but it was dripping with venom. It was not a voice Prez was used to hearing from his mother. He could feel himself clammy with sweat as the door opened and a middle-aged man in a shiny suit and thinning hair opened a door with a smile,

"Mr and Mrs Sinclair? I'm Mr Clarke, please come in and we'll set up your agreement."

Guy looks about as sincere as a crocodile and just as reptilian. What a profession, making money out of people's misery. Prez stood up and motioned that Edna precede him in to the office.

After around half an hour the moment arrived regarding the signing off of the agreement by Edna. *This is the part I've been dreading, we all have to sign the document handing power of attorney to me, agreeing that Mum is sound of mind.*

Clarke pushed the paperwork across the desk for Prez and Edna to sign, all the time looking at Prez, smiling,

"Don't worry Mr Sinclair, I've organised thousands of these, I know exactly how you are feeling." Clarke smiled thinly. It was coded language to let Prez know that everyone in the room knew that Edna was not of sound mind, but that wasn't how the game worked. The game worked by everyone agreeing a lie, so that Prez could control her estate. Edna could end up wherever she would end up and Mr Clarke and his organisation would get a nice fat fee.

S.O.S.

This is how society works, all a lie, a pretence. Sweep everything under the carpet and make a profit, money, money, money, right? All a corrupt lie and we're all part of it, everyone. Prez could feel his heart sinking as he signed the lie, because legally and for Edna it was the only thing he could do. She was obviously not in a condition or position to make important decisions anymore and he was damned if he was going to see her give her property away to some fraudster who might come knocking on the door for a "charity".

As Prez drove Edna back to her home she seemed like a small shrivelled little woman, but within that shell was a frightened little girl. He wished there was something he could do to reassure her, to help her but he feared that the impending visit to Dr Detlaff would result in a visit to a psychiatrist and that that would be the beginning of the end in every conceivable way. Prez felt helpless and impotent, as indeed in this instance he was.

What would a civilized society do? If the psychiatrist finds that Mum is suffering from dementia or is schizophrenic, or worse, what would a civilized society do? Put her in a home? Put her in a hospital? Drug her? Where is the dignity in that? The social services and their masters the politicians talk of dignity, but I see precious little of it. What about the right to die? Rather than live a life of fear, with only drugs to block out part of your suffering, shouldn't there be a way out? You wouldn't let an animal suffer such indignity, would you? Life is indeed sacred, yet when that life is merely a living death, a hell that is endured and no longer enjoyed, should it be encouraged to continue? Some enlightened societies advocate assisted suicide. It is a difficult and thorny issue. All I know is that my Mum is scared, her quality of life is disintegrating and all I can do is use the NHS who will probably ensure she gets drugs to remain functional. Sure, life is sacred, but only if there is a quality to that life. To become a shambling shell of your former self, not aware of your surroundings or even being self-aware, is that life? What is the definition of life? Are you alive if you're not self-aware, just because you physically exist? Sure, you're alive as an amoeba is alive! Is that what we want as a society for our old folk, the life of an amoeba? Because no one has the backbone to face facts and tell the truth? Because everyone is cosy living with the lie, except the very people who have to live through that lie, so others can remain comfortable with it? How do people sleep at night knowing what is happening? How do people work in institutions that prolong the agony of these old folk? I guess they're all caught up in the lie. The idea that perpetuating life is an all-consuming virtue, no matter what sort of drug induced hell you're putting these people through. As long as people think that they're "doing the best" for these folks, they seem happy, indeed consider themselves virtuous whilst condemning these poor souls to what must seem to them an eternity of suffering. Programmed by the great and the good to perpetuate existence, no matter how appalling the quality of that existence may be, with no hope of a cure, no hope of release, until the final demeaning trip to the hospital or hospice. Why can't people see how wrong all of this is? Prez was running through the whole gamut of emotions. He was angry over the way things were, he was angry over the injustice of what was happening to his mother, he was angry because he could do very little to help. But most of all he was angry because he was, despite everything he had done in life to live outside a rotten system, watching his mother becoming trapped within the rigid confines of the very system Prez rejected and he could see no way of moving forward. Perhaps the psychiatrist that would examine Edna would get to the root of the problem, perhaps Social Services would come up with a care package that would help Edna retain some vestige of normality in her life, retaining her independence and dignity. Prez felt that the harder he clenched his hand to retain the old Edna, her psyche, soul, essence, call it what you will was slipping through his fingers like grains of sand and he was powerless to do anything about it.

Two weeks later and Prez was sitting with Edna in the spacious office of the psychiatrist Dr Detlaff had referred her to. It was a soulless futuristic setting, with everything a gleaming white, apart from the numerous chairs scattered about the vacuous room. There was a desk but Mr Mortimer the psychiatrist never sat behind it. He reminded Prez of a stick insect, tall thin and with a shining pate. He had a strange predatory air about him that would have made him a casting agent's dream for any remake of the film *Nosferatu*.

"Edna, I'm going to ask you a few questions about yourself. I'll ask you some questions about where you've lived and what you've done in life. Then I'm going to ask you about some current affairs of the last few weeks. Are you happy with that?"

Edna nodded whilst Prez looked on. As the interview wore on it became apparent that Edna could remember incidents that had occurred years ago with crystal clarity. However, she could not recall what happened yesterday. She even struggled to know the present date and day. Prez was relieved that the chat was amicable and free from any aggression that Edna was now displaying with ever more frequency.

"Edna, that was all very good. Would you like to take a seat back in the foyer outside this office and I'll have a quick chat with Vincent." Mortimer grinned with the sincerity of a piranha.

As Edna left the room the smile faded from Mortimer's thin face,

"Mr Sinclair, how long is it since you noticed the issues that you reported to your mothers' G.P.?"

Prez slowly shook his head as he wracked his brain to try to remember when this had first started.

"Months ago. I really couldn't say when it started."

"Well it appears to me, having spoken to your mother and having read the report from Dr Detlaff and the evidence that you have supplied regarding her erratic actions that she is slipping in to a state of schizophrenia."

"I thought it might be Alzheimer's, or even dementia." Prez exclaimed, "Can she be treated? What can I do?"

Mortimer folded his arms and perched on the edge of his desk, exuding all the bedside manner of a vulture.

"Well, there are drugs I can prescribe to alleviate many of the symptoms and there is no reason that your mother can't lead a normal life. However, I must warn you that this is a degenerative illness and there is no cure or recovering from it. She will eventually need care and attention. Perhaps not now, or even twelve months from now, but at some stage, she will not be able to care for herself."

Prez nodded,

"Well she's eighty-one, so we figured that she would come and live with me and my wife at some stage anyway."

"Hmmm." Mortimer chewed his bottom lip, "You may find that other complications arise, it is not a role to take on lightly."

"What do you suggest?" Prez queried.

"Don't get me wrong, what you are suggesting is fine. I just want you to be prepared for what you are going to be undertaking. If you work full time it may be difficult as your mother may need care and attention on a full-time basis." Mortimer rubbed his chin, "I suggest together with Social Services we set up a care package initially and see how she copes with the medication I will prescribe. I shall arrange for them to contact you and with the details you have supplied regarding the nearest pharmacy to your mother, I will send the details of the medication to them. As with Social Services, the pharmacy will contact you as to when you can collect the prescription. How does that sound?" the piranha smile was back.

"Okay, whatever you say." Prez shrugged, standing up and proffering his hand to Mortimer. As they shook hands Prez felt like he was crushing a handful of damp twigs, "Thanks Mr Mortimer."

"A pleasure, don't forget to book in another appointment at the reception desk. Make it for a month's time."

"I'll do that, see you in a month." Prez smiled as he made his way to the door.

Maybe there is light at the end of the tunnel? Maybe these drugs can contain the worst of it and Eddie will get his Grandma back and me and Nessa will get our Mum back. I bloody hope so. Prez allowed himself the luxury of a smile as he walked to where Edna was sitting, staring out at the fountain in the communal garden.

"C'mon Mum, let's get you home, everything's going to be fine."

S.O.S.

Nessa sat at the dining table in Edna's lounge/dining room, looking out at the large and well-maintained garden that was Edna's pride and joy. It was two weeks since Prez had taken Edna to her initial meeting with the psychiatrist and now they were awaiting the arrival of Edna's health workers, who would administer the medication Prez had picked up from the pharmacy. Prez was in his usual chair by the window and Edna was sitting opposite Nessa. As usual, everyone was sipping tea. Prez spotted the car pull up on to the drive. Two portly middle-aged women wearing uniforms and sporting lanyards emerged and one knocked on the door. Prez was in "civvies", t shirt, jeans, cowboy boots. No need for club representation here. He opened the door,

"Hello ladies, come in." He grinned which was returned in kind by the two health workers.

They walked in to the room and introduced themselves,

"Hello, I'm Jill." Said the blonde one

"And I'm Irene."

"Hi, this is my wife Vanessa, and this is my Mum Edna" Prez swept his arm to encompass his mother and wife.

"Can we call you Edna?" cooed Jill, Edna looking quite flustered at the level of familiarity, it wasn't the Sinclair way.

"Yes, yes, would you like a cup of tea?" Edna spluttered.

"Oh, that would be lovely, wouldn't it Irene?"

"Lovely." Irene retorted sitting herself down on the sofa.

After twenty minutes of vacuous chat the health workers took the medication from Prez and explained that they would administer the tablets twice a day to Edna. One of them would call in at around ten o'clock in the morning and then again at three in the afternoon. They checked that they had contact numbers for everyone, gave Edna her first tablet and then in a flurry of handshakes and downing of tea, they were gone.

"Well they seemed nice enough Mum." Nessa beamed.

"Yes, I suppose so. What if I'm going out though?" Edna seemed unimpressed.

"Well just 'phone them on the number they left Mum. They're here to help, not tie you down."

Edna frowned,

"I don't like people telling me what to do Vincent. I don't like strangers in the house. They could be something to do with them." Edna pointed at the wall which divided her semi-detached house with next door.

S.O.S.

"Come on Mum, we've been through this, they're health workers, here to help, so that you can remain independent. That's what you want, isn't it?" Prez smiled.

"They are following me you know Vincent" Edna was beginning to take on a wild-eyed expression, Nessa piped up quickly, "Who is Mum?"

"They are, ssshhhh!" Edna put an index finger to her lips and gestured to the wall again. Prez knew he had been told to humour his mother's fantasies but he let his emotions get the better of him,

"How do you know Mum?"

"They're following me. Here, there, everywhere. They even watch me going to the toilet."

Nessa got up and tried to guide Edna to a chair,

"Sit down mum, you're getting agitated, we're here, so there-"

Edna shook free and turned to Prez, eyes blazing voice raised, but not shouting,

"I know what they're doing, they're following me!"

"How do you know Mum?" Prez pushed. Behind Edna and out of her line of sight Nessa frowned at Prez and shook her head but he persisted, as if common sense could somehow prevail.

"Because I know Vincent!" Edna barked.

"How Mum?" Prez wouldn't let it go, despite the black looks from Nessa.

"I know because I hear it when I'm walking to the shops."

"How? How do you hear it?" Prez held his arms wide.

"The airwaves, I hear it through the airwaves!" Edna turned and stomped in to the kitchen.

Prez and Nessa stared at each other dumbfounded. The confirmation of everything suddenly hitting them both like a tsunami of emotion.

That was it. The final confirmation that Mum was indeed, losing her mind. It was one thing to hear it from a trained psychiatrist. It was one thing to hear her talk nonsense about the police and the neighbours, but it was something else to hear it from the horses' mouth. She was hearing it from the airwaves..

Prez felt a yawning chasm open up beneath him, or was it a rug that had been pulled from under him? For what seemed like minutes he stood stock still, trying to process what he had just heard. Completely out of character he wasn't thinking of the impact the scenario had had on Nessa. Normally it was his first priority to protect her from everything............normally.

How does anyone process information like that? The person who gave you life, instilled their values in to you, fed you clothed you. The person you looked up to and took advice from, the person you respected and yes, occasionally had feared. The matriarch, the provider and tower of strength in a family where she became the breadwinner, the glue holding the whole thing together when times were hard. The person whose ideals and expectations you tried to live up to, although in reality those ideals were set so high, that you never could. The person you could never please, no matter what you did, yet you showered her with unconditional love, because of who she was and what she did for you and your family. The person who had now, in front of you and your wife stood up, looked you in the eye and declared their madness.

Prez felt sick and tears were welling up in his eyes. He was old school, *boys don't cry!* He fought the tears back and slowly realized that Nessa was standing beside him with her arms around him.

Prez looked down into his wife's deep green eyes,

"Well that's it then."

"Vince, come on, sit down." Nessa purred, "We knew Mum was ill, that's why she's on medication, that's why she's got a care package. Look, she's only just taken her medication, I'm sure it'll all calm down after a while. Didn't the psychiatrist say it was manageable?"

Prez stepped backwards and slumped in to his chair, all the usual strength and vitality having seeped through his body down to his boots and away. Nessa meanwhile darted to the kitchen to ensure Edna was alright. As it was, Edna was making yet another cup of tea, she had forgotten that the three of them already had mugs of the steaming beverage.

It was raining as they pulled up on the drive,

"Home at last Vince. Come on, I'll explain it all to Eddie, you try and relax." Nessa smiled at her husband as he killed the engine. As he did so the familiar rumbling of a Harley Davidson sounded, and Vince craned his neck to see BS pull up behind him on the drive.

"You go in sweetheart, I'll see what m'laddo wants."

Nessa smiled and disembarked waving at BS who waved back as he dismounted his 'bike. Vince locked the car and strode over to his Vice President who was clad in his leathers and patch, as indeed S.O.S. law demanded as he was on his motorcycle. He removed his helmet and adjusted his glasses, his face grim.

"BS, to what do I owe the privilege?" Prez grinned, determined not to let his VP see how he really felt.

"Bad news Boss."

"For a bloody change. Come on in" Prez motioned to the house and the pair trudged up the drive as the rain fell.

S.O.S.

Prez rolled his port around in its glass as BS sipped his coffee. Nessa was upstairs with Eddie, explaining the Edna situation, allowing Prez and BS to talk club business. BS leant forward as he put his coffee to one side.

"Okay Boss, first things first. Boalie is banged up."

"What, what's he done?" Prez raised his eyebrows, genuinely surprised.

"Well, y'know they had tried for ages to have a kid? Well, you know they were successful through IVF?"

Prez nodded.

"Apparently he's had a restraining order put on him a couple of months ago, can't visit the missus."

"What, how?"

"Dunno Boss." BS sat back in his seat with a resigned look on his face, "Me and Bear have tried every contact we can get hold of down south and we can't get any kind of a sniff of Jimi or Pretty Boy. No address, nothing. It's like they've dropped off the face of the earth.

"Probably in the Thames if they've been messing with the cartels down there, stupid bastards." Prez spat, angry and disgusted with both the ex-club members.

"Then there's this." BS fished out a sealed envelope from his jacket and handed it to Prez, who opened it and scanned the contents.

"Well, this is no surprise mate. It's a letter from Faceman requesting that he be released from the club." Prez sighed passing the letter to BS.

Boalie in jail, Faceman asking to leave and no trace of the dynamic duo, DJ changing sex and Mum sinking in to madness, what the Hell is going on? I must have been a complete bastard in my last life. Prez thought as he drained his glass of port and watched BS read the letter.

"See a problem with this Boss?" BS queried as he passed the letter back.

"Nah, not me. Out in Good Standing would be my recommendation. He's had enough, he's going places in his career, let him go." Prez murmured with an air of resignation.

"Think Bear will see it like that?"

"Probably not, but when he sees the Unholy Trinity giving their blessing, I think he'll vote with us."

"You think Oz will vote with us two on this? Face gave him a bit of a hard time back in the day, him and that hang around Steve, remember? That tall git who didn't cut it?" BS blew on his tea.

"Oz isn't like that, is he? He knows Face treated him badly but he's not like me, he doesn't hold grudges. That's what makes the 'Trinity work. You're a relatively laid-back guy who thinks things through, Oz is even more laid back and thinks things through then there's me, not being laid back and being a spiteful vindictive bastard. Who listens to you two and has enough common sense to usually take your advice, Christ help me!" Prez managed a genuine smile at his friend who chuckled in response.

"Don't think you'll get much help from Him!" BS grinned back.

"We'll bring it all up at the next Unkindness, when is that?" Prez queried.

"Tomorrow."

"Already, Christ I really am losing track of everything lately." Prez gazed in to the distance, unaware of the concern on his V.P.s face.

"How's things with your Mum?"

Now there's the rub. With all the things going on with the Club, does BS really need to know that my home life is falling to pieces as well? That Nessa and Eddie are my priority at the moment and that they needed protecting from the way Mum is acting. Prez took a deep breath and sat forward.

"Not good son, but I don't want this leaked to the Brothers. There's enough going on with all this shit without me going for the sympathy vote." Prez pointed at the letter.

"Yeah, I understand that Bro, but hey, we're here to help. Don't do a bloody Jimi and take on the world with you and Nessa, it doesn't work like that, right? That's the whole concept of the Club isn't it? Stand together, fall together?"

Prez forced a grin,

"Not sure I ever thought of us falling together."

"You know what I mean!" BS implored, looking more serious than Prez could remember.

"Okay, look, Mum is on medication, she's become paranoid and she's under a trick cyclist. She's got a care package via Social Services, but I figure that eventually, probably sooner rather than later, she's going to end up living here at Sinclair Towers. Not a wonderful option, but hey, she's not going in to a care home." Prez blurted.

"Amen to that Bro. Look, any way we can help, let me know, any way. That goes for me and Kel, not just the Club. If you want to keep it under wraps from the boys, I understand, but I think it's a mistake. Either way, it's your decision and they won't hear anything from me."

S.O.S.

Prez stood up and placed a hand on BS's shoulder in recognition of his help as he walked beyond the seated Vice President and replenished his port from the bottle on the table.

"Much appreciated Bro. I think I'll just keep it within the 'Trinity, at least for now."

As he sat back down Nessa entered the room, poking her head around the door,

"Okay if I come in boys?"

"Yeah, we're pretty much done Kid." Prez smiled.

"Hi Nessa, sorry about your Mum. Just been telling the Boss here, anything me and Kel can do, let us know." BS stood and hugged Nessa as she closed the door behind her. Then he turned to Prez,

"I'll leave you to it Boss, you look like shit!"

"Gee thanks mate! Thanks for calling." Prez stood and the two shook hands in the S.O.S. tradition by grasping forearms.

"Tell Kelly we'll have to meet up." Said Nessa as she held the door to the porch open for BS to pass through.

"I'll do that Nessa." BS nodded as he collected his helmet and gloves, "See ya tomorrow Prez" he called over his shoulder. Prez appeared behind his wife and waved as BS fired up his 'bike and paddled it out of the drive backwards before roaring off down the road. The couple returned to the front room and Prez slumped back in his chair whilst Nessa perched on the sofa.

"How did the boy take it?" Prez asked, rolling his eyes to indicate Eddie's room upstairs.

"Okay, he's like his old man, doesn't say much. Honestly though, I think he's handling it okay."

Suddenly it was all too much, Prez sat forward and put his head in his hands. He could feel hot tears in his eyes and bile rising in his throat. Nessa was immediately beside him with her arm around h s shoulder, "It's okay, it's okay." She purred, "We'll get through this, we're all in it together. We've dealt with stuff before. Your Dad passing away, my Mum passing away, we've got the three of us and we're strong. You've got, the Club too, they'll rally 'round!

"Rally round? The bloody Club is falling apart. Boa ie's in nick, Face is leaving, and Jimi and Pretty Boy are AWOL." Prez mumbled. Nessa pretended not to be surprised that Prez had disclosed Club business to her. She put it down to shock. It had had to express itself somehow and now it had. Nessa stood up and Prez stood with her holding each other close. Nessa then pulled away and looked him straight in the face.

"Now look Prez, share your doubts with me now, but tomorrow at that Unkindness, you go out there and be the man they all expect you to be!"

Prez smiled at his wife. She never used the "P" title and he was wryly amused by her. But the steel in her voice reminded him of one of the reasons he had plighted his troth with her. *Not only is she stunning, with shining red hair passed her shoulders, not only does she have legs up to her neck, not only does she have a cute upturned nose, and not only does she still have a great figure, it's all these things plus the fact she's one tough cookie, a tower of strength which I draw from. The perfect woman.*

"C'mon Red, lets hit the sack." Prez smiled.

"Not until I've got the cat in!" Nessa smiled back.

Committed

Prez gazed out of the window of the clubhouse awaiting the arrival of his brothers. The rain pattered gently on the glass, Spring had arrived. BS was already sitting at the table, hanging on Prez's every word.

"It doesn't seem like any time at all since Mum was allocated that useless care package. Now she's in a care home, I feel like I've stabbed her in the back." Prez spoke without facing his friend.

"Don't be so hard on yourself. It wasn't you hiding the tablets, was it? People with these conditions are cunning. Just because they're mentally ill doesn't mean they aren't all there." BS replied not realising the irony in his statement.

"Shit, you sound just like Oz!" Prez grinned. Finally taking his seat at the table, "Just 'cause you're nuts, it doesn't mean you're crazy!"

"You know what I mean!" BS scowled back, "So, I've got the agenda here, wanna go through it?"

Prez shook his head,

"Nah, surprise me as we go along!"

S.O.S.

A knock on the door announced the arrival of the awaited Brotherhood as Bear and Oz strode in. Prez raised his eyebrows after glancing at his watch,

"Is this it? No one else at the bar downstairs?"

"This is it Boss." shrugged Oz.

So, this is what we've come to now, an Unkindness that can only muster four members. Bloody pathetic. Prez mused as he watched Oz and Bear take their respective places.

"Okay Gents, we're here to discuss a couple of things. Firstly, the charity Wirral Egg Run, we all good to go with that?" Prez looked around the table as his crew nodded and gave thumbs up in affirmation. It was a bike run that had once boasted tens of thousands of riders but was now much diminished due to red tape and hassle from the police and local council, despite it all being for charity.

"Bear, can you get a few bodies on board?"

"I'll give it a go Prez. But we're pretty thin on the ground at the mo."

Prez smiled thinly back. *Master of the bloody understatement.*

"Any word on Chinner?"

"Still over in Ireland I think." Oz piped up," He went and hasn't come back after palling up with Irish Kev at the Wild Hunt last year as far as I know." Oz looked uncomfortable, Prez knew the signs.

"Go on mate, spit it out, what else?"

"Well, Boalie's in hospital over the water in Liverpool. He's had a tracheostomy"

The three others glanced at each other, BS being the first to address Oz,

"What the Hell? What happened, how long have you known? Is he okay?"

"Today boys, only found out today. Years of hitting the sauce I guess. He didn't take too kindly regarding that restraining orcer either."

"Shit." Prez shook his head, "I should've seen this coming. He's been drinking like a bloody fish lately......" BS interrupted his President,

"C'mon Prez, he's been drinking like a bloody fish for years, I can't say I'd noticed any bloody difference lately."

The company nodded in unison. *It's true enough, Boalie had always been a heavy drinker, when does a heavy drinker or a party animal become an alcoholic? Should I have spotted it, could I have spotted it? Could anyone? It's part of our culture. I guess we all thought he could handle it, maybe no one can really.* Prez cleared his throat and addressed the Unkindness,

S.O.S.

"Okay, we'll have to pay him a visit lads. Who's up for a ride over to Scouse Land on Friday?"

He was greeted with a resounding chorus affirming the brotherhoods intentions to visit their fallen comrade.

"Okay Oz, find out the visiting times and then text the rest of us and we'll meet up in New Brighton and then take the tunnel from there."

"No probs Boss." Oz replied, then looking rather sheepish he addressed Prez again, "Have you had a look at the agenda?"

Prez turned his mouth down at the corners and shook his head,

"Nah, surprise me!" he smiled.

"Well I'm afraid the accounts aren't looking good."

Prez leant forward on the table,

"Go on............"

"Well, err with the fallout from London and New York and no dues from Chinner or Faceman and the general rising in prices and everything, looks like it's going to be tough keeping the clubhouse." Oz was sweating profusely now, worried that as the messenger in chief he may incur the wrath of the assembled bikers, especially Bear. Prez sat back and stroked his moustache,

"I s'pose I've seen this coming. I know the royalties from the band aren't what they used to be."

"Hey, if we find Jimi we could do a farewell reunion tour!" BS quipped, nobody laughed. Prez grimaced,

"Yeah, more than likely we'll find him propping up the North Circular, we could call it the Lazarus tour!" Prez retorted.

Bear leant forward his brow creased in confusion,

"Hey, I thought we *owned* this place?" he growled.

"Yeah, we do, but it's the upkeep mate." Oz pickec up a sheaf of papers that lay in front of him and waved them at the assembled throng, "it's not the building, it's the council tax, the electricity, everything. All this stuff has been effectively subsidised by the royalties from *Hanoi Jane* for years. BS and Prez have kept this place running as a hangout for brothers and dues from outside chapters and the membership have helped with the everyday running costs." Oz waved the papers at the empty places at the table, "Take a look around Brothers, we're almost done, there's only just enough of us to form a chapter according to our own constitution. One more loss and we're effectively disbanded."

Say it like it is brother, say it like it is. Prez smiled an ironic grin at his treasurer's outburst. He was proud of him for making at least a verbal stand in the face of Bear.

S.O.S.

"Let me have a look at the books and I'll give it some thought Oz." Prez held out his hand and Oz passed the papers to him, then added,

"Maybe we should have a charity run for ourselves!" Oz snorted.

"What about Dazzler and Greg The Vet, where are they tonight?" Bear rumbled.

"Dazzler's been given a bye as has Greg, nippers are both unwell." BS replied. Prez stroked his moustache,

"Greg I can understand, but Dazzler? If we called in his dues for every missed Unkindness, we'd be in bloody clover. How many did he miss last year?"

Oz put his hands to his forehead as if in thought, Prez shook his head,

"I don't need an answer, I just mean we'll have to increase the fines on brothers who can't attend. I mean he uses the gym facilities here often enough, but when the nitty gritty needs sorting, where is he?"

"Dog dating websites Boss." shrugged Oz

"Christ, he's not still using them, is he?" BS looked bewildered as Oz nodded in the affirmative.

"Well he did have a long relationship about a week ago................" Bear muttered, causing a ripple of unexpected laughter around what had been a morose table. Prez sat up straight,

"Okay, I know it's tough, I know we're all the wrong side of fifty and we've all got wives and kids, even the younger guys like Greg and Dazzler have got family obligations. Having said that, isn't that what we're about? In these times of transgender nonsense being sold to kids at primary school, aren't we just an act of rebellion by being straight, married with children? "a ripple of agreement confirmed his audience's affirmation of his position. "Let's get the Brothers to bring in some hang arounds and friends of the club, I'm thinking maybe Troll, Jack Shit, Johnny H. We'll make a change for this Egg Run and wear club colours, to make a statement. I know in the past we didn't want to make it a political thing at the Egg Run, but we need to remind the great unwashed that we are still actually around. Do I have a seconder for that?"

"Yay, Prez." Bear raised his hand.

"All for?" Prez continued and was followed by a resounding "Yay" from the collective.

"Okay, that's April boxed off. We'll all meet up on Friday to see Boalie, Oz will be in touch with the details. I'll have a look at these bloody accounts and see if there's any other funding stream we can tap in to. Any other business Brothers?" Prez looked around the table, it was a short look.

"Okay, business closed." He brought the palm of his hand down with a slap on to the table top signifying the end of the Unkindness. The Brothers filed downstairs to the bar. *At least the bloody bar is still well stocked.* Prez thought as he poured himself a port. Oz sidled up to him as he took the first gulp, mobile 'phone in hand,

"Prez, Nessa's been trying to get hold of you, something's gone on at the care home with your mum, not sure what."

"Cheers mate. Can I borrow your 'phone?" Oz nodded in agreement and passed the item in question to Prez who stepped in to the gym for a little quiet. *Shit, I've really got to get one of these bloody things. It's all well and good hanging on to my principles, but with things the way they are, it's not fair on the Brothers that they're the ones taking my messages for me.* He mused as he punched in Nessa's number.

"Hello?"

"Hi Ness, it's only me. Sorry for not getting back to you, we've been in an Unkindness and Oz has only just picked up his messages."

"Vince, you've got to get a 'phone, I can never get hold of you." Nessa sounded upset,

"Yeah, I know babe, I will, I guess I'll have to the way things are going. Hey, enough about that, what's happening?"

"It's Mum, she's attacked someone in the nursing home, bitten them."

"What?" Prez was stunned, even with what he'd gone through in the last twelve months there seemed no end to the downward spiral of bad news. He put his hand to his temples.

"So where is she now? What's the score?"

"They've taken her to St Cath's."

St Catherine's, the bloody nut hutch. Prez brooded. *The holding area for those who are assessed before finally being sent somewhere to spend their days in a secure environment, drugged up to the eyeballs. Of course, that's not what the state will tell you. It'll tell you that it's a home where the elderly can spend their final days in contentment and peace, with dignity and security, yeah, right. Whilst they're secured to chairs, drooling in to their soup.*

"Can we visit?" Prez kicked himself metaphorically at the inanity of his question to his wife.

"Just come home Vince!" Nessa spat down the 'phone.

"I'm on my way, see you in half an hour. And stay calm babe." Prez tried to sound as supportive as he could as he heard Nessa clicking the 'phone down at the other end. He walked in to the bar area, handing the 'phone back to Oz.

"Problems Boss?" enquired the Treasurer.

"Is there anything else?" Prez sighed and turned to BS who was pouring himself a vodka.

"VP, you're going to have to organise the Boalie thing on Friday, looks like I'm going to be tied up with some personal stuff."

"Your Mum? What's the problem?" BS furrowed his brow.

"Whole thing's gone tits up, she's attacked someone, bitten them I think. I'm not sure really, I've gotta go and see Nessa for the full s.p." Prez shrugged, feeling light headed and extremely tired. The bad news just did not seem to stop.

"Leave the Boalie stuff to me Prez." BS put his hand on his president's shoulder, "Me and Oz have got this. We'll sort the club stuff re the Egg Run too. Don't worry, we can function without the main man for a while!" he said, forcing a grin. Oz came in to Prez's view nodding like an enthusiastic schoolboy,

"Yeah, no worries Prez, the old Unholy Trinity, err minus one, we can keep a lid on things 'til you're in a position to step up. Honestly, anything you need Brother."

It's at times like this you know who your friends are. In earlier times I'd have spoken to DJ, bounced a few ideas off him, used him as a sounding board, as he would with me. Happier times. Not in that position anymore, time for me to finally stand alone, well sort of.

"Cheers lads. Let me know if you need me." Prez picked up his gloves and helmet from behind the bar and stepped out in to the night.

As the door closed behind him Prez felt genuinely alone. *Is this how everyone feels who deals with this stuff. When your last parent becomes mentally ill? When your best friend becomes transgender and betrays the club that it's taken years to build? Sure, there's still a handful of Brothers left, but has it all really been a fantasy? Were our ideals just too lofty to really put in to practice? Can anyone really take on the "establishment" and expect to win? All I know is that I'm tired, my family is tired, and my Brothers are tired. Is this just old age? Is this the time to just jack it all in and admit defeat?* Prez swung his leg over the flame encrusted *Landwaster* and reached up to the apehanger bars to fire up the engine. He coasted past the Wheelwrights pub, the sound of the engine reverberating back from the building like a Panzer tank advancing through France. Then it was on to the motorway and the white lines flashing past, illuminated by the headlamp in the dark and drizzle. The speedometer climbing with every twist of Prez's grip.

Sod it, I'm not beaten. What doesn't destroy you DOES make you stronger! Adversity doesn't break character, it defines it! I'm going to beat this thing and the S.O.S. are going to come out of it stronger. Nessa's going to get through it, Eddie's going to get through it and they're all going to need me to lean on to do it. To hell with the traitors and the backstabbers and the nay sayers. To hell with the hands we've been dealt, I'm going to take the losers hand and come up thumping trumps! That damned amulet around my neck stands for something, like the tattoos on my body and the colours on my back, "No Justice, Just Us".

"No Justice, Just US!" Prez shouted as he twisted the throttle and *Landwaster* surged to over ninety miles per hour in the dark and wet. Once again being united in speed with his iron steed the problems that had appeared insurmountable moments earlier within the confines of the clubhouse now seemed conquerable. Prez grinned as he saw the lead off ramp from the motorway approaching.

Prez and Nessa pulled the Focus in to the car park to the hospital. Prez was not wearing his club colours. *This is strictly a civilian matter, no need to spook the good staff at the hospital with what they would perceive as gang colours.* He smiled to himself. Cutting the engine, he looked over at his wife who smiled weakly back. He placed his hand on hers in an attempt at reassurance, feeling that it was he who needed the reassurance.

"Don't know what we're going to find here kid, I'm here for you, whatever." Prez smiled. Nessa squeezed his hand her eyes sparkling with emotion,

"I'm here for you, you daft thing! C'mon, let's get in and see Mum."

After checking in at reception a matronly nurse, all uniform and waistline took them in to the main living area. Prez could feel his stomach churning as if a knot had been made from his intestines and someone was pulling them as tight as possible. He and Nessa held hands tightly as they walked in to the room. It was a large area, with huge floor to ceiling windows on one side which revealed a garden. There were several smaller rooms that were light and airy due to the fact that there were windows everywhere. There were old folk sitting around reading papers, watching television and sleeping. Prez's initial reaction was that the place wasn't the Bedlam he had been expecting. The nurse turned to speak to them,

"If you want to wait in the room over there, I'll get your Mum" she said with a smile that never reached her eyes. *If she'd said, "have a nice day", I wouldn't have been surprised.* Prez thought grimly as he smiled back. Exchanging glances with Nessa told him she was thinking exactly the same. As they walked towards the room allocated, a short old woman clutching a cuddly panda stepped in front of them, smiling.

"Hello, you're nice. You're new too aren't you?" she said, looking up at Prez and Nessa.

"Yes, we're here to visit my Mum." Prez smiled back. The woman thrust the panda at him,

"This is my panda, he likes chocolate." At that moment Prez realised that the woman had a chocolate bar in her other hand and that the toy had chocolate all around its mouth.

S.O.S.

"Would you like some dear?" the woman addressed Nessa.

"No thanks, I'm on a diet." She smiled back gently.

"Oh well, more for us then!" the woman shuffled off to talk to someone else. Prez's positive feelings about the place were swiftly evaporating. He began to realise that most of the old folk were asleep, or worse drooling as they stared in to space. One or two were talking to themselves. *All these glass partitions everywhere, they're not there to make the place light and airy, they're in place so that there's no way anything can happen without it being spotted.* He pointed his grim realisation out to his wife who nodded in agreement,

"That's a good thing though, isn't it? If anyone needs help, then a nurse will spot it straight away, won't they?" Nessa replied, positive as usual. Prez smiled back as they sat down in the room,

"Think positive, I always knew there was a reason I married you, apart from the stunning good looks of course!"

At that moment the nurse returned bringing a hunched shuffling figure with her,

"There you are Edna, here's your son and daughter to see you." Prez stood up, as he would whenever a lady entered a room. He could feel his palms sweating with apprehension as his mother shuffled in to the room, smiling weakly, yet all the time her eyes searching the area. Nessa jumped to her feet and gave Edna a hug,

"Hi Mum, are you okay?" Edna continued smiling weakly and slumped in to a chair opposite Prez who smiled at her,

"Hi Mum, you alright?" he asked as he sat down, leaning forward his elbows on his knees.

"I'm fine Vincent. How are you both, how's Eddie?" Edna asked, her eyes still scanning the room as she did so.

"Eddie's fine, he sends his love" Nessa smiled back warmly.

"Don't bring him here, I wouldn't want him to see me here." Edna suddenly focussed on Prez with panic in her voice.

"Don't worry, we won't bring him Mum. Are you okay here?" Prez smiled gently.

"Not really" Edna lowered her voice, "They're all 'round the bend in here you know." She whispered conspiratorially,

"They've all gone funny. Do you know there's a woman in here that thinks her cuddly toy panda is alive! She keeps feeding it chocolate you know."

"Yes, we've met her!" Nessa smiled back. Edna suddenly leaned closer to Prez,

S.O.S.

"You've got to get me home son. How is the house? Don't let them take the house off me." Her eyes were now wild and staring. Prez remained calm and tried to sound reassuring,

"Don't worry Mum, the house is fine."

"I tried to get away you know, over the wall, but they caught me, I want to go home son, take me home, please." Edna was pleading like a small child and whilst it was breaking her son's heart he remained calm and strong. He knew that his wife was crying inside but she too was bearing up and displaying her usual fortitude in the face of adversity.

"You're just here for some tests Mum, so they can work out the best medication for you." Prez smiled. Nessa leant forward and took Edna's hand,

"Is there anything from home that I can bring you?"

"Yes Vanessa, could you bring something to get rid of this?" Edna rubbed her chin which was starting to sprout whiskers.

"Of course I can, anything else?"

Edna turned from Nessa to address Prez,

"The house Vincent, you must take me home so that they don't take my house away from me!" she was breathing quickly now and obviously in a state of panic. Prez smiled back, masking the pain he was really feeling. He leaned further forward and uncharacteristically put his hand on Edna's, the Sinclair's had never been a tactile family,

"Don't worry Mum, the house will be fine."

At that moment the nurse returned and addressed Prez as he stood up,

"Mr Mortimer will see you now Mr Sinclair, if you and your wife would like to come with me." She turned to Edna, "If you want to go in to the main room Edna, I think there's something nice on the telly." Edna glared back slowly standing and muttering to Prez as she shuffled past,

"Don't let them take the house son."

Prez and Nessa sat across the large white desk in the office currently (but obviously only temporarily) occupied by Mr Mortimer. It was a makeshift affair, used Prez was sure, by many of the staff who required a meeting with relatives. Today it was Mortimer's turn to meet the family of the deranged. He steepled his fingers and looked sombrely across the desk, first at Nessa, then at Prez.

"I'm afraid I am the bearer of grave news Mr Sinclair." Mortimer let the words hang in the air for a moment, a moment of pure theatre enhancing the drama, then he continued. Prez realised grimly that Mortimer had delivered this speech to dumbfounded and uncomprehending relatives and loved ones a thousand times before,

S.O.S.

"I have never seen such a rapid medical decline in a patient's state of mind. Despite our excellent care package and medication, it appears that Edna, your mother, has slipped in to a state of paranoid schizophrenia." He paused again.

At last, in a way it's a weight off everyone's mind. Finally, a medical diagnosis, instead of us trying to guess what the problem is. Prez nodded awaiting the next instalment of Mortimer's macabre delivery,

"I'm afraid I suspected as much from the outset, which was why I was against you taking your mother in to your home. Patients like her, at this heightened state of development of the illness, are completely irrational and given to violent outbursts. I must tell you, that she is going to have to be committed, sectioned, if you will."

The sentence hit the ear drums with a huge impact and the silence following it was excruciating. Prez looked across at Nessa who held one hand to her mouth. Whilst the news should not have come as a shock, Prez found himself dumbfounded and his wife was obviously stunned. He leant forward, having to clear his throat to address the mantis like Mortimer,

"So, you're saying she'll be kept in a secure unit for the rest of her life?"

"Yes. It will not cost you anything." Mortimer grinned in a sibilant reptilian way as if this news compensated for telling Prez and Nessa that

Edna was completely raving mad. "Because she is a danger to herself and others, the State will fund her stay within an institution." Suddenly he stopped grinning, realising perhaps that delivering such news as he had done in such a joyous fashion was not, in hindsight, sensible or respectful. He sat back in his chair awaiting questions with his eyebrows raised.

"I take it we'll be liaising with Social Services again regarding where Mum will be sent?" Prez scowled.

The same Social Services who we liaised with to get Mum the original care package which failed. That package which had taken months to set up as the Social Services had to liaise with the Health Service. The fact that I discovered the two members of staff from these departments actually sat opposite each other in an office made it even more difficult to comprehend why it took an eternity for them to liaise with each other. A period of huge stress for Nessa, Eddie, Mum and of course myself!

"Yes, exactly." Mortimer beamed back as though Prez should be turning cartwheels of joy at the prospect of handing Edna's future back to the same incompetents that had completely and utterly failed the family thus far. Prez turned to Nessa who was as pale as a sheet, her eyes brimming with tears. He stood up, taking her hand and guiding her from the chair to the door, his arm around her waist. He shot a glance at Mortimer who wore a confused expression, almost suggesting he expected gratitude for the news he had delivered. Prez opened the door for his wife and nodded at Mortimer as his wife left the room,

S.O.S.

"Thanks very much for all you've done." It was a flat monotone delivery, but it was the best Prez could summon.

Back at home Prez sipped his tea, whilst Vanessa sat opposite him with a mug of coffee.

"I'm going to have to discuss it with Big Sis, but I think she'll be in agreement if we put the house on the market." Prez mumbled to his wife who nodded in agreement. Despite his sister being six years his senior, Prez had always taken charge of helping his mother and indeed, his father when it was required. His mother and sister had never got on and whilst Edna had never been the easiest woman to deal with, Prez found it difficult to understand the deepness of the animosity between them. Maybe there were things that he just didn't know, or indeed would never know.

"I'll get a valuation from some estate agents in Heswall and see what they think. I reckon we're looking at around £200,000."

Here we go again, why do I feel like I'm betraying my Mum, again? First the deception to get her treatment and now going against her express wishes by flogging the family home?

"I know what you're thinking." Nessa leaned forward and wrapped her fingers around her mug, "But you're not letting Mum down." She smiled at Prez reassuringly.

"If she was in a position to make rational decisions, she'd be agreeing with you. You're making tough decisions, but they're the right ones Vince. Mum isn't Mum anymore. Sure, she is in body, but not in mind. She's going to say and do some hurtful things from here on in, but just like the stalkers and the murders and everything else she's been coming out with it's all just the condition. She's a paranoid schizophrenic Vince, nothing she sees or feels or thinks makes sense in the real world."

Prez nodded, grimly smiling in agreement as Nessa continued,

"No more guilt then. Put the house on the market and let's be rid of it and move on. We'll tell Mum we're looking after it, she doesn't need to know. It's not lying or deceitful, we're playing by a different set of rules now and I don't want to see you punishing yourself anymore. Give me a hug!" Nessa stood as Prez crossed the floor between them and embraced her.

This is why I married this girl! Well, that and the long straight hair and legs up to her neck!

Suddenly the 'phone rang and Prez jumped at the sound. For so many months it had been Edna on the 'phone with tales of the police and neighbours spying on her, so much so that both Nessa and Prez had come to detest the 'phone as an actual entity. Prez broke from the embrace and noticed that Nessa was smiling at him in an amused way that told him they were thinking the same thought.

No, you idiots, it can't be Mum. Prez grinned back and moved in to the hall to answer the 'phone.

"Hello."

"Prez, it's me." Oz's good-natured voice was bursting with positivity as he blurted out his message,

"I know you're dealing with some crap, but I've used a bit of nous and done some stuff off my own bat and hope it'll be okay I-"

"Oz, mate, no worries, where are we at?" Prez interrupted to put his Treasurer at ease.

"Well the Egg Run, I've got you an interview with the local free press. Thought the publicity might do us some good, since we're gonna be wearing colours for this one. Plus, I've got hold of Chinner and Irish Kev and they're gonna be there too! Irish is bringing some mates from over the water. Faceman said he'll ride, without his colours of course."

Nessa popped her head around the door to see who was on the 'phone to which Prez smiled and gave a thumbs up.

"Good work Oz, really good work."

"We're gonna have a really good turnout Boss. You, me, BS, Bear, Chinner, Kev, Greg The Vet, Dazzler, Faceman, Troll, Johnny H, plus a whole load of hang arounds that we haven't seen for a bit, even that prat Gimpo!"

*Gimpo, JJ's mate, Christ I thought he was dead. An odd couple of guys if ever there were. I never understood how they were mates, love of 'bikes I guess. JJ, the ultimate fantasist and Gimpo who just liked being his sidekick I s'pose. JJ had been drummed out of the club and his club tattoo "removed" as he was too much of a liability and consummate liar. He'd got the club and myself directly in a number of scrapes, one even involving a fight with a mob of yobs in Chester that resulted in him, me and another member being hospitalized. He came off worse, there's karma for you. I only collected a couple of cracked ribs whilst he was royally rewarded with a number of stitches to the head. One occasion where the boys in blue actually helped us out! When we kicked that idiot out it was the first time I'd seen a queue of guys **wanting** to do ironing! Even with his mate excommunicated Gimpo still can't resist what he surmises to be the "glamour" of being associated with the club. Idiots like that never learn, the man makes the patch, not vice versa.*

"Excellent work my Brother, hey, maybe I should hand the President patch to you! Just make sure that Gimpo behaves himself, I'm sure Bear will."

"It's not all good news Prez." Oz's voice took on a sombre tone, "Boalie is in a right state in hospital. He'll be okay, but he's got to knock the sauce on the head and start looking after himself. He'll be out in a few weeks. Maybe we should go and see him again when he's discharged?"

"Sounds good Oz. Thanks to you and the guys for nipping over to see him. So, what's the score with the local rag, where's the interview?"

"The journo's going to send you an email introducing herself, I gave her your e mail address, is that okay?" Oz sounded perplexed but Prez calmed any fears,

"Yeah, that's fine as long as the Missus doesn't think I'm compiling a number of female admirers!"

"She said she'd be in touch to let you know the where and when's of the interview. Err, can't think of much else going on. Err, how's it been with you?" Oz sounded a note of concern in his voice now that he had delivered his news.

"Tell you Bro, I'm a lot happier now I've heard your news. On the Mum front, we're doing all we can. Complex business, but with the love of a good woman, I'll get through it. Let's hope this journalist is a good woman!" Prez smirked as a hand displaying a solitary raised index finger appeared around the door, from where Nessa was listening to the conversation.

"Tell the Bros that Prez is back in the saddle and I'll be at the next Unkindness! Get those Eggs collected 'cause this Egg Run is going to be the best ever."

As Prez replaced the receiver Nessa emerged from behind the door,

Robert C. Holmes

"Now *that's* the man I married."

Angel

The thunder of four v twin engines rumbled through Heswall as the four bikes turned right at the crossroads at the centre of the village. A left turn and it was straight up the hill to the Jug and Bottle pub. Heswall being a relatively affluent area the Jug and Bottle was a regular to some of the areas movers and shakers. The S.O.S. were tolerated as they had been using it as a watering hole for years. At least, the Unholy Trinity of Oz, BS and Prez had. Before that, Prez and DJ had regularly met up there, once their original stamping ground the Victoria Hotel in Lower Heswall (where the really well-heeled drank) had been bulldozed to accommodate domestic dwellings. The four powerful machines lined up outside the pub and the bikers cut their engines. BS was riding his newly constructed Triumph America custom. He'd stretched the front forks and lowered the frame, finishing it off with a pink and yellow polka dot paint job. With that sort of a look it was christened *Mr Blobby* immediately. As BS and Prez removed their helmets Bear called to them,

"Now we've made an entrance, me and Oz are off!"

Prez acknowledged his Sergeant at Arms with a thumbs up as he and BS made their way in to the pub, removing their gloves as they went. BS quietly spoke as they approached the doors,

    "Do you think our journalist lady will have been impressed by that arrival?"

Prez shrugged, "That was the plan, but who knows? Sod it, I was impressed. Maybe she's too young to remember *Mr Blobby*!"

The couple strode to the bar and Prez ordered their usual tipples of a J.D. and coke for himself and a pint of bitter for his V.P. BS scanned the dark interior of the place, his eyes still adjusting behind his round spectacles. Prez addressed the barman as he paid for the drinks,

    "Anyone here from the press mate, we're s'posed to be meeting someone."

The barman, all neat haircut and trimmed beard with the dress sense of the lesser spotted hipster motioned to a booth in the corner,

    "Looks like it's your lucky day gents. Don't worry though, she's out of your league!" he smirked. In a parody of flicking the finger Prez held up his left hand with just the third finger lifted in salute,

    "It's always my lucky day pal, I'm married." His white gold wedding ring shining on said finger.

S.O.S.

"I'm always up for it though!" BS smiled sarcastically at the barman. Prez snorted, knowing that Kel would geld BS if she thought he was chasing other women. The two bikers strode over to the booth and realised that the barman had been right. Awaiting them was a young woman with mousey long straight hair, a good figure and long legs. All displayed via a short skirt a matching plunging neckline attached to a too small white tee shirt. She looked over the glasses perched on her nose and grinned at them, revealing a set of perfectly white teeth.

Shit, it is our lucky day! Prez stifled a grin and placed his drink on the table, extending his hand.

"Hi, I'm Prez and this is BS, he's the Vice President of the club. And you are?"

The girl half stood and offered her hand before slipping back down on to her seat with a feline fluidity that wasn't lost on the grizzled bikers as they sat on the opposite side of the table. They were only just noticing the lap top that the girl had been using, as it now blocked their view of her cleavage.

"Angel, Angel Dubois. Nice to meet you boys. My, was that you outside, I thought you had arrived via helicopter." The smile was perfect as was the diction, a faint hint of student twang, but no trace of a regional accent.

"No, no helicopter today, that's only for Tuesdays." Grinned Prez. Angel turned her attention to the lap top and then back to the bikers,

"I spoke to, Oz? Was it? Yes, Oz. He told me that you're supporting the Egg Run this Easter but you're wearing your, is it colours, this year?" her eyebrows arched as she put the question, looking at Prez then BS.

"Yeah. We've supported the Egg Run almost since it started, way back when. We've never worn our club patches to a run though. We've always thought it too political, and as the event was set up as a charity, it isn't the forum to make statements." Prez replied.

"Ahh" Angel purred tapping information in to the lap top with perfectly manicured long red nails, "So why now then?"

"To be honest we've been around this town since the eighties. We've seen it all. We saw the Council and sponsors take over this Egg Run and we've seen the Council and the police try to ban it. We've been hassled on it by the forces of both and we've been cheered on by the local populace. Folk 'round here know they can count on us if they've got a problem and can't get help." Prez smiled.

"What you're like vigilantes?" Angel's eyes sparkled but Prez wasn't falling for the trap.

"When I say help I mean help. Say there's a cat stuck up a tree, well, we're your boys. Don't bother the brave fire brigade, they've got a game of cards to finish at the station, we'll rescue Tiddles for you." Prez grinned.

"Pussies in need, we're your boys." BS grinned leaning forward as he did so.

"It must be a great comfort for the locals, knowing that you provide that kind of service." Angel smirked back.

"Never had a complaint yet." BS replied sitting back and swigging his pint. It was Prez's turn to lean forward, forcing himself to meet Angel's eyes rather than look elsewhere,

"We have our own charity run in November. The Wild Hunt Run, where a group of us ride up to Scotland. This year the Egg Run has come round and we just want to remind Heswall, the Wirral, the World, that we're still around."

Angel nodded and then looked puzzled, lines creasing her forehead,

"Tell me, S.O.S., what does it stand for?"

Prez leant forward encouraging Angel to do so also, so that their foreheads almost touched, BS grinned as he watched them.

"If I told you, my Sergeant at Arms would have to kill you." Prez whispered.

They both flopped back in their seats with Angel looking less than impressed at the fact that there had been no local scoop forthcoming.

"Look Angel, we're not the kind of club that you see at the movies or on T.V. We don't pack firearms or run drugs or kill rival club members. All we want is to live by our own rules and hey, if we can help ordinary guys and gals along the way, we will. The charities we help support the kind of things that can strike anyone. Anyone could get cancer or need a blood transfusion or need the air ambulance, right? If your editor has sent you to get us to tell you about how we tattoo our women *"property of"* or how I can get you twenty kilos of Columbian Red or put a hit on an ex-boyfriend, you're going to be disappointed sweetheart."

Prez wasn't sure what made the most impact, the information about the club or the use of the term sweetheart. The frosty reply answered his unasked question.

"You are dinosaurs though aren't you? I mean *sweetheart*? Come along, how sexist is that?"

"Well, last time I looked the dinosaurs were extinct." BS smiled, then hit Prez hard on the arm, "But no, we're still here, which puts that issue to bed doesn't it?"

Angel visibly stiffened, which to the delight of the bikers put a further strain on her white tee shirt,

S.O.S.

"I mean your attitude is prehistoric. The way you treat women, all this macho stuff."

"The way we treat women? We're mostly all happily married men." Prez sighed. "We love women, we respect women. A lady walks in to a room we stand up, a lady walks to a door, we open it, a lady needs a seat on a bus, she can have mine. You see where society has got it wrong is that it wants everyone to be equal in a literal sense, the same." Prez was warming to his theme,

"You see a sphere and a cube can be equal. They can be the same colour, same mass, same density, etc, etc, but they can't *be* the *same.* They can't literally be equal because one's a cube and one's a sphere. A sphere makes a great football, a cube makes a great die, but they're not interchangeable. Men and women, they're different. Sure, there's many ways they are interchangeable and don't get me wrong, I'm all for equality of opportunity, but the Politically Correct Czars don't mean that. They want us all wearing Chairman Mao boiler suits and singing from the same asexual hymn sheet. I mean take the B.B.C., it's started forcing this gender-neutral stuff down our throats. An actress is now an actor, how crazy is that? You see they're not consistent. If they're going down that stupid gender-neutral route, why don't they call Princess Anne, Prince Anne? But they won't do that, will they? It's crazy. What the Hell's wrong with gender anyway?" Prez paused as Angel stared at him then started typing on her lap top. "Forgive me, I've made an oversight, would you like a drink Angel?"

Angel shook her head furiously and looked up from her typing,

"I can get my own drink thanks."

*I'll bet you can, but I bet your paper's picking up the tab. Same way I bet you used your looks to get your job and to get your shot at us. It'll be Fleet Street, then T.V. for this lady. Don't get me wrong, I'm not knocking it. Use what you've got, that's what I say. But don't bloody **pretend** that looking gorgeous or being handsome doesn't open doors, because it does, end of. Like money and contacts. All the P.C. bullshit is just propaganda, so that the ugly sods like me are brainwashed in to thinking that we've all got a shot at being Prime Minister or a date with the girls from the Pirelli Calendar! Somehow the ridiculous notion of entitlement has corrupted society, scream and shout if you don't get your own way, protest, sleep with the right people and above all win over the media. Win them over and you're sorted. It doesn't matter how you get your money or influence, just make sure you get it so that you can then use it to rewrite how you got it! Perfect. The more money you've got the better looking you can become and the more you can access the media to ensure that what you say is the way it should be. Completely disenfranchising the majority of wage slaves, who can only aspire to your giddy heights. You can lay the trail of breadcrumbs and the disenfranchised will just gobble 'em right up! Everyone's a politician now!* Prez thought as BS sidled past him to get another round of drinks, turning as he did so for a peek at Angels cleavage before she looked up and he added,

"Sure I can't tempt you, Miss?" BS grinned.

"It's Ms, and no, thank you." The reply reminded Prez of a blast of cold air when a fridge door is left open. Angel looked up from the laptop and resumed her questioning in what was now becoming an aggressive and patronising tone,

"You say you "represent the people," but you don't work, do you?"

"Well, firstly, I didn't say I represented anyone, although I do represent anyone who wears our colours and they represent me. As for citizens, I'll help where I can, if I can. As for working, running this club is a full-time job. Wirral is only the Mother Chapter, we have numerous others throughout this country and beyond."

"So where does all the money come from?" Angel slipped back in to her friendly journalist mode, hoping to eke out a response she wanted to hear.

"All the money.........." Prez rubbed his chin and stared out of the window before returning Angel's gaze,

"I don't know who's done your research kiddo, but I can tell you the club gets by on subs, fines, donations and the back of the band BS used to front as Nikki Michelle, *Hanoi Jane*. Maybe you've heard of us? "

Angels fingers flitted over the keyboard again and she looked up,

"Ahh yes, *Hanoi Jane*, you had a couple of albums that sold well in the eighties and then folded, yes?"

"Yeah, that was us. We made good money from those albums, they did really well in Germany for some reason. Anyway, I made some sound investments and here we are. We're not awash with cash, but we get by."

"You were in the band too, weren't you?"

"Yeah, but BS was the front man, they always remember the front man." Prez smiled as he shifted in his seat to allow BS to return to his window seat, plonking the drinks on the table. Angel looked up and wrinkled her nose,

"Wasn't it heavy metal?"

"No." Prez sighed, "It was heavy rock, not metal, but you can call it what you like."

"Nothing too challenging, then?" Angel pursed her lips waiting for the bikers to bite. Prez shrugged as he sipped his drink,

"Challenging if you wanted to get airplay or appear on the B.B.C. We weren't P.C. you see."

BS jumped in,

"Yeah, we weren't the bloody *Clash* or *Tom Robinson Band*."

"Anyway," Prez interjected, "That was where the money came from."

Angel tapped away at the keyboard again Prez noticed she was slowly shaking her head as if mentally scolding the bikers as mischievous little boys, a fact confirmed by her next remarks,

"Don't you think you're all a little old for all this now? Boys and their toys?" She smiled sweetly.

"Every time I shave this face, sweetheart." Prez smiled back, "But you don't choose this life, it chooses you. You can either hack it, or you can't."

"Most can't." BS added wearing a deadpan expression.

"You think that makes you special?" There was a hint of a sneer in Angels reply, just a hint,

"Special, no. Different, yeah, definitely and proud to be so." Prez replied.

"Better?"

"Yeah, better. Who would differentiate themselves with a patch on their back to announce they were worse than mainstream society? Nihilists Are Us?" Prez laughed humourlessly. Angel spotted what she perceived as a chink in his armour and dived in,

"Nihilist, that's a big word for people like you." Prez had been holding back but reckoned now was the time to put the young journalist in her place,

"People like us...............hmmm, just who do you think *people like us* are?" he hesitated as her brow furrowed slightly, then before she could formulate her reply he continued on, "Dubois, that's a Norman surname, so I s'pose you can trace your lineage all the way back to William The Bastard? Your family probably owned huge tracts of land way back when, handed out to all the Norman nobles. Maybe your family are still landowners? Perhaps you are from a wealthy family and have had a good education and are now reaping the benefits of that? Or am I just stereotyping, as you are?"

Angel was for the first time on the back foot, Prez had hit a nerve and when on a roll there was no stopping him,

"I'll give you some decent material for your article if you want to know about me." Prez leaned back in his seat as the young journalist attempted to type all the information down as quickly as possible, all thoughts of a reply to the bikers queries gone, "I've got an honours degree in humanities with classical studies. A library at home which has my wife tearing her hair out 'cause it takes up so much space. I've rowed as part of the crew of the *Harald Draken Harfagre*, largest Viking ship reconstruction ever built. I've got a stunning wife and a son who is at university. I'm elected President of the S.O.S., an international club, which

S.O.S.

as President I represent, although each chapter is democratically run and thus autonomous. I appoint the Mother Chapters' officers, who are responsible for the smooth running of the club locally. These positions range from Treasurer to Sergeant at Arms and carry big responsibilities." Prez stopped for a moment giving Angel time to catch up, the moment she raised her eyes form her laptop he continued,

"I work out three times a week and support St Helens Rugby League Club. My ride is a Harley Davidson Wide Glide, which I've customised with ape hangers, drag pipes and more chrome than you can shake a stick at. I've written for Motorhead's fan club, I've never had a criminal conviction unless you count a parking ticket, I don't think that made any headlines. I manage the assets of the rock band *Hanoi Jane* who're still big in Germany, and oh yeah, I used to play bass guitar. Is that the stereotype you had of me?" Prez raised his glass in salutation and drained it. Before the young journalist could reply Prez delivered the coup de grace,

"Oh, and just to confound your stereotype of me further, I do the cooking, the washing up, the housework and myself and my wife do the shopping together. Not quite the rough, tough, misogynistic macho existence you had me down for, eh? I only beat her up if she's been a really naughty little girl.........." Prez smiled mirthlessly.

Angel was flustered now, the cool composure gone. Her research had not included any of this, she had been armed with the usual half truths about bikers and heavy rock bands on the road. Apparently based loosely on a working knowledge of the films, *This is Spinal Tap* and *Easy Rider*. Sex and drugs and rock and roll...........................BS leaned over as he placed his pint to one side,

"Seems to me that you've come here expecting us to be knuckle dragging misogynistic Neanderthals love." He grinned. Angel looked shocked,

"I'm sorry, I, didn't know, I......." her professionalism crumbling, Angel was reverting to the spoiled little girl that Prez had thought she might be, although he had remained cautious of stereotyping her, he had been on the end of such stereotyping for as long as he could remember and wasn't about to start operating under those illusions himself.

"Time for that drink?" Prez smiled gently, standing up and placing his hand on hers. She looked up nodding.

Prez pulled up on the drive of his mother's house and cut the engine. He'd ridden there straight after the conclusion of the interview with the local press to help Nessa with clearing items out from the house. He looked around as he dismounted.

S.O.S.

A typical snapshot of middle-class suburbia, all prim lawns with well-manicured hedges and trees. Typical seventies hacienda style bungalows with lawns with low ranch style fences, this had been a nice place to grow up in. The problem was, as a family we hardly spoke to our neighbours and vice versa. It seemed to be a soulless place, with no community spirit at all. Of course, that could have just been the attitude of my parents, but we never integrated with anyone really. In her later years, Mum put her trust in a few folks but if Dory next door was an example of her idea of a nice guy, then her judgement has been impaired for much longer than anyone realised.

The glass door of the porch opened, and Nessa poked her head out,

"Typical! I've done all the hard work already!" she called out grinning as Prez strode towards the house.

Once inside he placed his gloves and helmet on the dining room table. There were two large boxes on the floor. Prez raise his eyebrows and addressed his wife,

"This it?" he stared, incredulous.

"Yes, I know." Nessa nodded, "This is all the personal stuff I could find. I'm taking Mum some clothes tonight, they're in the back of the car."

Prez shook his head,

"Not much for a lifetime, is it?"

"No and I'll tell you what's odd." Nessa looked concerned, "There's absolutely nothing I can find to do with your Dad."

"What do you mean?"

"Nothing, no photos, letters, nothing. I can't even find their wedding photos."

Prez frowned,

"I'll nip up in the loft." he said but Nessa shook her head,

"Already been up there, nothing."

Prez put his hand to his moustache, deep in thought,

"Hey, wasn't there a photo of Dad, taken in the Lake District years ago, on the dresser? Thinking about it, I haven't seen it for a while."

The next half an hour was taken up with a thorough search of the house from top to bottom, even the garage wasn't spared. Alas, it was all in vain as neither Prez nor his wife could find a trace or any sign that Edna's husband had ever existed. The crushing truth of the matter appeared to be that in her anguished mental state she must have turned upon the memory of her husband and removed any physical evidence of his existence.

More than any other symptom, the biting, the paranoia, the change in character this was the most heinous. To be married to a man for decades,

S.O.S.

nursing him through tuberculosis, to bear his children and be a matriarch to the family home and then for whatever twisted reason to then loathe that man. To rewrite your past in a terrible and toxic way. For your cherished memories of your entire life to become tainted with whatever loathing and hatred Mum now had for them, must surely be the cruellest blow dealt to anyone with a mental illness. To not even be allowed the succour of treasured memories in one's darkest hours. I can think of no greater indignity, save perhaps to be completely paralyzed. Where is the compassion, the justice, vindication, reason? Of course, there isn't any. If there is a "Great Scheme of Things" then it is woven in such an arbitrary way that we mere mortals will certainly never understand it. When I was a little boy, I used to think that we were merely creatures being studied in a laboratory. Each planet and solar system separate from the other, to ensure no cross contamination. Then, as I got older I pondered that perhaps we were all merely part of one great entity. I wondered at the fact that we could be like atoms, planets circling and agitating like electrons and atoms, millions of them reaching out in to what we perceive as infinity. My Mum had ironically said that "people who think about these things go funny". I guess we only get the answer when we pass away, or perhaps we never get the answer? I am certainly older but no wiser regarding the subject. I feel that fate is fate and beyond our comprehension. One should live well and attempt to do good, not out of any desire to rack up points to stand and be judged before some deity but out of a sense of self pride and the knowledge that you did what you could to enrich the lives of others, because we only get one shot at it. In my case

I hope I've done that, at the very least I've touched the lives of my Brothers in a positive way and tried in some small part to share my values with them. All you can do is give it your best shot. Either way someone somewhere will judge you right and just as many, if not more, will judge you wrong. It's the way of things. Prez brooded.

"How did the interview go?" Nessa broke Prez's introspection as she handed him a box to take to the car.

"Good, I think. They'd sent this pretty young thing, straight form University, all teeth and legs, y'know the sort."

"I know *your* sort!" Nessa called back over her shoulder as she picked up another box.

"Yeah, well, we put her right on a few things, so when the article's printed we shouldn't come out like child molesters and cannibals. Who knows though?" Prez noticed Mr Dory scuttling in to his house as he placed the last box in the boot of the Focus and shut it. He and Nessa exchanged glances,

"Nice folk Mum's neighbours, always there for her." Prez growled sarcastically.

"Well, they aren't her neighbours anymore." Nessa patted Prez on his arm and locked up the porch whilst Prez slipped on his gloves.

S.O.S.

"Vince. I did find one thing." Nessa purred softly, a note of concern in her voice, as Prez was about to put his crash helmet on. He placed it on the seat of the 'bike and raised his eyebrows quizzically,

"What was that?"

"An envelope addressed to you. I haven't looked inside. I think your Mum left it for you, should it come to the worst. It was down the back of her bedside cabinet, trapped behind one of the drawers. That's why we didn't find it earlier." Nessa looked visibly upset as she reached in to her coat pocket and drew out a small envelope with the name "Vince" written in Edna's handwriting. It was strange as she barely ever called him Vince, it was usually the full Vincent. They exchanged glances, then Prez took the envelope and placed it in his jacket pocket. He smiled reassuringly at his wife.

"We'll have a look at it after tea." He smiled matter of factly, trying to play down the importance of Nessa's find. She smiled back and nodded eagerly as she moved around the side of the car to get in. Prez fastened his helmet and fired up *Landwaster*.

Prez walked in from the kitchen and set a mug of coffee down on the table for his wife, then set his own mug of tea down before taking his seat. He picked up the envelope from the table and looked at it. Nessa had returned from visiting Edna and was as depressed as such an event would make anyone. Neither of them had enjoyed their tea, a black cloud hung over proceedings.

Well, here goes..

Prez opened the letter. It contained five items. One of the items was a reading by Henry Scott Holland, the Canon of St Paul's Cathedral 1847-1918, it was on a printed card. Strangely it had been written out again in a handwriting Prez did not recognise. Prez read it out,

"Death is nothing at all. I have only slipped away into the next room, I am I and you are you.................Whatever we were to each other, that we are still. Call me by my old familiar name. Speak to me in the easy way which you always used. Put no difference in your tone. Wear no forced solemnity or sorrow. Laugh as we always laughed at the little jokes we enjoyed together. Play, smile, think of me, pray for me. Let my name be ever the household word that it always was. Let it be spoken without effort without the ghost of a shadow on it. Life means all that it ever meant. It is the same as it ever was. There is absolutely unbroken continuity. What is this death but a negligible accident? Why should I be out of mind because I am out of sight? I am waiting for you for an interval. Somewhere just around the corner. All is well."

Prez took a deep breath and Nessa crossed the floor to put her hand on his shoulder. Below the reading in Edna's handwriting it said, "Hymn. The Lord's My Shepherd (Crimond)". Prez looked at two of the other pieces of paper, one telling him to get copies of the death certificate and send it to

S.O.S.

Edna's insurance companies, the other requesting the funeral director she preferred. It also requested that the curate or vicar of Barnston or Pensby conduct the service and read the piece Prez had just read out. He took a deep breath as he read the final piece of paper:

"Dear Vincent,

When you receive the cash from the sale of my house, I do hope you will be able to repay your mortgage in full, and if you keep on paying the endowment mortgage you should receive the money when it reaches full term, and I hope you will be able to enjoy what's left.

Love

Mum

XXXX"

Prez sat, head bowed. Edna was practical until the end. The letter was dated 2003, before anyone had known about her mental health issues, before perhaps they had even existed.

Her eyes filled with tears, softly sobbing, Nessa looked at her husband,

"Come and sit on the sofa for a hug."

Prez complied, hugging his wife, yet keeping a stiff upper lip as she cried quietly.

Robert C. Holmes

Thunder In Spring

The bikers dutifully filed in to the room to commence the Unkindness. It was the Tuesday before the Sunday of the Wirral Egg Run and time to ensure that everyone knew the importance of turning up. Prez failed to suppress a smile as he noted the numbers present. His gaze swept the table. BS, Bear and Oz were naturally present, all as constant as the Northern Star. What was really making Prez smile was the rest of the crew. Greg The Vet, Dazzler, Irish Kev and Chinner. A plastic "Mr Potato Head" was put on the table at an empty seat. Prez raised his eyebrows as he looked at it. Oz explained as the bikers took their seats,

"Boalie's still laid up Boss, so I took the liberty of bringing his effigy in." The assembled bikers rumbled their consent and a ripple of applause then washed over proceedings.

It's the first Unkindness in months that has had a light-hearted feel to it. This is what we're here for, not to carry the weight of the World on our shoulders. Prez thought to himself.

"Okay Gents, I declare this Unkindness open." Prez called out, "Oz..." he gestured to his Treasurer,

S.O.S.

"Okay Boys. We all know we've got a good turnout for Sunday; weather forecast is good and you all know to wear your colours. I've got a little item here you may enjoy." Oz reached below the table and produced a copy of the Wirral free newspaper,

"Hot off the press, the delightful Ms Angel Dubois interviews Prez and BS. To quote: "Hell raising Bikers with hearts of gold!" unquote!" Oz had a grin from ear to ear.

"How did you manage that? Did you get her pissed?" Bear rumbled. Prez and BS shrugged their shoulders in mock humility.

"Just were our natural selves!" Prez grinned.

"It's all good press Brothers, I've left some copies downstairs if you want to read it. Suffice it to say that Ms Dubois sounds like she wants to have your children guys!" Oz chortled. BS waved a hand,

"What can I say? A young woman of taste and refinement!"

"It was worth an afternoon in the pub." Prez nodded, "You've all seen the pile of Easter Eggs downstairs on the way in, over a hundred of 'em, donated by various folk. Kel and Nessa will be at the final destination of the Run with the eggs you can see and to collect any others from the riders. Then it'll be on to Clatterbridge Hospital to hand 'em in."

"We're going to make the dentists of Wirral happy bunnies." Bear growled to the amusement of the assembled throng. Prez cleared his throat as the laughter died down,

"Oz, any news on that rogue drug dealing family in your neck of the woods?"

"Gone Boss, evicted by the landlord eventually. At least that's the story!" Oz gave a thumbs up.

"Y'see, one application of S.O.S. and the stains are gone!" Dazzler called out once again causing the eruption of laughter around the table.

"Hearts of gold, balls of steel, eh boys? You English lads aren't just a bunch of pussies then?" Irish Kev called out over the laughter.

"We get by." Bear rumbled back. Dazzler raised his hand to speak and Prez acknowledged him,

"So boys, was she fit this Dubois bird?" Dazzler asked earnestly, causing the bikers to spontaneously burst in to laughter and then a moment of applause.

"Daz, she was gorgeous." BS grinned, "Totally above your pay grade matey!"

Prez decided to introduce a hint of gravitas without wishing to bring the buoyant mood down,

"I'd just like to say on a Club level, that I know a lot's gone on lately and not all of it good," a low murmur of agreement rumbled around the table as the bikers nodded, "But we're on the up now boys. This Egg Run will raise our profile as the good guys and Ms Dubois has given us a leg up."

"I don't give a fuck about being the good guys." Bear growled. Prez shot him a smile back,

"Good P.R. never hurt anyone, and I don't know about you guys, but I'd rather have people cheer at me than try to get me locked up."

"Amen to that Bro." Agreed BS and the assembled crew nodded their affirmation. Again, Dazzler raised his arm,

"So when she gave you a leg up, did you give her anything lads?" He crowed, still unable to shake the image of Angel Dubois from his fevered imagination. Prez shook his head as BS grinned and replied,

"Christ Daz, can you put something in your bloody tea to calm down, the bloody crack of dawn isn't safe with you around."

"Don't tell him where Dawn lives!" called out Greg the Vet, as once again laughter filled the room.

After the Unkindness, Prez joined BS in the back garden of the clubhouse. BS rolled a cigarette whilst Prez cradled a mug of tea. It was a typical spring evening, cold, yet with a hint of freshness in the air that promised the rebirth that was to come. Prez turned to his Vice President as he lit his roll up,

"Thought that went well."

BS nodded after taking a draw,

"Yup."

"Can't wait 'til Sunday now and get the show on the road."

"Yeah, should be good Prez." BS exhaled and looked up at the clear sky where stars were emerging, his breath steaming in the cooling air, "How are things with your Mum?"

"She's in a new place in Upton now." Prez sighed taking a sip from his mug, "Bloody hateful place, if I'm honest. You go in and it's such a cloying atmosphere, in every sense of the word." Prez took a deep breath and continued, "It reeks of lavender, but beneath it you can make out the stench of vomit, even decay. You look around and you can see where it all ends and how."

"Christ."

"Yeah, I know, bloody horrible mate. They're all drugged up to their eyeballs. Mum too. They're not supposed to restrain them but me and Nessa have visited on a couple of occasions where Mum's been strapped to her wheelchair."

S.O.S.

"What, tied up?" BS looked aghast.

"Yeah. When we challenged 'em about it they told us it was to stop her falling forward out of the chair." Prez shrugged. "The staff, I feel for them. You can see some of 'em really care, they're the ones who suffer. You can see there's others there because they can't get a job anywhere else. They're the ones who end up in the news for all the wrong reasons. They're on piss poor wages and suddenly find themselves empowered over people for probably the first time in their miserable lives. That's when you get the horror stories in the media. Someone said once that you should judge a society on how it treats its prisoners. Well, I reckon you should judge a society on how it treats its pensioners. I mean, most people hope to get there, don't they?"

BS exhaled in to the sky and crushed the remnants of his cigarette between his fingers,

"Shit, not exactly a happy ending is it?"

Prez drained his mug and turned to walk back in to the clubhouse, as he did so BS grabbed his shoulder,

"What about DJ?"

Prez turned back and pulled a face illustrating his frustration,

"DJ doesn't exist mate. It's Nigella now. I've had some communication with him via e mails, but every last vestige of the man we knew has been erased. Sad thing is I've got a collection of air mail letters at home from when he was in H.K. Norway and the States. All red blooded male talk, no hint of what was going on. Think I'll have to burn 'em"

BS shook his head,

"What makes that happen to anyone?"

"Who knows? I'm convinced it's a mental thing myself. I was reading in the press the other day that a Professor at some university had his funding pulled because the powers that be didn't think what he was doing was appropriate." Prez sneered as he finished his sentence.

"What was that?"

"He was looking in to Transgender reassignment."

BS's eyes widened,

"What, you mean turning someone back again?"

Prez nodded,

"Yeah. It turns out that there's a huge number who take the plunge and then aren't happy and want to return to what they were." Prez put a hand to his temple, "I can't remember the exact proportion, but it was pretty high."

An uncomfortable silence fell, the music in the clubhouse rumbling away in the background as AC/DC informed everyone *"It's a long way to the top, if you want to rock n roll!"* Prez answered the question that was hanging between them,

"I don't reckon we need to vote him out."

BS nodded sombrely as Prez continued,

"Pointless. The NY Chapter's gone, as has HK, they were autonomous anyway, so any debts they racked up were theirs to settle. He's not a he anymore, so as such can't be a Club member, so no need to get rid of the ink, although I'm sure that's been done anyway. Might as well just let it all go." Prez sighed and looked up to the sky,

"Y'know, he was my best friend. We were like brothers. Now I can't decide if he was a very good liar or demented or what." Prez shook his head, clearly upset by the turn of events, "It was a real stab in the back, bloody hell, he was riding a 'bike before I was!" he turned once again to head indoors, "I think we should just let sleeping dogs lie mate."

BS nodded in agreement and followed his President in to the clubhouse. He wasn't convinced Bear would see it the way Prez did, but as long as DJ wasn't in the U.K. he would be safe from any ursine retribution.

Typical Egg Run weather! Bright sunshine, blue sky and a cool breeze. Thought Prez, as he surveyed the scene along New Brighton waterfront. Thousands, literally thousands of bikes were parked in the slip roads which lined the large grassy areas where burger vans and even some tents were pitched. The gleaming machines reflecting the bright sunshine like snaking lines of metal clad mercenaries from the Dark Ages, awaiting the call to arms. Prez didn't attempt to suppress the smile which spread across his face beneath his wrap around shades as BS approached from a burger van with a burger in each hand.

Not sure what's the most pleasing aspect, the weather, the numbers or the tight group of patches that surround me, yet are mingling with the public. Prez pondered. BS passed him a burger,

"There you go Chief, botulism in a bun!"

"Cheers mate." Prez beamed," "Did you expect this turnout?"

"Nope" BS replied between mouthfuls. Prez was suddenly aware of Oz at his side,

"Okay Treasurer?"

"This is brilliant isn't it boys?" Oz capered like a dog with two tails, then dropped his voice in conspiratorial fashion, "I've gotta say though, there's a bit of resentment about our press coverage. I mean it's not our run, is it?"

Prez shook his head and swallowed down a chunk of burger,

"No, it's not our run. But the feedback I got from the organisers was that anything that lifts the profile and brings in more money for the charities we're supporting has got to be good." He shrugged, "There's always going to be some bruised egos, and we're never goin' t'be everyone's bosom buddies, shit, I wouldn't want to be, would you?"

"Nah." Beamed Oz, "Just saying..........Nothings gonna put a dampener on this for me, it's great. Someone said there was a film crew at the starting point. Want me to check it out?"

Prez shook his head,

"No, it's twenty minutes before we roll off, I'll take a walk to the front of the queue for myself."

"I'll come with you." Agreed BS to which Prez raised his eyes to the heavens,

"Christ, anything to get your bloody mug on the TV!" to which BS fluttered his eyelashes.

As the pair made their way to the head of the ranks of parked bikes, appraising each machine as they went, they noticed that there was indeed a large crowd gathered at the start point.

"Yeah, it's a camera crew and a sound guy." BS remarked as they got closer, then Prez dug him in the ribs with his elbow,

"Never mind that, there's our girl!" Prez exclaimed pointing at the familiar figure of Angel Dubois. Decked out in a pink leather jacket and black leather jeans, with high heeled boots, she was, understandably, the centre of attention. Spotting the two bikers approaching she tossed her mane back and held her arms open as if receiving two long lost friends,

"My Boys!" she called out, hugging first BS and then Prez. The assembled crowd watched on, many envious, many respectful, many just glad to be there. Prez broke from the embrace,

"Hi Kiddo, how are you? Great to see you here. "he smiled. Angel beamed back from beneath her Ray Bans,

"Wonderful to see you both, and what a turn out! I think half the 'bikes in England are here!" Angel enthused, her poise and self-assured manner to the fore, "I'm here with a friend from London." She looked around attempting to locate her friend in the crowd, then spotting him she pointed for the benefit of the bikers.

"There's Oliver, the one on the Road King."

BS and Prez followed the perfectly manicured finger to its target. There, all square jawed, fashionably stubbled, encased in black leather, sporting shades worth more than the entire ensemble of cow that he was wearing, sat Oliver.

"Come and meet him, I've told him all about you!" enthused Angel.

If she'd added "jolly hockey sticks" to that statement, it wouldn't have seemed out of place. Prez thought as he looked across at BS and nodded assent to meet Oliver.

"Olly, Olly, these are the bikers I told you about." Beamed Angel as they approached. Oliver dismounted the Road King and smiled to reveal flawlessly perfect teeth. He offered his hand to Prez and his grip was strong when they shook. He looked about thirty-five and was a good two inches taller than Prez.

"Quite a little party you've arranged here." He grinned, the plummy tones mixed with a subtle urban bite. *Giving Oliver instant street cred amongst his friends in Chelsea.* mused Prez.

"Alright mate. Glad you could come and see us at our best." Prez smiled as BS shook hands with Oliver.

"Yeah, we do our best, in our quiet understated northern way." BS smiled mirthlessly back.

"I'm a little taken aback that charities would have anything to do with the Hells Angels." Oliver smiled back. Prez looked to the floor, shaking his head, then addressed Angel who had now slipped seamlessly under Oliver's arm,

"Angel, babe, what have you been telling this gent?" then he addressed Oliver, "Sorry pal, but we're not the Hells Angels."

Oliver frowned,

"But you're all the same, aren't you?"

Prez looked at BS who looked away over the horizon and blew out his cheeks. Yet before Prez could reply Angel pulled away to look Oliver in the face.

"Olly! You know they're not the Hells Angels, remember what I told you about them." She sounded like a petulant child stamping her foot. Then, just as suddenly she slipped underneath his arm again and gazed up at him as he smiled at her.

"Oh gosh, you're just teasing, you pig!" she hit him on the chest playfully. He looked at Prez.

"Just a jape my friend. I've read Angel's piece about you. In fact, she's written much more about you than the item that appeared in that ridiculous provincial publication she works for up here."

"All good I hope?" Prez smiled back.

"Well, it may be rather good for you fellows." Oliver replied, his modulated vowels as smooth and dark as molasses.

"In what way?" Prez raised his eyebrows and BS leaned in further to listen.

S.O.S.

"Well, I work for a firm in the City, I have friends in the literary world, many of whom find the tales Angel has been spinning about you fellows, quite intriguing. Naturally such things have a shelf life and would have to be pitched at the right moment. However, I would like you to meet some people to see if there's any, forgive the pun, mileage in it."

Ahh, now it's all beginning to make sense. Angel is currently the latest girlfriend of this guy, albeit she's many years his junior. They come from similar backgrounds and everything these characters do is related to making a buck or self-promotion. Unlike us, they can speculate to accumulate, because they're rolling in brass already. So, if a little deviation from the mainstream path goes wrong, chalk it up to experience. If, on the other hand, a little dabble in to the left field comes up trumps and makes everyone a shed load, enhancing their already burgeoning piles of gilt, well it's much kudos all around. They make some money they don't need, and their status is enhanced as they've unearthed this week's next big thing! Not to mention there's the raucous excitement of going to where no man has gone before, in to the belly of the beast! Just think of the hours of fun that could be had recounting their tales about the barbarians on wheels over a glass of champers, or a hip flask whilst watching the rugger. Pass the bloody stirrup cup. Prez fumed but remained outwardly calm, his shades ensuring that his usually expressive eyes gave nothing away.

"That sounds like a plan Oliver." Prez smiled, "To be honest, we've got rather a lot on at the moment. If you could leave me your number, I could get one of my officers to get back to you."

The look on Oliver's face was priceless. *He'd obviously expected the grubby little plebs to take his arm off at the very sniff of a few quid which might be in the air. Typical of his type!* Prez inwardly sneered. Angel jumped up and down with excitement,

"That would be wonderful, wouldn't it Olly?"

Oliver produced a smile which slipped in to place as if by magic and replaced the dumbfounded expression that had come and gone in the blink of an eye. Having dealt with some slippery customers in the music business Prez was not about to be bowled over by false promises and a slick sales pitch. He had seen it many times before. Not that there might not be an equitable outcome beneficial to all parties. He'd be damned if he would take the first bait cast by the angler though. Perhaps Oliver could get his after-dinner revelations to impress his rugger playing mates and posh totty, whilst the Club gained some good press and a vitally required shot of cash, if the situation was handled correctly.

"Boss, we've got to get back to the 'bikes, we'll be starting soon." BS reminded Prez who offered his hand to Oliver,

"Nice meeting you Oliver. I'm sure we can thrash something out."

"Indeed, likewise, I'll be in touch." Oliver replied although there was a frostiness in his tone that Prez had not been aware of previously. Angel broke away from her beau and again hugged the pair of bikers.

S.O.S.

"This has been wonderful. You two just *must* come to London to see me." She bubbled. Prez and BS broke free and smiled back at her, Prez as aware as BS that they weren't the only people being used in this arrangement.

"Yeah, that'd be great kiddo. Have a good ride!" Prez said raising his hand to wave goodbye as he turned away whilst BS ensured he got another exuberant hug. As his Vice President caught him up Prez turned and growled,

"That kid's being used by that bastard."

"Yeah................................." BS murmured thoughtfully, "But that's the way those types are. She probably knows it and will be on to some other Roger or Timothy before the year is out. Don't worry, she'll be okay."

"Different bloody world mate, different bloody world." Prez nodded as they walked to the bikes. BS pointed to the knot of S.O.S. patches huddled around their 'bikes talking to some civilians,

"Hey, isn't that the Brokeback Boys?"

Prez squinted in the sun and held up, his hand to keep it from his shades. Sure enough, it was indeed Dave and Phil, christened the Brokeback Boys, due to their close relationship regarding motorcycling. It was a tongue in cheek nickname and was taken in good humour, both men being staunchly heterosexual, making a mockery of their moniker. They were what Prez would call "serious motorcyclists", due to their penchant for taking their touring 'bikes all over the country. They were also dab hands on the off-road circuit. When Prez and BS arrived at the group, they shook the hands of the two men.

"Good to see you boys." Prez grinned.

"Good turnout Vince, belter of a day too!" The stocky individual called Dave grinned back, his bald pate dazzling in the bright sunlight. Phil smiled back,

"We thought you needed some support after reading that stuff in the papers!" he scoffed.

"I've even seen bloody Troll!" Dave snorted. Prez nodded,

"Yeah, I don't think he's been seen outside of his shed since 1066!"

A shrill whistle announced it was time to saddle up and the assembled group immediately fractured in to individuals, as they moved to their machines and began slipping on helmets and gloves. When the massed throng fired up their engines it sounded as though Armagedcon had arrived. The thunder reverberated through rider's chests and must have been audible for miles around *Makes me think of the Heavy Metal Holocaust gig headlined by Motorhead back in '81, where a guy living three miles away complained to the police that he couldn't hear his television! Largest outdoor rig ever used in Blighty, actually took out a power relay station. Great gig!* Prez grinned to himself. BS noticed and as he lined up *Mr Blobby* next to *Landwaster*, he gave a thumbs up. Words would have been pointless in the rumbling thunder all around.

The ride in itself snaked around the Wirral, culminating in a rally at a local farmstead. There Easter Eggs and donations were made. A small idiotic minority, mostly riding scramblers or quad bikes rode irresponsibly and as usual such buffoons shot off to Wales, rather than give a donation.

Having parked up, Prez approached each stall, giving five pounds to each charity. He could see Nessa and Kelly standing at the Easter Egg stall, relieving bikers of their chocolate eggs. There was already a mountain of the goodies protected from the sun by the shade of the stall's canopy. They had been brought to the site in advance by the girls earlier. Oz approached, prerequisite bacon sandwich in his hand,

"Prez, what a bloody show, great isn't it?" he beamed between mouthfuls,

"Yeah, better than I'd hoped, to be honest. Even had a chat with Angel beforehand."

"Bloody Hell, don't tell Dazzler!" Oz coughed on his sandwich theatrically.

"I think she'd be able to handle him!" Prez smiled. BS strode up from behind him and joined in,

"Don't tell Daz that, I think that's what he's after!" he chuckled as the bikers nodded agreement. Prez glanced at his watch,

"Give it another three hours and we'll start telling everyone to move out. Some of 'em are going to The Tap, others in to Wales, think I'll just head home." He couldn't mask the tiredness in his voice. It was a hot day and what with all the shenanigans with Edna he was feeling exhausted. He didn't feel like another round of backslapping and small talk. He'd let BS and Oz deal with it. He knew things were safe in their hands.

"I'm going for a bevy." BS replied, Oz nodding furiously,

"Yeah, I'm with you V.P. Hot day like this, brings on a fair old thirst!"

"I think that's probably the bacon sarnies sunshine." Prez grinned. Kelly and Nessa strolled over from the mountain of eggs they had been collecting. Kelly grabbed BS by the arm,

"Look! Our very own chocolate pyramid!" she breathed excitedly. Nessa linked arms with Prez,

"Don't get any ideas, Vince! They're for the kids!" she hissed then laughed. It was well known that Prez had a weakness for chocolate, although his slim build maintained by his three times a week workout routine, made a mockery of his vice.

"Yeah, okay!" he smiled, "Look, we're giving it about another three hours, then I'll help you load up Cheops over there and we'll take 'em to Clatterbridge Hospital and they can keep' em."

Prez put his arm around Nessa's shoulders and walked her back to the eggy pyramid,

"Thanks for this kiddo. I really appreciate you and Kel helping out with this stuff. Gives the club a human face." He looked closely at his wife and shrugged, "Well, *almost* human!" he grinned wickedly. Nessa retorted with a swift kick to his shin, which immediately changed his face from a grin to a grimace,

"Guess I asked for that!"

Nessa pulled a mirthless grin back at him then burst out laughing.

This whole gig hasn't just been good for the Club, it's been good for all of us as people. A shot in the arm. Funny how just doing good things for others can give you a rush. It's not just that though, it's the whole shebang. The charity stuff, sure, but the weather, the camaraderie, the lightness of it all after all the heavy shit we've been going through. Gives you faith in things. I'll have to watch out or I might become a glass half full person! Prez smiled to himself before limping theatrically and leaning on Nessa's shoulder for support, whilst she carried on giggling like a schoolgirl.

Reality Check

Prez padded in to the bedroom after performing his morning ablutions. Vanessa had already gone to work, leaving him to make the bed and ensure the housework was completed.

Hardly the rock'n'roll biker lifestyle. He mused as he slipped his silver rings on to his fingers. He pulled on his jeans and spent five minutes surveying his amassed Motorhead and Harley Davidson t shirts in his chest of drawers before selecting a shirt from Motorhead's "Inferno" tour. Pulling it on he opened the curtains and shook his head at the sight that greeted him. He'd already been outside in his dressing gown earlier to remove the thin layer of snow from Vanessa's car, enabling her to head off to work, but it had thickened since then. Prez gazed out of the window, his thoughts swirling,

November, don't you just love it? I guess it was the right thing to do, cancelling this year's Wild Hunt Run. It's almost as if this is the Fimbul Winter we've been waiting for, ha, bring on Ragnarök! I hated putting the motion to cancel to the guys at the Unkindness, but they all knew it was coming. The weather's been awful and according to the media, it's set to get worse. No reason to take a bunch of over forties and fifties to the bloody frozen wastes. It's been cancelled a couple of times before after all. Prez took a sip of his hot tea and grimaced ruefully. *Yet there was a kind of finality about this cancellation, almost as if by cancelling our traditional run, it was a kind of admission, not of defeat, but that the club has almost run its course. Not quite the last rites but a definite feeling of finishing a chapter of one's life. We're all too old, with different commitments and to be honest I'm not sure that anyone actually believes in what we started out to do. I reckon it's true that idealism fades as you get older. What's that saying, the young are socialist and the old are conservatives? Something like that. I've never liked change really. So, few things that we're told are "progressive" and "better" turn out to be so. I mean, you don't require intelligence to amass knowledge any more. All you need to do is ask your mobile 'phone to find out the answer. Then, as soon as it's answered the question, you can forget it and move on. People are enslaving themselves to modern technology and they don't even know it. Or more worryingly, they do know it and they just don't care.*

The success of the Egg Run earlier in the year was a fading memory and as winter had begun to arrive early, all Prez's doubts and uncertainties that he kept locked away were surfacing once more. As always, the year appeared to have flown by. Good things had happened, a wonderful holiday week in Scotland, spent with Eddie and his girlfriend Samantha. The wildlife was incredible and the whole family had enjoyed spotting woodpeckers, Red Kites, hares, deer and various flora and fauna. It was an ideal stress buster as it temporarily removed both Vanessa and Prez from the arduous chores of Club duties and visits to Edna. It was fairly full on for Prez though, as he took it upon himself to drive the family everywhere, putting a couple of thousand miles on the car at least. However, it was still a wonderful holiday, a brief respite at least amidst the chaos that was threatening to swamp Prez and Nessa at home. Now, however, it was back to reality with a bump as Prez mulled over Edna's condition.

It's a Tuesday which means we'll be visiting Mum again tonight. I hate these visits. She's either sitting there, barely responsive or she's lying in bed, not responding at all. I don't know whether it's the drugs, the condition, or what. I do know it's no way to live. I'm sure there's no quality of life for her. If only I could get inside her head and reassure her that everything is okay and that she can live out her days in peace That though, isn't on the agenda. We've just got to keep her alive until the torment is finally over. Not good.

He made his way downstairs into the kitchen and after making himself a mug of tea sat in his armchair and watched the snow gathering pace in the front garden. Star hopped up onto his lap, purring enthusiastically as she treaded on his jeans to make herself comfortable before curling up on his legs. The final act in her settling down was turning upside down so that her head pressed against Prez's leg.

She'd sit there all day if I let her. Actually, if reincarnation is the real deal, I'd like to come back as a cat. Only if I could live with a family like us though! Prez thought to himself as Star sank in to an even deeper sleep, her whiskers twitching as she pursued some prey in her dream.

There's a load of e mails I've got to wade through regarding the band, the Club, bills and demands mostly, but also queries from hardcore fans, curse of the internet again, all demanding an immediate response.

Prez drained his mug and shifted his legs which prompted an immediate reaction from his feline legwarmer who bounded to the floor and started washing. After placing his empty mug on the kitchen worktop, he turned and made his way back through the living room and in to the hall to go upstairs to his study. Before he had taken two steps on the flight of stairs there was a heavy knock at the front door. He opened it to be faced with a tall young policeman. His nose red in the cold, breath snaking from his mouth as he spoke,

"Mr Sinclair?"

Prez nodded and stepped aside,

"That's me, do you want to come in, it's not too good out there is it?"

The policeman shook his head,

"Property in Sandham Grove, I believe it's your mothers, but she's currently-" Prez interrupted,

"In a nursing home, yeah that's hers, well, mine and my sisters really, since Mum won't ever be coming out. Mental health issues."

The policeman nodded slowly and continued,

"I'm afraid there's been an accident. Her neighbour a Mr, err...." he produced a notebook and tried to thumb through it with his gloves on, Prez helped him out,

"Dory? Mr Dory?"

The policeman smiled back,

"Yeah, that's him. He reported a burglary at your Mum's. Don't worry, it wasn't a burglary, but I'm afraid the ceilings fallen in. Water tank we reckon, although we've only looked through the window, you understand."

Prez blew out his cheeks,

"Bloody hell, I didn't think to drain the damn thing!"

"Happens a lot in empty properties Sir. I advise you to get down there asap, turn the water off, assess the damage. It looked fairly comprehensive I'm afraid."

"Sure you don't want to get a warm and a drink mate?" Prez queried.

S.O.S.

"No thanks, I'm off duty in half an hour and I've got stuff to do. Thanks anyway, sorry to be the bearer of bad news."

"No worries mate. Thanks for your time, I'll get right on it." Prez smiled weakly back as the policeman turned to walk back across the thickening snow to his car at the end of the drive.

Good news, you just can't get enough of it! My own damn stupid fault, I should've drained the tank when I knew Mum wasn't ever coming home again. Shit.

It was worse than Prez had imagined it. He looked up at what had been the ceiling in the living room, it was merely wooden planks now, he could see through to the bedroom ceiling, or what was left of it. Most of what had been both the ceiling to the front room and the front bedroom, plus the rear bedroom and the dining room now lay in a heap on the ground floor. The kitchen had escaped the worst of the devastation. Prez could feel the urge to cry, a feeling he'd become accustomed to over the last couple of years, something which was new to him however and that he did not like one bit. All caused by a complete lack of control over given situations, things he always thought he could deal with through strength of will. He blinked the moisture back, fighting back the memories of how the rooms used to look. He'd never liked the house, but it was just one more thing that was now erasing the memories of Edna, how she had the place decorated, how it had in its own way, exuded her personality.

Where's the justice in this, the natural justice? This woman, who never hurt anyone, is now being wiped out of existence. She's already lost her mind, now her home as she would've known it has gone as well. No fairness or justice. I guess there never was any. I just hoped there was. No justice, just us.

Prez grinned tight lipped at the irony of it all. He picked up some of the sodden plaster board and then pulled up the edges of the soaked carpet. Everything ruined. He would now have to call Julie of course and let her know the situation. She would doubtless wish to help, but her financial position would mean there would be little monetary help there. She was retired and her husband, Bear, was hardly in a well-paid job as a hospital theatre technician. As usual, it would be down to Prez to sort it out. His own financial situation was hardly rosy, and he knew it would probably mean securing a bank loan, just to get the property in a state to sell. It had been Prez and Nessa looking after Edna for the last few years. Taking her on holiday, visiting at least twice a week, taking her shopping. Once again, it would be the pair of them stepping in to set things right, as best they could.

First thing I'd better do is tell the estate agents, not that they've been any good. They keep contacting me at weekends asking if I'd show prospective buyers around because they're short staffed! What am I paying them for? Useless! Then I'd better contact someone with dehumidifiers and then a builder, a plumber and of course, Nessa. Another quiet day in S.O.S. land.................

S.O.S.

Hours later Nessa and Prez stood evaluating the damage, surrounded by workmen unloading heaters to dry out the house. Prez had engaged their services, despite the cost, as he was sure the bank would come across with a loan. He had always been a good customer and had never defaulted on the few loans he had taken out over the years. If they wouldn't lend to him, he was sure Nessa wouldn't have a problem. She was shivering as she hugged his arm and Prez realised she was crying,

"Vince, what are we going to do? Look at it, how are we going to fix this?" she sniffled. Prez put his arm around her shoulders,

"Look Ness, we're not going to let this beat us after what we've been through the last couple of years. I'm going to call the bank when we get home and sort out an appointment. If they won't lend to me, I'm sure they'll lend to you. Can't see it being a problem with the investments I've got and you having a regular income. What could go wrong?" Prez smiled back. He hoped he looked more confident than he felt.

"Hey, look," Prez injected a note of optimism on to his voice as he turned his wife around to look him the eyes, "Maybe a facelift will help sell the place. It'll be fresh and new and a blank neutral canvas for some punter to put their own mark on. Before this, it was always a dated, old ladies house, wasn't it? But now, prospective buyers will see a fresh new opportunity!"

Nessa smiled back and nodded,

"I s'pose you're right…………………..But you sound like you've been watching too many of those house buying programmes on T.V.!"

"Only 'cause I fancy Kirstie Alsop……not!" Prez forced a laugh and for a moment had convinced himself that he'd turned a disaster in to a positive.

"It's just like us to grab victory from the jaws of defeat!" He beamed. At that point the senior labourer approached him,

"Well, we're done here. It'll take a couple of days to dry out at least. Just leave these heaters on. We'll come back then and give you a price on what needs fixing, you okay with that?"

"Yeah, thanks for coming out so quickly. You've got our number, so give us a call and we'll come out and meet up here again when you're ready mate." Prez smiled back.

Nessa and Prez followed the labourers outside and looked back at the house. From the outside, you would never know the carnage that had occurred within. Nessa looked at Prez,

"Vince, I can't face seeing Mum tonight. Not after this. Would it be okay if you went on your own?"

"Yeah, of course, no worries." Prez smiled back as they climbed in to the car.

S.O.S.

A great end to a perfect day.

The journey to the care home only took about twenty minutes normally, but with the snow fall having made the roads akin to ice rinks, it had taken Prez nearly an hour to get there. It was dark now, visiting hours being from six until seven thirty. His headlamps picked out a couple of vehicles in the small car park, far fewer than usual.

The weather. An ideal excuse not to put yourself through the torment of seeing people you care for reduced to something not unlike zombies. Prez thought grimly as he stepped out of the car. Even walking up to the foreboding building filled his heart with dread. He rang the bell and as the door opened the familiar stench of vomit, desperation and thickly scented lavender, with just a hint of sweat assailed his nostrils.

"Mr Sinclair?" A young girl of around twenty greeted him in her slightly stained uniform, Beverly announced her name tag.

"Hello. Yes, I'm, here to see-"

"Edna, isn't it?" Beverly smiled from under her fringe of bright purple hair. Being around four feet nothing tall she craned her neck to look up at Prez,

"We've moved her to a more suitable room."

"Okay, where do I go?" Prez smiled back.

"Follow me." Beverly led Prez along a corridor, they passed the main living areas and stopped at a flight of stairs,

"Fourth floor, room number seven. There's a lift just further down the corridor if you need it." Beverly smiled.

"No, that's okay." With that, Prez began his assent. By the time he reached the door to Edna's room he was breathing deeply.

How on earth can it be sensible putting an old person with mental health issues on the highest floor in the building? They know she's had falls before, what are they playing at?

It hadn't escaped his attention that Edna's room was the only bedroom on this floor. There were a couple of bathrooms and a door proclaiming "staff only" other than that, there was just Edna's room. Prez knocked on the door,

"Mum....................." silence enveloped him, "Mum? Can I come in?" more silence. "Mum, it's Vince, I'm coming in."

Prez opened the door and entered. He was shocked by the small dimensions of the room. The roof was slanted so he had to be careful that he didn't hit his head. Naturally that wouldn't bother someone of Edna's stature, nevertheless the room was tiny. There was a small bedside lamp that dully illuminated the room. A wardrobe and a chest of drawers. Sparse to put it mildly. Prez looked towards the bed. There swaddled in the sheets lay Edna, her back facing him, her face to the wall. There was a chair beside the wardrobe which Prez pulled over to the bed and sat upon.

"Mum, how are you?" Silence again. "It's snowing outside, really cold, are you okay?" more silence. "Mum, are you okay?" Prez put his arm on her shoulder but Edna roughly pulled her shoulder away and buried herself deeper in the bedclothes. Prez sat back and took a deep breath,

"Eddie sends his love, he's enjoying university." Silence, "Vanessa sends her love as well. We're all thinking of you. I see you've got a new room, what do you think?" silence. After fifteen minutes of trying to instigate conversation Prez patted his mother on the shoulder, returned the chair and left the room. He felt drained, all his energy had been sucked from him, this then was truly the feeling of despair. He trudged back down the stairs and spotted one of the senior orderlies. A thick set woman in her fifties, who looked as though she had just walked off the set of *Carry On Matron*. Prez quickened his pace to catch her.

"Excuse me."

The lady turned her ample proportions and looked sternly at Prez,

"Yes?" she was curt and exuded the warmth of an alligator, without the charm.

"I'm Mrs Sinclair's son. I was wondering why she's been put in that little room at the top of the building, she's got a his-" before Prez could finish, Sarah, for that was the name on her uniform butted in sharply,

"Your mother is proving to be a danger to staff and others. We've put her up there so that we are more able to ensure the safety of staff and other residents."

Prez was only half surprised,

"She seems pretty uncommunicative. I've been up there for about twenty minutes and couldn't get a word out of her."

"That's the way she is I'm afraid." Sarah gruffly replied, "She is an extremely difficult personality to deal with, despite the medication. As you're aware, we are running on tight budgets and schedules and we have to do what is right for *all* the residents within the property. It may seem harsh, but there is nothing else we can do for your mother. Trust me, she's in the best place." Sarah attempted a reassuring smile but ended up just screwing her face up. *Looks like she doesn't get much practice.* Prez thought to himself.

"That's not good news."

"No Mr Sinclair, there's rarely good news for children of patients suffering mental illness." Sarah announced as if she thought Prez had visited on the off chance that he might be informed Edna had been cured.

"Yeah, I get that." Prez smiled grimly, "Thank you, I know you're doing your best." he didn't want to antagonise staff looking after Edna, God knows what they could do to her as an act of retaliation, it didn't bear thinking about.

As the door closed behind him Prez took in great gulps of the crisp snow filled air. He was grateful to be out of the cloying atmosphere of lingering desperation that the building reeked of. Yet he felt the guilt of that feeling of gratefulness. The guilty fact that he could walk away from the problem, the problem that was, through no fault of her own, Edna. The staff, it seemed to Prez, were as desperately trapped as the residents. Those residents, whose only final liberation would be, shockingly, death itself.

You wouldn't treat an animal you loved like that. What's wrong with this bloody society?

It was twelve thirty at night, Prez had been working at the computer for hours. It didn't matter how he examined the ledgers, the hard facts of the matter were that the clubhouse was no longer financially viable. Unless the club received an injection of cash, the clubhouse would have to be sold off. Oz had been his usual efficient self when he had brought the bad news to that Unkindness all those months ago. With everything that had been going on Prez hadn't had the opportunity to immerse himself in the club's finances. Now he wished he hadn't. Still, the nettle had to be grasped and the club would have to know the bald unpalatable truth of the perilous state of the finances. Nessa had gone to bed, he'd ensured she remained oblivious regarding the activities at the care home. *Poor kid's been through enough for one day. In fact, she's been through enough crap for a couple of lifetimes!* Prez thought as he finished replying to a fan's email on screen. He stretched in his seat, his lower back clicking as the discs realigned themselves from his position at the keyboard. *Let's see what's on the agenda for the wonderful Wirral Peninsular as we head towards Christmas............................*

Prez clicked on to a local "What's On in Wirral" webpage. What greeted him was akin to a cold slap in the face. Not quite believing it, he did a double take and then re-read the site more closely. It was announcing the launch of a book at Heswall library on Wednesday. This in itself was fairly unusual but not unknown. What had shocked Prez was the book and its author. He re-read the article yet again:

"Heswall Library welcomes author and international broadcaster Nigella Carter as she launches her book *"Free To Be Me"*. Nigella, formerly Nigel, a successful radio broadcaster, presenter and Heswall resident, has taken time from her busy schedule to leave New York and visit her hometown to sign copies of her book. It deals with the trials and tribulations of transgender transitioning in the modern day. All are welcome at what promises to be a thought provoking and enlightening event."

Prez slumped back in his chair.

S.O.S.

So, Nige is still doing what he always did best, selling himself! I'm not surprised, as looking back, I'm not sure anything he said or did was grounded in reality. It makes me feel like a complete dupe to think that I put one hundred percent faith in that guy. At times it even put a considerable strain on my relationship with Nessa. What a bloody fool I'd been to even put him on any kind of par with her. Turns out he's just a fantasist on the make, who's made enough money to actually live out his fantasy, with some not inconsiderable financial help from his poor old Mum, of course. He represents the kind of folk he and I had always railed against. Maybe in hindsight he got some kind of sick kick at hearing me espouse my views against such folk, when he secretly knew he was one such individual himself. What to do then? Should I go to the book launch? Our friendship having ended acrimoniously with e mails winging backwards and forwards. Should I do anything? Prez rubbed his jaw, trying to ascertain the most respectful course of action, what was the *right* thing to do? He grimaced as he pulled his chair closer to the keyboard and typed an e mail to his excommunicated club brother,

"Hi DJ. Just saw you're in Heswall on Wednesday. Well, despite our differences, I'd just like to say good luck with the book launch."

   Prez.

I hope that doesn't make me too much of a hypocrite. I really do hope his book is successful and in truth, if he's the sort of person I think he is, he won't give a monkey's what I say or think anyway. Still, there you go, I

meant what I said, and I hope he's good with it. I'll pop in to the library to have a look and see if they've got a copy I can scan through. I've no intention of fattening DJ's coffers by buying the finished article, hey, you never know, I might even feature!

Prez turned off the electronica in his study and quietly made his way downstairs to make a much-needed cup of tea. It was always a source of much amusement when, many years ago Eddie's first words as a baby were "Cupoftea, cupoftea, cupoftea". It had taken them all a while to work out what he was saying, although it should have come as no surprise to a family of "teapots" like the Sinclairs. The soothing "cure all" and stress buster, the herbal miracle that is tea.

Prez found a secluded area in the library and took a seat. He looked at the cover of the book in his hands. It seemed to show a young woman sitting on a flight of stairs in a house. He assumed this was a representation of "Nigella". Prez was a quick reader having the ability to speed read. It was not something he would do if he really wanted to enjoy a novel, but it was a useful tool to scan books merely to extract information, such as this one. Much of the early chapters dealt with Nigel's growing up on the Wirral, which for some unknown reason he called a suburb of Liverpool.

I guess that's for the States and foreign market. Everyone knows (or thinks they know) where Liverpool is, don't they? Gives the whole thing a much more intimate feel, who's your favourite Beatle? Ironic that I can't ever recall DJ having a good word to say about Liverpool. Still, like everything else, if he can use it to his own advantage, it's all fair game to him.

So, the groundwork done, it was time to introduce some characters. Chapter thirteen, "Vinny the Biker". Prez sat back further in his chair and poured over the tome. No longer speed reading but digesting every syllable and piece of punctuation. Here, in microcosm was his friendship of forty years laid out, in one chapter. Initially Prez was genuinely surprised and flattered to see that his old friend had even mentioned him in the book. However, as he read on, it was obvious that he featured merely as a knuckle dragging bigot. A creature not fit to reside with the rest of humanity, wilfully refusing to see the wondrous opportunities and freeing of shackles for people "trapped" in the wrong body through pioneering surgery. Prez was feeling tremendously uncomfortable now. Shifting his position uneasily as he continued to the end of the chapter. DJ was whining about how the e mails between them had been hurtful and in some cases showing prejudice. Prez was beyond angry with that.

Prejudice? No, no, my old friend, prejudiced I'm not. Prejudice is when you make a judgement with no facts and no rationale. Prejudice is not liking someone for looking the wrong way in your eyes or acting the wrong way. Prejudice is basically ignorance and one thing I am not, is ignorant. Throughout my life I have amassed mountains of information (either through first-hand experience, the benefit of age, or by immersing myself in the writings of others) on issues before making decisions upon things. I have never been hasty to make judgement calls. My major failing (if failing it is), touched upon in DJ's book, is that once my mind is made up, I'm very difficult to shift! Now, some may look at that and call it stupidity, I naturally think it shows strength of character and a belief to stick to your guns. Once you've invested time and energy researching something and you've formed an opinion, based on what you have read and experienced yourself (always better to have first-hand working knowledge of something), why, barring a Damascene conversion, should you change your mind? If you are, for whatever reasons, totally opposed to a course of action, should you then change your belief because someone close to you takes that course of action? Of course not. Everyone thinks they hold the right opinion, or they wouldn't hold it, would they? Nobody (or at least very few sane folk) go around acting out their lives in a way they don't believe to be correct. Apart from those at the top of the food chain such as politicians of course! It's second nature to those snake oil salesmen (and women) to say one thing and do another. So much so that the whole of society is now becoming permeated with that kind of thinking, which can't be good for anyone, can it? Surely the right-minded thing to do is to attempt to convince the person close to you that what they are doing is wrong. Despite what the liberals and media will tell you, there is still a right and wrong, yes, there is! However painful it might be, no matter what the sacrifice may be, one should stand up for what one believes to be right. One must be prepared to make the ultimate sacrifice for one's beliefs. That was the mantra of liberal Britain through the sixties seventies and onwards. Although., like most things pedalled to the plebeians, it was all a lie. What the establishment really meant was, stick to your guns and stand up for your beliefs, if they are of liberal or leftist leanings.............otherwise, forget it! Well, I bought into their mythology of standing up for my beliefs, trouble is, they weren't the kind of beliefs that the liberal left wanted to hear! I think of all those young souls lost at Ypres, Passchendaele and then again in World War Two and I think, is what we've ended up with really what they fought for? For, in this instance a man to choose to become a woman, because after forty years of womanising existence he now decides that he is a woman and not a man? Is that really what folk sacrificed themselves for? Madness, utter madness.

Prez concluded his reading of chapter thirteen (aptly his favourite number) and placed the book back on a shelf. Having read how DJ felt about him, or more to the point, was prepared to put in to print about him, all the feelings of being betrayed and stabbed in the back returned. Prez had a busy day ahead of him. Returning to Edna's house to ensure that things were drying out and later in the evening holding court at an Unkindness. Not to mention the housework! In an instant Prez suddenly decided to finish the book and grabbed it back off the shelf. Settling himself back down he speed read the remaining chapters and found the medical treatments, both surgical and drug related a tale of pure horror. It reinforced his belief that only someone with mental issues would undergo such a procedure. Before he set the book down he flipped to the pages preceding the start of the story proper. Typically, there was a dedication from Nigel to his Mother.

Unbelievable! Nigel cites his Mum for her support and waxes lyrical about how wonderful she is. That being so, I remember watching this strong woman in bits, because of what Nigel had decided to do. Her whole world was in tatters. Not what you really need when you live alone in a large house, your mobility restricted to use of a walking frame and you're in your eighties. Initially I visited her on a regular basis, trying to comfort her but in the end, she forced herself to come to terms with her son's choices. She went thought the entire DADA process I guess. Perhaps that is a failing on my part, that I have only managed the "Denial, Anger and Depression" part, can't quite make the leap to "Acceptance"? I realize now that Nigel was only ever part of the club to use it for his own devices. Whatever perceived kudos it gave him in the world of entertainment. His Mum has been used in the same way, a cash source for him to reinvent himself, literally. To the casual reader of his tome, whom one would imagine would have some empathy for the subject matter anyway, he would appear like the perfect son/daughter. Struggling with moral issues and his love for his mother. The Great struggle for Nigel to be "herself" rather than "himself". All very noble. I view it somewhat differently. The shabby act of betrayal by a person, so driven by the cult of the individual that everything in his life has been focused on one thing only, himself! I am disgusted with my own stupidity for trusting and even admiring a man who, now I can evaluate the situation clearly, was obviously only ever pursuing the "main chance".

S.O.S.

Who ran roughshod over everyone who extended the hand of friendship and used these people as stepping stones on the long and convoluted journey to wherever it was he intended to go. He took things to extremes, whether it be to promote himself in the entertainment world or to exploit his poor mother in funding his hare-brained fantasies. He fulfilled his ultimate fantasy of living the true bohemian lifestyle. Rather a departure for a guy who always wanted to be James Bond!

Prez stood up, shaking his head to himself and returned the book to the shelf.

Maybe I shouldn't have sent that e mail, I'm not really sure I do wish him well. Oh well, I've sent it now, should've read the damn book first..

Prez glanced at his watch and exhaled loudly. It looked as though the foul weather had taken its toll on the numbers showing for the Unkindness. Naturally the die hards had made it. The ever-present BS, Oz and Bear, but that was it. Excuses had been received from Greg the Vet and Dazzler. No one had heard anything from Boalie for weeks and Chinner was back visiting Irish Kev in Eire. Prez decided to press on,

"Well, the weather outside is frightful!" he half sang, Bear and the others shaking their heads in disbelief at his attempt.

"Well, just thought I'd introduce some levity guys!"

BS looked aghast,

"No wonder it's bloody sleeting outside!"

"Okay, to business." Prez decided to get serious, "Here's the way it is. I've been through the books with a fine-tooth comb and barring any new injections of cash, this good old clubhouse will have to be sold off."

The silence was palpable.

"We've got a falling register of members and despite the good press we got from the Egg Run, all those months ago, we've had very few interested in joining and to the best of my knowledge, no one is sponsoring anyone?" Prez looked quizzically around the table. The bikers shook their heads. Bear raised his hand,

"Look boys, I've had a couple wanting to join, but they've just been kids, no idea of the life, just not worth sponsoring, they'd be out within a week." he rumbled.

Prez was surprised that anyone would approach Bear, in his mind the least approachable of those seated at the table, so perhaps Bear had been too hasty in rejecting them. He kept his counsel however, that's the way it works. To join you need a sponsor and if things go awry, then the sponsor is in the frame for any comeback. Oz raised his hand,

"What about other Chapters, Prez?"

S.O.S.

"All feeling the pinch Oz. International Chapters are now zero, as you Know, only what we've got in Blighty and they're all feeling the pinch too." Prez rubbed his temples, "To be honest, I think we're coming to the time of some rather large decisions gentlemen."

BS raised his hand,

"Well, I for one ain't ready to give the club the last rites yet! What about you guys?" he declared triumphantly. Oz and Bear banged the table enthusiastically, but to Prez the sound of them doing so only emphasised the small number present in the room. He rubbed his chin,

"Well, any suggestions, greatly appreciated." he sighed. At which Oz raised a tentative hand,

"What about getting in touch with that journalist girl?" Oz shrugged, "Might be some mileage in articles, might be some coin there Boss?"

BS nodded in agreement,

"Oz has got a point Prez, maybe she could get something printed in the nationals, or one of those lifestyle mags, or even the music press?"

Prez grimaced,

"Even if that's the case, what do you think they'd print? Raking over old *Hanoi Jane* news? Our fan base age group must be well over forty. Who wants to live the bloody nostalgia trip?" Prez knew he was being negative, but all the events of the last couple of years were now weighing heavily upon his shoulders. There seemed to be a finality to things, a winding down. BS could sense the pressure his old friend was feeling and took control,

"Look, it's been a hell of a couple, of years for all of us. Prez, you more than most. You've had a lot to deal with. Why don't you let me and Oz get in touch with Angel and see what's what? Can't hurt, can it?" BS smiled at the assembled crew with boyish enthusiasm. Prez regained his equilibrium and shot back in jest,

"Sure it's just a desire to see the club back on its feet and not Miss Dubois, flat on her back?"

"You know me Prez, a missionary zeal where the Club's concerned!" BS retorted, the bikers chuckling at his wordplay. Prez shrugged,

"Okay, it's worth a shot. I reckon that we can keep this place ticking over for another six months. But seriously, if there's no extra cash forthcoming, we'll have to hold Unkindness's in someone's living room!"

Bear barked out a laugh,

"Not in our bloody house, you can't swing a cat in there!" he roared. Oz and BS looked askance at each other, not quite sure whether Bear had actually tried that or whether he was indeed using a figure of speech. At which point the big man leaned over to them,

S.O.S.

"Don't worry lads, y'know I love animals!" he grinned wolfishly. Prez couldn't resist a retort,

"Yeah, skinned and slightly salted!" which raised a gale of laughter, even Bear saw the funny side to it.

Prez glanced at his watch, aware that he and Nessa were due to visit Edna. He inclined his head to the window behind Oz,

"What's it doing out there now?"

Oz stood up and walked to the window, pulling the curtain back to see out. He turned back with wide eyes,

"Bloody hell, looks like we might be here for the night lads!"

The three other bikers joined Oz at the window and sure enough, the snow was thick on the ground. They had all arrived in cars and in truth they would not be snowed in. However, Prez realised that it might be appropriate to end proceedings so that everyone could get home safely. If riding motorcycles had taught each of them anything, it was that there were some absolute barn pots out there on the roads and inclement weather didn't improve the driving of such individuals.

As the bikers descended in to the main room on the ground floor Prez used the telephone on the wall. *I'd better let Ness know that I might be a bit late to pick her up for our visit to Mum.* He thought as he punched in the number. Moments later his wife answered the 'phone,

"Hi Vince, I know, you're snowed in!" she chuckled.

"No, not at all. It's pretty bad here though, just letting you know I'll be a bit late."

"Don't worry, I'll take my car. I'm, going in a few minutes as it'll take me longer to get there in this. You take it easy and just come straight home. We'll eat when I get in if you fancy cooking something?"

What a girl, positive, constructive, supportive! Prez thought, in truth relieved that he would be spared another tortuous visit,

"Yeah, that's great, thanks kiddo. Would spag bol do you?"

"Yep, there's mince in the fridge. Look, I've got to go, sooner I'm there, sooner I'm back. Drive carefully and say hello to the guys, bye!"

"Bye. Drive carefully." Prez replied as he heard the receiver click down. BS walked up to him wearing a long coat and a large smile,

"Spag bol is it? The tea of champions!" he grinned, patting Prez on his shoulder.

"Sure is V.P." Prez smiled as the bikers passed him and exited the building, leaving him to lock up. They helped remove the snow from each other's vehicles and after the customary club handshake Prez watched as his brothers drove away. He had already started the engine whilst removing the snow, so the car had warmed up as he slid in to the driver's seat.

S.O.S.

Home James and don't spare the horses!

The bolognaise was simmering nicely in the pan whilst Prez checked on the bubbling pasta. It was a small kitchen, but that ensured that everything was in easy reach, including his glass of red wine.

Eat your heart out Keith Floyd! He chuckled to himself. He took a look at his watch. *Nessa should be home any time now.* The thought had barely entered his head when he heard the front door close.

"Tea in ten Ness!" Prez called out. Moments later his wife's head poked around the doorway. It was obvious she was upset; her cheeks were reddened. Her mascara had run, and it was obvious she had been crying. Prez quickly reduced the heat on the stove and stepped out in to the dining room to give his wife a hug.

"What's going on Ness? You okay?"

Vanessa buried her head in his shoulder hugging him fiercely, then pulled away shaking her head,

"It's no good Vince, I can't keep going there. She was babbling about them trying to poison her."

Prez stepped back and took hold of Nessa's shoulders, looking her in the eye.

"C'mon kiddo, this isn't like you......" Nessa took a step back,

"You don't understand Vince, she hit me!" she said sniffling back tears. Prez looked aghast,

"What? Hit you?" he spluttered.

"Yeah, because I told her not to be silly, she hit me." Nessa babbled, "Across the face." She tilted her head sideways and Prez realised what he thought had been a rosy cheek from the cold was in fact the afterglow of a slap to the face. Prez put his arm around her waist and guided her in to the front room,

"Come and sit down. I'm sorry, I should've been there." Nessa sat down and related the whole sad tale. About how Edna was now convinced the staff were trying to poison her and that they had been doing so since she had taken up residence. It appeared that whatever psychotropic drugs she had been taking were now proving totally ineffectual. Prez folded his arms,

"I'll go and see them tomorrow. Maybe I should see if I can get an appointment with Mortimer, see what he thinks we should do. If there is anything anyone can do." Prez sighed and gave his wife a hug," You're not visiting her anymore Ness, I'll go."

Nessa shook her head,

S.O.S.

"No Vince, she doesn't mean it, it's not Mum really, you know that." Nessa replied earnestly.

"I know that kiddo, but you're not going to be slapped and upset anymore. I'll do the visits and see what can be done. Mum would understand if she were herself. As it is, we've got to stop feeling guilty about her being in a care home and looked after. She's someone else now, not Mum, she's someone who barely knows us. We've got to face up to the facts and realise that Mum has been gone a while now." Prez hated himself for what he said next,

"We need to remember her the way she was, 'cause that Mum is never coming back." The sentence hung in the air between them. Both knew what he said was true but that didn't make the facts any more palatable.

Neither of them ate much of the bolognaise that Prez had cooked. In fact, neither spoke to any degree for the rest of the evening. They both had nothing to say, what could anyone say that would improve the situation? Prez stared at the television which was showing some American Football, whilst Nessa flicked through some equally mindless nonsense on her 'phone. Both lost in their thoughts. Prez sucked his upper lip with his teeth. *Maybe I should book us a holiday somewhere. I could have a word with Eddie to look after the pets, make it a week he's not in university. Nessa deserves a break, Christ, she needs to get away from this stuff. It's not fair that she's having to deal with this. It's not fair anyone has to deal with it! We had a great week in Scotland during September in a rented holiday cottage. Eddie and his girlfriend Sam had been with us and although I found the driving a bit tiring, it was great to get away from everything. She's always loved Barcelona, a week, or even a long weekend there might cheer her up, at least it would be a break from everything that reminds her of what's going on here. Yep, that's what I'll do, book it on the Q.T. and then just lay it on her!* Prez smiled to himself. He knew it was not an answer, merely a diversion but a pleasant one at that. After all, he knew what they both knew, there was no answer.

S.O.S.

Yul Brynner

Prez studied the quotes in front of him whilst sipping a mug of tea. He was awaiting his Vice President at the clubhouse and was using the time to decide which builder to go with regarding the repairs to Edna's house. He was glad to be sitting down, shocks are always best absorbed when the knees are relaxed. Any hope of taking Nessa away on a weekend break had been dashed by the figures he was looking at. Getting a loan would be tricky, since he had no regular employment. Although he had banked with the same company since he was seventeen and they had gladly taken his money and managed his growing investment portfolio, Prez knew the loan scenario may well not play out favourably. The quotes he studied made it clear that the cost would be in the tens of thousands. Prez knew that he would recoup the money once the property was sold, however, that would take time as he had already discovered. So, as he put the paperwork down on the table in front of him he let out a long sigh. He looked around at the wall hangings around the room within which they held the Unkindness each week. The empty seats either side of the table reminded him of absent brothers and he felt a cold shiver run up his back.

The door opened and snapped Prez out of his brooding. BS walked in brushing sleet from his long overcoat before slipping it off and hanging it up on the back of the door. He was, as usual, wearing a denim jacket, shirt, a t shirt and of course the obligatory jeans. Naturally his patch was over his denim. Prez smiled at his V.P., whom he noticed had put a mug of coffee on the table,

"Turned out nice again V.P.?" he joked.

"Yeah, not even bloody December yet and it's awful out there. Good job we didn't do the Wild Hunt this year Prez!" BS replied as he made himself comfortable at the table, "More bad news re the accounts?" his eyebrows rose arching. Prez shook his head,

"Nah, quotes for Mum's place. Just killing time 'til you arrived to be honest."

BS smiled back pulling himself closer to the table and cradling his mug. He reminded Prez of a cartoon cat who just got the cream. BS smiled again, nodding as he addressed his President,

"I don't like to think I've got all the answers-" he started but Prez interjected,

"Yes you bloody do!"

S.O.S.

"Err, well, maybe I do, but you're gonna like this Vince." BS continued, through a wide grin, "We've not had much good fortune lately have we? Well, that may be about to change Boss."

Now it was Prez's eyebrows which arched in surprise as BS continued his tale,

"I have, as we agreed, been in touch with the lovely Angel, purely as V.P. of the club and with no personal agenda." he smiled, "And I reckon that we may have the embryo of an idea. "BS sipped his coffee whilst Prez sat forward on metaphorical tenterhooks, "Her Egg Run report and her tales from the event were a big hit in her social circles. Y'know the kind of hooray Henrys who think that we're all drug taking hitmen with Playboy Bunny girlfriends, remember Oliver?"

"Yup." Prez replied, nodding as his friend picked up the pace, his enthusiasm brimming,

"Well, he's history now, our girls got some other character in tow. Anyway, to cut to it, she reckons she might be able to get some more stuff published about us. Y'know, memoirs, that kind of thing. Either the S.O.S. or possibly even the band. Nostalgia baby, it's all the rage! What do you think of that?" BS sat back sipping more coffee. Prez reclined in his chair, mulling it over, a half smile on his face. He sat forward nodding,

"Sounds like a plan. I've been writing bits and pieces for years. Being in Motorheadbangers, I had quite a few things published in their mag. Hell, I even got a letter published in a weekly comic called TV21 when I was about seven, always an early starter, see? Not to mention being published in The Caldean, my grammar school's magazine." Prez chuckled," I remember getting beaten up by a bunch of dipsticks at school for that, 'cause I advocated using live ammo instead of rubber bullets against pro IRA demonstrators." BS looked mystified,

"Didn't know there was such support for a united Ireland on The Wirral" he scoffed. Prez rolled his eyes,

"Just another example of the media programming gullible idiots mate. Hey, this sounds great, I'm sure I could get something together. Does she mean she'd be writing it, or I would, or what?"

"Dunno, we didn't talk about that. I mean, you've always been a good writer yourself, why not give it a go? I'm sure she'd support you and with her contacts, who knows, could help out our cash flow issues if you end up with a Pulitzer Prize winner................" BS gazed theatrically at the ceiling, "then there's the screen play, sound track..........."

"Yeah, yeah, let's keep our heads here, I've got to write the bloody thing first! Y'know, I have kept a series of diaries over the years, never thought they'd really be of any interest to anyone else. Just kept 'em up for posterity, I guess. Could be that I could use them as a framework. They cover the whole lifespan of the Club. Then there's those scrapbooks I kept of the Band, photos, reviews, all that stuff."

S.O.S.

"You'll have to change a few things, on a, ahem, legal basis." BS snorted.

"Yeah, the old favourite; *only the names have been changed to protect the guilty!*" Prez suddenly felt a wave of optimism hit him, something that awoke all the positivity he remembered bathing in when he founded the club and indeed when he'd been in the recording studio with *Hanoi Jane*.

At the end of the day, it was me who created the Hanoi Jane logo, me who sent out the demos and got us signed, me who thought up the album titles and artwork, me who represented the band on a management level. Then there's the Club, I'm in charge of just about everything, from the Clubhouse to the design of our patches. The Brothers elected me President, so I've got the responsibility that no one else wanted. Nessa always reckons I want to be in control, but she's wrong, what I want is the responsibility, that's a whole different ball game. Besides which, if I was a control freak, I certainly wouldn't have married her would I? I remember years ago, whilst unemployed for about six months when I first finished school at sixteen, I wrote a book called "Shattered Dreams of Youth". I always fancied myself as a writer, just never had the opportunity, what with the Club, family, the band and latterly Mum. Maybe, this is that time? They say everyone has a book in them. Prez cleared his mind,

"So when can I hook up with the delightful Ms Dubois?" he queried.

"Well, it's gonna be next year now. It's a busy social season down in the Smoke and the Home Counties don't you know Old Boy?" BS attempted his best Old Etonian accent with little success. Prez chuckled,

"Yeah, I guess there's a lot of halls to be decking and stirrup cups to be supped. But I bet Angel won't be decking many halls!"

"Probably drinking a few stirrup cups though!" BS grinned back.

"I want you to carry on liaising with her and next year you and I will pay her a visit, what do you think?" Prez paused looking thoughtful, "Maybe she'll be up for the Egg Run next year?"

"Hope so." BS exclaimed eagerly, a faraway look in his eye as he thought back to Angel's figure-hugging leather jeans worn during her previous visit to the aforementioned event. Prez smiled to himself,

"Whatever, it'll give me some time to get my diaries together and maybe put some stuff down that she'd like to have a look at." Prez saw his Vice President's eyes light up, but held up his hand to stop the forthcoming remark from him,

"No! I don't want to know what you'd like to show her, draw a veil over it mate!"

Maybe, just maybe there is light at the end of the tunnel……………….Or maybe it's just a train coming towards me…………………………………

S.O.S.

Prez took a sip of red wine as Nessa finished her tea. West Country Hot Pot was one of Prez's signature dishes. Potato, bacon, onions, salt, pepper, cheese and of course, cider. Apples were optional, but Prez never included them. Nessa placed her knife and fork on to her empty plate and looked at Prez,

"That was lovely, compliments to the chef." She smiled.

"Cheers kiddo. Not bad, if I say so myself."

"How did it go at the bank?" Nessa purred, trying to keep the question low key, although both of them knew the importance of the meeting that Prez had attended earlier in the day. Prez shrugged, raising his glass again,

"Seems like you can have saving portfolios of tens of thousands of pounds and have banked with the same robbers since you started earning a living, but if you don't fit in................." Prez let his words tail off. Surprisingly Nessa sounded upbeat,

"Don't worry Vince. I've been thinking. Why don't we just cash in some of your shares and pay that way? Sure, I know we didn't want to, but we'll still have a fair amount to play with and barring a financial crash, we'll get it back when we sell Mum's house, won't we?"

Prez nodded in agreement, relieved that his wife was so supportive, and level headed.

"Yeah, I was going to put it to you, but didn't know how........"

"What! The President of the S.O.S. and leader of *Hanoi Jane* didn't know how to ask his wife what to do with his own money?" Nessa rolled her eyes.

"C'mon Ness, y'know that it's *our* money. The fact that it's earnings from the band that we've saved for years doesn't mean it's mine! Christ we've got joint accounts in the building society and our shares are in joint names too aren't they?"

"I know, but it's still your money."

"No, it's *our* money woman!" Prez snarled playfully. Nessa giggled across the table,

"Anyway, once you've written your best seller, you'll be repaying it back in spades!"

"Yeah, if I can get it together and Angel comes through."

"She's quite a woman this Angel." Nessa muttered, her coolness noted by Prez.

"C'mon Ness, BS saw her first!" Prez grinned.

"Yeah, and Kelly would kill him if she thought anything was going on!" Nessa chuckled. As she did so a faint look of concern crossed her face, "I ran in to Glenys today. She's working in a clothes shop in Chester."

"Well, tell her old man to start hauling arse to an Unkindness, we haven't seen him for over a month and he owes us some serious wedge in fines for it!" Prez smiled, before realising that Nessa had more news.

"That'll be a bit difficult, since they're not together anymore."

"What?" Prez was genuinely surprised that Greg the Vet and Glenys had split up. They had seemed rock solid and he was as loyal to her as a puppy to its master.

"I know, I was shocked. Just goes to show, I guess..............." Nessa rose from the table and after taking their plates in to the kitchen sat on the sofa in the living room. Prez followed, sitting in his chair with his red wine in hand.

"I'll get Oz to get in touch with him." Prez said," I know him, he'll have taken it hard. That guy thrives on loyalty and commitment. He may have been a hero in the forces and been rightly decorated for it, but he's a sensitive bloke all the same. We'll need to rally 'round for him and let him know he's not on his own with this stuff."

Greg had not touched alcohol for years. None of the brothers had ever asked him why. I always assumed it was to do with his experiences in Afghanistan. He was the kind of bloke who never really talked about it, which made it all the more surprising when he appeared in an article regarding his heroic exploits on the front page of the Chester Chronicle a few years ago. If any of the brothers had ever had any doubt as to Gregg's value to the Club, they were dispersed upon reading that article. He was a true hero, in a world where the term is much used and abused. Anyone who risked his life to go back for a fallen comrade in the full knowledge he could get himself killed is more than welcome to share a patch with me! Especially when he shares our ideals. Prez thought, then added,

"Any idea why they split?"

"Yeah, like I'm going to ask!" Nessa snorted as Prez nodded realising the stupidity of his question. He suddenly downed his remaining wine and smiled at his wife,

"So, we've got some positive things going on Babe. We've got the possibility of some work getting published, we've made a decision on how to finance getting Mum's place refurbished so that we can sell it and we know why Gregg's been M.I.A. for weeks." Nessa smiled back,

"I'll 'phone the builder's that we picked from those quotes in the morning and you can meet up with them at mum's place to go through the finer points." Nessa said, taking charge as only she could. Prez walked to the kitchen and poured himself another glass of red, calling through to Nessa,

"Do you want a drink kid?"

"I'll have a coffee if you're making one." She called back.

S.O.S.

As Prez returned with his wine and Nessa's coffee he was wearing a soppy grin.

"What's up with you?" Nessa smirked.

"Well, it's just that after months of crap, it looks like we're finally getting over it all." Prez paused and sat down, taking a sip of his wine, "I know that Mum's still ill and that I've got to keep up the bloody visits and I know that we'll be out of pocket for a bit and I know it's bloody horrible weather!" he grinned "But Hell, this is gonna to be a better bloody Yule than the last one!"

"I'll drink to that!" Nessa raised her mug and Prez did likewise.

"Skol!" he exclaimed as glass and mug clinked together. Meanwhile, sat on the pouf next to the radiator Star the cat slept on, oblivious to the World and the trepidations and celebrations of what she considered to be bipedal felines.

Prez and Nessa gazed around the room, both beaming with delight. In less than a month, Edna's home had been transformed by the contractors that they had selected. Instead of an old lady's house being put back on to the housing market, the property would now be being sold as a blank canvas for anyone with any foresight. The contractors had finished the rooms to a high standard, keeping the colours neutral. The kitchen was the greatest revelation, with new fixtures and fittings bringing it in to the twenty first century. Prez put his arm around his wife's waist and gave her a squeeze.

"Can't recognise the place, can you?"

"They've done a really good job Vince." Nessa smiled back, "I'm so pleased, it's better than I could've imagined, really!"

"Yeah, me too."

Now is not the best time to put the property on the market, what with Christmas weeks away, but who knows? Maybe some rich parents may want to splash out, or at least help a son or daughter gain that first step on the property ladder? Prez thought as he and Nessa walked out of the front door. Their nostrils still fizzing with that new house odour of paint and plaster. Nessa looked at Prez as they settled in to their seats in the car,

"Do you think this is it? Do you think we're finally getting through the bad luck?" she asked. Prez smiled back, involuntarily touching his Odin amulet hidden beneath his t shirt,

"Shit's in the rear-view mirror now babe!" he grinned, "This isn't luck either, we've bloody earned this!"

"And paid for it!" Nessa's eyes sparkled. They both knew that their savings had taken a hit, but it was the only way to get the property in a reasonable condition to make a profit on the housing market. Prez still felt uneasy about it as the domicile had been his mother's pride and joy. She was of that generation whose mindset meant that owning property was everything. Not just in terms of financial security, but also of social standing. Some in her Liverpudlian family had felt that when she had got married and moved down south to Watford to her cockney professional husband that she became a snob. Prez didn't know anything of that. Indeed, he put it down to regional stereotypical jealousy. *Let's face it, the south has everything, the best theatres, the major sporting venues, the busiest airports. Not to mention Buck House and the Royals. Besides, she came back up north after eight or nine years, didn't she?* Prez chuckled to himself as he reversed the car out of the drive and drove towards home.

"What are you chuckling about Mr S?" Nessa purred. Prez grinned back shaking his head,

"Just glad to be alive sweetheart. And enjoying the love of a good woman!" Nessa snorted at that statement.

"I'm glad you think that Vince, because I've just bought a new Christmas tree." Nessa grinned.

"I like the old one!" Prez protested.

"Don't worry, we'll still have the old one where it always goes in the lounge. This new one is a white one and it's a narrow one. Just enough room for it in the dining room." Nessa held up her hands stopping Prez's protests before he could make them," I know, you don't like white trees.

Look, you know all those miniature bobble hats I've been knitting? It's for them."

"What? Why does a tree need a bobble hat?" Prez looked quizzical.

"Well, it doesn't but I thought they'd look good on it. I've bought blue fairy lights and, well, it'll look great!"

Prez liked it when Nessa was enthused over a project. From a Club point of view, it didn't hurt either. Lately she had taken up various charity runs and walks. Local folk knew she was the wife of the S.O.S. President and a little bit of good publicity goes a long way when you are a back-patch motorcycle club. Prez sighed back theatrically,

"Okay, okay. Hey, are you still doing that Santa Dash from Neston to Parkgate this year?"

"Yes, me and Agnes are doing it, it's okay isn't it?" she replied, referring to a work colleague. Prez nodded,

"Of course, I just wasn't sure if it was still on your agenda." Prez smiled, "What with all this tree felling, decorating and knitting going on!" he grinned back as Nessa pulled a playful face.

"I've got the Santa hat, I just need to get a tutu."

"Sounds good to me!" Prez grinned salaciously, for which he received a none to gentle punch on the arm.

"Serves you right!" Nessa retorted, before changing the subject, "When's the next Unkindness?"

"Few days. I'll get the guys to sort out the decorating of the Clubhouse. You up for that? Hey maybe that white tree............................" Prez received a second thump on the arm.

"The white tree is for our dining room, not your Clubhouse!" Nessa spoke firmly.

"Okay, okay! "Prez whimpered before continuing," You and Kel be able to help out as usual? The Yule bash will be in a couple of weeks. You two can get together and do the shopping as usual if you like."

"You mean **will** you two do the shopping for our party **please**!" Nessa growled.

"Err, that's what I said sweetheart." Prez grinned sheepishly.

"Yes, suppose so. Have you made a list of what you all drink and the volumes?"

"Yup, err, well no. But I will after the Unkindness, honest."

Nessa looked to the heavens,

"You blokes couldn't run a knees up in a brewery!"

Prez smiled back,

"That's why I always leave the finer details to you girls Babe."

Nessa realised that she had been outfoxed and conceded defeat.

Prez gazed around the table and allowed himself to feel a warm glow of satisfaction. It never failed to amaze him how the festive season could bring the brothers together at an Unkindness. In their usual seats were Bear, BS, Oz, Dazzler, Greg The Vet and Chinner. Prez spread his arms widely,

"Yo, ho, ho gents, a merry festive season to you all!" a ripple of applause went around the table, then Prez continued.

"Oz is going to audit you all on what we need to stock up the bar for our Yuletide Bash. First though, he's going to give us a short report ion the accounts." Prez shot a quick smile at Oz, "Make it quick and painless, it's nearly bloody Christmas after all!"

Oz cleared his throat before referring to a sheaf of papers in front of him,

"Well the good news is, we saved a shed load of pennies by not having a Wild Hunt Run in November. The hoteliers kindly waived their fees because of the inclement weather."

"Really……………….?" Prez raised a quizzical eyebrow at his Treasurer who blushed back,

"Well, Bear and I persuaded them that although they were losing our prebooked business, they'd still make a mint out of all those skiers they'd be able to lure in early as a result of all the snow they were having up there!" Oz beamed, "They seemed to agree and as I said, waived our booking fees, so nothing to pay boys!"

"So, although we didn't make any money from The Run, we didn't lose anything?" growled Bear, playing devil's advocate, to which Oz grinned back.

"Exactly Brother. We could've taken quite a hit, but you and me sorted it!"

"I think that deserves a round of applause!" Prez grinned as the assembled bikers thumped the table and whooped their consent. As it subsided Oz continued,

"We've had some substantial payments from brothers who've been, err, somewhat lax in their attendances of late........." all eyes turned towards Dazzler and Chinner who shrugged and shook heads respectively. No one stared down Greg The Vet, as all knew he had had good reason for missing Unkindness's. All the same, he had paid his fines.

"So Brothers, at the moment, there are no outstanding fines." Oz beamed at the throng again as he shuffled his papers in to some semblance of order.

"So, we're in clover now?" BS looked astonished. Oz harrumphed,

"Err, well, not exactly, but we're not broke. The Clubhouse is still on borrowed time, but we may have longer than we thought."

Prez decided it was time to help his Treasurer out,

"It's true, the situation has gone from critical to stable, inasmuch as we're not expecting to have to sell anytime soon. The money we've clawed back from the Wild Hunt and from brothers who owed dues has helped but it's not a long-term solution. We need a fresh revenue stream and I'm working on some stuff which might help us out next year. I don't want to say too much in case it goes pear shaped, but have faith guys. BS and I reckon we may, and I stress, *may*, have a way forward, but we can't really expand on anything until after the festive season."

"Is this to do with that posh bird?" Dazzler piped up, his interest piqued. BS nodded back,

"Yeah, remember a while back we thought she may be able to get some stuff published? Well, I've been in touch and that may still be a viable option."

"I don't mind putting a word in Boss." Dazzler grinned, Prez rolled his eyes,

"I'm sure that's the last thing you'd be thinking of putting in Daz!" the assembly guffawed,

"Stick to your on-line dating mate, she's out of your league!" BS added to the amusement of the others. Prez raised his hand to call some order to proceedings.

"Okay guys." He turned to BS.

BS raised his hand and was acknowledged by Prez,

"More news, Brothers. Remember the Bulldog Bash this year?" the Club always attended the annual biker festival hosted by the Hells Angels in Stratford Upon Avon. They never wore their patches in deference to their hosts but always enjoyed the event. Due to his commitments with Edna, Prez had been unable to attend the last Bash but most of the Brothers had rocked up and partied hard as expected. The Bikers nodded with various degrees of enthusiasm, "Well, I don't know if any of you were sober enough to recall running into some Nomad S.O.S. brothers at the gig?" again there were some nods and some blank stares. "Well, I got talking with some of 'em about this and that." BS stood up and putting two fingers in his mouth let out a piercing whistle. The door to the room opened and three Club members strode in. The first a shaven headed six foot four thirty-year-old, the second a portly six foot fifty something and lastly another six-footer plus, built like a heavyweight boxer, in his late twenties. The three stood by the door awaiting permission to sit at the table. BS announced their arrival,

"Okay, here we have Stevil," the shaven headed biker nodded, "Tommo," the dark haired thick set biker nodded "and ATV" the boxer winked back.

"ATV?" Oz raised his eyebrows.

"Andy The Viking, scourge of the boxing ring mate!" Prez obliged with the answer before either BS or ATV could reply. BS continued his address,

"These guys are all Nomads, but they're looking for a new home." He retrieved a piece of paper from his cut, "Big John informed me at the Bulldog that he was stepping down as President. He's knocking on and as you probably know, his missus has been ill for years. Well now he's got to devote his time to her. The guys in The Nomads voted him out in Good Standing, as you'd expect. So, what with the chapter folding a number of the crew needed to relocate. These three reprobates are the most local to our chapter, so I invited them to our Unkindness tonight. ATV and Tommo know Dazzler through their jobs in security. Prez knows Stevil from a previous life I think?" Nodding, Prez spoke up,

"Boys, take a seat. I've known these guys since before they went Nomad, and some of you know 'em too." Dazzler and ATV were already grinning at each other in recognition, "Well, I've got no qualms welcoming them to The Mother Chapter. "Prez turned to the newcomers, "Gents, we're having our vote as to whether you're in or not in front of you. We don't believe in secrets at the Mother Chapter. If you're not welcome, we want you to know who's got an issue and why. No backstabbing in this Chapter!"

The bikers all nodded in agreement, Bear banging the table enthusiastically. The Mother Chapter prided itself in honesty and integrity.

"I move that we accept the three Nomad Brothers present." BS announced.

"Anyone got any issues?" Prez scanned the table, no one spoke, "Okay then, I second the motion. All those for?"

The usual creeping death around the table began with Bear who nodded,

"Yeah, 'bout time we had some more muscle in this outfit." He winked at ATV.

Chinner nodded,

"Yeah."

Dazzler beamed back,

"Sure, someone else to work out with in the gym!" Greg The Vet grinned back,

"I know Tommo and ATV, they've got my vote."

"Me too." Oz confirmed, and BS nodded in satisfaction. Prez slammed his hand down on the table,

"That's unanimous then boys, you're in! I for one am glad to welcome some new blood to the Chapter."

A raucous cheer went up from the assembled throng as Prez produced three bottom rockers emblazoned with the word "ENGLAND" in red Old English script which would replace the "Nomad" rockers currently on the newcomer's patches. He passed them out to each of the Nomads as he walked around the table. Each one standing and hugging him as he welcomed them to the Mother Chapter. Finally, as he sat down Tommo raised his hand,

"I'd just like to say, on behalf of the three of us, we're glad to have a new home. Just in time for Christmas!" he grinned.

Again, the table erupted in to shouting and hammering of fists on to its surface. Oz raised his hand as it died down,

"So that's more good news, more dues." Oz announced rubbing his hands together in a fair approximation of a modern-day Shylock. He looked hard at the newcomers, "And more fines!" again the room erupted in to uproar as the bikers laughed and cheered with equal abandon.

This is exactly what we needed. Some new blood to invigorate the Chapter. What with losing Faceman, and Irish Kev and Boalie out for the foreseeable future, we needed a shot in the arm. Like Oz said, it'll bring in more revenue and it'll bolster the show we put on at things like the Wild Hunt and the Egg Run. More actual patches, as opposed to us with hangarounds and supporters. Prez thought to himself, involuntarily touching his amulet, *Things really do seem to be turning around, let's just hope things keep on doing just that, this Club deserves some breaks.*

Prez again raised his hand to restore order,

"I'm also proposing that we add some new Runs for us next year, starting with a Lee Rigby Memorial Run. What do we think?"

"Seconded Prez. That poor guy who was hacked to death in London just because he was white and a soldier, terrible!" Bear shook his head. Prez addressed the table,

"Anyone against?" he scanned the assembled bikers none of whom raised an eyebrow.

"All those for?" once again there was a roar of agreement and a hammering of fists on the table as the bikers voted in the motion unanimously. Once the furore subsided Prez spoke,

"We're also looking at a Manchester Run to commemorate all those poor buggers affected by that bomb blast at Manchester Arena......................"

"Seconded, Prez." Oz quickly spoke up. His President then put it to the vote. Again, the vote was unanimously in favour and again the result was greeted with cries of approval.

Excellent, we can get out there and start doing some good. It'll raise our profile too. It's about time folk started to stand up and do something positive, instead of moping around lighting candles. If we can make these events as big as the Egg Run, we'll have done a good job. Prez smiled.

The Unkindness over, the bikers milled around the bar downstairs, music blaring from the jukebox in the corner. Prez and BS welcomed the new trio of ex Nomads before adjourning to the patio in the back garden. Cold as it was, a fire pit had been lit and it was emanating enough warmth to encourage the two friends to stay awhile whilst finishing their respective drinks. Prez held his glass aloft in salutation to his old friend,

"Skol, my Brother! And bloody good work with those newbies, I owe you one!"

"No worries Prez. I know that they're all known to you and they're dependable married with children guys. No loose cannons there. I reckoned they'd get voted in, just glad it's worked out for them and us." BS returned the salutation, clinking his glass against his Presidents. Then he lowered his voice,

"How're things on the Mum front?"

"As bad as ever mate, although we've got the house back on the market." Prez smiled, his breath forming great snaking plumes in the cold air.

"Well that's something. I guess it's the only good to come out of the whole thing. I know you'd rather have your Mum around, but at least if you can get rid of the house it'll generate some cash."

"Yeah, that makes me sound like a right mercenary bastard." Prez grimaced and BS realized he had made a mistake,

"Christ, engage brain before opening mouth! Sorry mate, that didn't come out as intended." BS blew out his cheeks, flushing in embarrassment.

"No worries son, I think I've known you long enough to understand what you mean, even though it's not often what you actually say!" Prez patted him on the shoulder reassuringly. At that moment Oz bounded out to join them, a steaming mug of hot chocolate cupped in his hands,

"Bloody hell lads, it's freezing out here!" he smiled, his face painted a vivid red from the fire pits blaze.

"Ozzo!" Prez smiled, "Hey, did you ever hear any more about those drug pushing bastards?"

"Yeah." Oz nodded, moving closer to the heat," They set up back over the water, someone else's problem now Boss."

"Whole thing made me feel like we're *The Magnificent Seven*." Prez grinned. Oz frowned, Prez explained,

"Well, the locals can't handle the bad guys, so they call in outsiders, who they don't like either, to sort the mess out. Once it's done the locals go back to not knowing if they like their saviours or not!" Prez grinned. BS blew out a plume of breath,

"And there was me thinking you thought we were *The Magnificent Seven*, just 'cause I remind you of bloody Yul Brynner!" he said rubbing his bald head to emphasise the point.

Prez grinned back holding his arms out wide, displaying himself in his biker finery, the silver rings the jeans and cowboy boots, the tattoos, the plaited hair and of course, the colours.

"Hey c'mon Bro, fashion may go out of style, but style never goes out of fashion!"

S.O.S.

The Sound of Silence

Prez hunched over his monitor as he reread the work he had just finished typing. He'd been working hard on the project since BS had told him of Angel Dubois' interest in him producing some work regarding the Club. He'd gone back through his writings and musings, all the way from 1983. He was a natural hoarder and had kept clippings about the band and fan mail from that time. He had also kept up an erratic journal, throughout the "band years" and then onwards through the creation of the S.O.S. to the present day. Now he was sifting through the information to create a narrative of his time within the Club. It was hard work and he had scrapped entire chapters upon revisiting them, but it was rewarding, cathartic in a way. *Hanoi Jane's* first album blasted from the CD player in the study where Prez was working. He chuckled to himself as the bands hit single *"Sweet Addiction"* roared from the speakers, remembering how BS used to introduce the song as "The Dentist's Number", although naturally, the song was about an addiction to a member of the fair sex and nothing to do with confectionary. That was BS for you, a veritable card.

Prez sat back and took a sip from his mug of tea before dunking a chocolate digestive and nibbling it. As he washed it down with another gulp of tea the 'phone rang. Prez made his way downstairs, fully expecting it to be another nuisance call, they had been receiving many cold callers, at least twice per week. With this in mind he picked up the whistle that Nessa had left beside the 'phone and prepared to give it a blast down the handset.

"Hello." He brought the whistle to his lips. Yet instead of the usual delay before the inevitable Asian voice confirming that he wasn't about to sell you anything, he received an immediate reply,

"Mr Sinclair?" a woman inquired.

"Yep, that's me."

"Hello, I'm Marion from Woodland, your Mother's nursing home. I'm the Manageress." She sounded professional, yet concerned.

"Hello, what can I do for you Marion? Is everything okay with Mum?" Prez felt that now familiar sinking feeling in his abdomen. He had almost got used to Edna being either totally non-responsive, or conversely heatedly telling him that the staff were trying to poison her, when he visited, almost.

"I'm afraid she's been taken to Arrowe Park Hospital, A and E."

Prez could feel the anxiety rise up, but remained calm,

"What happened?"

"Well, she was complaining of stomach pains," Marion's voice dropped a little as if sharing some sort of conspiratorial secret, "But as you know, she's been saying things like that for a bit."

Prez nodded as he listened to Marion continue,

"We didn't think too much of it, but when lunchtime arrived we couldn't get her to leave her room. She was rolling on her bed in apparent pain. It was then that we called an ambulance." Now Marion's professional voice returned, "Our main concern is for our resident's welfare, as you know Mr Sinclair."

"Thanks for letting me know." Prez sighed, "I'll get over there right away."

Prez raced upstairs and got changed in to jeans and a sweatshirt. He jogged back down picking up his bomber jacket from the back of a chair. It was cold outside for March, but the worst of the winter was gone. All the same, he took the car rather than go through the time-consuming effort of moving it so that he could gain access to *Landwaster* and then remove the padlock from the beast and wheel it out. Besides, it would have taken him twenty minutes to put on his 'bike gear and time was of the essence.

Arrowe Park Hospital, Prez grimaced as he walked through the entrance doors to And E. *Where did they put the sign saying, "Abandon Hope All Those Who Enter Here"?* He stood in the queue for reception and surveyed the usual motley crew of pensioners and children waiting to be seen in the large waiting area. *All that's missing is a kid with a saucepan on his head.* He thought as he scanned the crutches and plaster casts. Surprisingly quickly he arrived at the head of the queue, there were two women staffing reception, which had undoubtedly sped up the process. Prez smiled at the woman who faced him.

"Hi, my name's Sinclair, my Mum has been brought in from Woodland Nursing Home........"

The woman whose name badge declared her to be Monica surveyed the screen in front of her. Without raising her eyes, she spoke to Prez in a tone that suggested she really wished she were somewhere else,

"Through the doors in front of you, turn left and then left again. That's reception, they'll see you." She lifted her head, "Next." Prez was already gone.

Walking briskly, he arrived at the second reception desk. A pretty young brunette name badge reading Prue smiled at him. He smiled back,

"Hi, I'm Mr Sinclair, my Mum's been sent here from her nursing home. I've just come from reception."

Prue nodded and asked him to take a seat. She was obviously aware of Edna's arrival, as she didn't use her monitor to check on anything. As Prez sat down she called over,

S.O.S.

"A doctor will give you a call shortly Mr Sinclair."

Prez gave her a thumbs up and smiled back as he settled in to the surprisingly comfortable chair. There were six of them arranged in two rows, but he was the only person present. Apart from the ever-present comings and goings of the medical staff that is. He spotted a 'phone on the wall and thought it prudent to alert his sister Julie of the situation. She and Edna may not have been friends, but they were still mother, and daughter and Julie had a right to know what was going on. *No point in contacting Nessa at work, she won't be able to do anything, and it'll only worry her.* He thought.

Thirty minutes later and Prez was woken from his thoughts as his sister entered the room. Upon spotting him she bypassed the reception desk and came to sit with Prez. She was swaddled in a large pink coat which made Prez think of marshmallows. She looked concerned,

"Well, what's the problem now little brother?"

Little brother! There I am six-foot-tall and her being around five foot nothing and I'm still "little brother"! Prez thought to himself,

"Dunno, I've been here for half an hour, waiting for a quack to have a chat."

At that moment a door opened and a red headed man who looked around twenty but was obviously older walked over to the pair.

"Mr Sinclair?"

Prez nodded,

"This is my sister." The doctor acknowledged Julie,

"Hi. I'm afraid it's not great. Your Mum has been brought in complaining about stomach cramps, so we've had some scans done and there appears to be some sort of blockage in her bowel."

"Can we see her?" Prez asked.

"Yes, briefly. We have sedated her, but it hasn't taken effect yet." His cheeks flushed slightly, "She's talking rather oddly, be prepared when you go in........"

Prez and Julie looked at each other, fearing the worst. Prez stood up and followed the young Doctor,

"You do know about her condition?" he asked.

"Yes, the nursing home told us about her mental health." He motioned to a bay with drawn curtains, she's in there.

Prez and Julie pulled back the curtains to find Edna on a bed with two female nurses in attendance. They were attempting to calm her down, effectively restraining her as she struggled, wild eyed. The nurses looked sheepishly at Prez and Julie who both leant over the bed to make eye contact with Edna.

"Mum, it's me and Julie, we're here to see that you're okay." Prez said in a voice that he hoped sounded reassuring.

Edna shook her right arm free and stared beyond Prez in to space, obviously focussed on something no one else in the room was aware of. She looked pale and drawn, her false teeth were missing, and her hair matted. She tried to thrash about, then a truly hideous voice emanated from her lips,

"The children, what about the children?" Prez and Julie looked at each other, their skin crawling at the sound. It certainly didn't sound like Edna. For a moment Prez thought about the idea of demonic possession, in that split second, he realised now why people believed in such things. Then he settled for the fact that this was just another illustration of Edna's condition. He composed himself and drew closer to her,

"Mum, it's me and Julie, we're here." It didn't help as Edna grew more violent, staring blindly at whatever it was only she could see,

"The children, what will happen to the children?" Edna was close to raving now. Julie leant over the bed from the other side and took her arm,

"We're your children Mum." she insisted. Prez had never seen Julie concerned about Edna like this, she was obviously as shocked as he was. Suddenly all the tension left Edna's body and her eyes fluttered shut, her breathing, although shallow became steady and relaxed. The elder of the two nurses a portly woman in her fifties lay the arm of Edna's that she had been gripping down beside her. She stood up and spoke to Prez and Julie,

"I'm sorry about that, it takes a while for the sedatives to kick in. Your Mum's a real fighter." She smiled. Prez shook his head,

"What happens now?"

"Well, Doctor Bentley, the red-haired gentleman who brought you in, he thinks that they'll have to operate, probably tomorrow."

"That soon?" Julie asked agog.

"Yes, it looks serious and Edna must be in considerable pain. You can't take a chance with these things. If you keep in touch with our staff, they will keep you in the loop and let you know when the op is going to take place."

As they walked back to the car Prez was the first to break the silence,

"I've got the house back on the market. Cost a pretty penny, but when it's flogged I figured you'd let me take whatever I've had to fork out on top of splitting it?"

"Of course. We couldn't have helped you get it refurbished, could we?" Yeah, you skim off whatever it's cost you over the last few weeks or so, the heaters to dry it out, the work that's been done, all that." Julie replied. She recognised that Prez and Nessa had taken a financial hit and had performed miracles to get the work completed and paid for so quickly. Someone else might have pointed out that Prez should have drained the water tank initially and that would have prevented the need for all the work in the first place. Yet Julie was not of that mindset. She realised that her brother had stepped up to the plate and taken charge of the situation, in a way that she just didn't feel able to. If he was willing to shoulder the burden, let him, she thought.

"Cheers Jules. Has Bear mentioned anything re the clubhouse?" Prez enquired. He knew that it was club policy not to disclose what went on at Unkindness's, but he knew that his Brothers were human beings and that Bears relationship was, like his own, with a strong-willed woman. There was little point in keeping secrets from either Nessa or Julie, so Prez had expected that the financial difficulties of the Club would have filtered back to his sister.

"Yes, he's mentioned it. What are you going to do?" Julie asked as they arrived at her car. Prez shrugged,

"Not sure, really. I've got a few ideas. If we get Mum's house sold, I might be able to direct a few quid from the sale to the Club. I'd have to run it past Nessa, obviously."

"Don't go blowing it all on that, little brother! How old are you? Fifty-seven? "Julie queried,

"Yeah, don't look a day over sixty!" Prez smiled back.

"Just make sure you sort your own finances out first." Prez was about to reply but Julie held up her hand," I know, it's all about 'bikes and brotherhood, how you'd all die for each other, yeah, yeah. Look Vince, this is the real world. No one's going to ask you to die for each other, but someone's going to ask you to pay the bills matey!"

"I know, I know," Prez shot back exasperated, "sometimes you've just gotta have faith in people. Christ knows, I've little enough faith in society as a whole, you know that. And I've seen enough of human nature and its frailties within the Club itself to realize that even Brothers can let you down but bloody hell……………you've got to hang on to something, haven't you?"

Julie shrugged as she opened the door to her vehicle.

That's one of the few similarities between Julie and me. We barely trust anyone. She's got more faith in animals than people! I guess you can't have an ideological argument with a domestic pet, can you? Well, you can, but you win 'em all. Knowing Julie, that's just the way she likes it. Bear, I salute you!

Prez smiled to himself as he thought of his long-suffering Sergeant at Arms. It certainly helped explain the taciturn nature of his officer. Still, when all said and done, no one enforced the rules like Bear and Prez was grateful that he was in the same metaphorical corner as the big man.

S.O.S.

Just two days later and Prez and Julie were back at Arrowe Park hospital. They both realised that the prognosis was not good. They had been ushered in to a small room and sat on a trolley bed, hardly a great scenario for the delivery of what they both knew would be bad news. Prez had tried to keep things light with some excruciating jokes, but Julie could see the strain he was under and played along. As they swung their legs which couldn't reach the ground from the trolley, the door opened, and a young female doctor walked in.

"Hello, you are Mrs Sinclair's children?" she asked in her sing song Asian accent.

"Yeah, what's going on Doc?" Prez asked, assuming the woman was a doctor, although she had not introduced herself. Without even batting an eyelid or showing an ounce of compassion the young doctor delivered her news,

"I am afraid your mother has come to the end of her life."

Prez sat bolt upright,

"What? She's died?" he gasped, the doctor shook her head,

"No, no, no Mr Sinclair. She is alive, but she has contracted sepsis, and with her mental health being the way it is, we do not feel that it would be correct to put her through any more undue trauma."

Julie spoke whilst Prez wrestled with the morality of the whole thing,

"So, what does that mean exactly?"

"We run a programme called the Liverpool Pathway. It is recognised nationally as the very best in palliative care. In effect it will provide a dignified end to your mother's life. She will be kept sedated until nature takes its course."

Sedated until nature takes its course? What exactly did she mean by that? This Liverpool Pathway is supposed to be a dignified death, so what's involved? Prez thought, but he discovered that frighteningly, he could not put his thoughts in to words. The doctor continued in her emotionless monologue, showing absolutely no compassion or feelings for the two individuals sat on the bed opposite her.

"We will assign her to her own room, where you may stay with her as long as you like, whenever you like."

"How long are we looking at?" Julie asked.

"Probably a week or so, it's difficult to be accurate. Any questions?"

Prez sat dumbstruck.

So, this is how it ends, this is how you're treated as the soon to be bereaved. Stuck in a room no bigger than a broom cupboard, sat on a

trolley bed and being spoken to by someone with all the sensitivity and bedside manner of a bedside cabinet. What the hell is going on?

Taking the now horribly familiar walk through the car park Prez and Julie exchanged frank views over the manner in which they had been told of their mother's imminent death. They both agreed that it had been a woeful way to tell anyone such news. Prez knew that Nessa and Eddie would be heartbroken. Edna had been like a mother to Nessa and had spent many afternoons playing with Eddie as a child, a good Grandma.

Driving back from dropping Julie off at her house in Heswall, Prez found himself thinking strange thoughts.

It's weird, but I don't feel upset. I'm upset about the way the doctor was so callous, I'm upset that we were told bad news in a broom cupboard, I'm upset at the NHS. But I'm not upset that my Mum is going to die. Maybe that's because we've all already done our grieving. Maybe we did our grieving when we really lost her, when she lost her mind and identity. When she stopped being Mum and became something else, which no one understands, least of all herself. Of course, we never stopped caring. But it reached a point where there was nothing to care about. A visit to be grunted at or ignored, just checking she was alive. She wasn't Mum though, she was, horribly, just a lump of flesh. Surviving, eating, sleeping, unable to hold a decent conversation and living in a hideous world of pain, paranoia and illusion. Maybe that's why I'm not upset. Maybe Nessa and

Eddie won't be upset either. I've got to make Nessa realise, it's a release for Mum. From all the suffering, the fear, the humiliation. It'll be over at last. Not just for her, but for all of us. In a strange way I was pleased. Pleased that it would be over. Not in a selfish way, it had taken up years of our lives, all of us, but pleased for Mum. I don't know what comes next any more than the next person, but I'm pretty sure that it must be better than what Mum had been living the last few years. Torment and anguish, fear of living itself, and the desperate feeling of isolation. The horrible feeling that no one else can understand you or believe anything you say, because actually what she believed and what she was saying was complete madness. Someone once wrote "No man is an island" but when you're afflicted with paranoid schizophrenia, that is exactly what you are. You can see things no one else can, hear things no one else can and it's you who are right and they who are wrong. You are the only person who knows the truth and even loved ones you've known all your life are exposed as liars and cheats, working tirelessly behind your back to promote your downfall from grace.

Once home Prez delivered the news. Firstly, directly to Nessa, who, like Prez did not experience the outpouring of emotion both had expected she would. They both realised that over the last few years the emotions that had flowed had, in effect, all drained away. They had already got over the shock and the grieving regarding Edna. All that was left was the ending of the horrible saga. Both of them had loved Edna deeply but they no longer felt such empathy for the entity which now inhabited Edna's body. In fact, the end could not come soon enough, as a release for everyone. Prez then contacted Eddie who was at his university digs in Ormskirk. Prez found it difficult to gauge his son's reaction, but he seemed to take it well. When he put the receiver down and entered the front room Nessa handed him a mug of tea.

"How was he?" she purred.

"Okay I think. Christ, I don't know. He sounded alright, you can't tell, can you? I didn't want to do that over the blower, but better that he know now than find out later." Prez replied as he slumped in his chair. "I think we should take it in turns to sit with her, us and Julie and Bear."

"Yes, I think so." Nessa agreed.

For the next two weeks most of Prez's time involved looking at his prone mother lying on a hospital bed. The room was small, with enough room for the bed and four chairs. Its only window looking out onto the rest of the hospital buildings, including a large chimney set back from the rest. Prez grimaced as he thought of the myriad of gruesome reasons for that chimney's existence before turning from the window and sitting down in his plastic chair. Comfortable it was not. The only sound in the room was Edna's rasping breathing, which occasionally became a full-on snore. The air stank of human waste, her natural functions being siphoned off into a container beneath the bed.

I once read something somewhere regarding Heaven and Hell. Heaven contained long tables with benches on either side. People sat on these benches and food is set down opposite them, out of reach. They are given long spoons to feed themselves, but it is pretty much impossible to bring food back on the spoons from the bowls. In Heaven they circumnavigated this by feeding each other with the long spoons. In Hell the setup is the same, but because all the selfish horrible folk go to Hell, no one was willing to feed anyone else, so they are all perpetually starving. I used to think that a pretty good analogy of Hell. This room is a better one though. The stink of waste, the stale sweat, the bare walls, the absolute hopelessness of the situation. The grim wait for the rasping to stop, to signal an end to it all.

Prez glanced at his watch, which had moved a full five minutes since his last look. He had brought a book in one day, only to find that reading was impossible as the wheezing and snoring played havoc with his mental state. Bear and Julie had done their bit regarding visiting, as of course had Nessa, who was due any moment. As Prez walked to the window to look out for the hundredth time, the door opened, and his wife walked in.

"Hi Babe, happy St George's Day." Prez spoke quietly.

"Hi, you okay?" she whispered as she entered the room. Prez gave his wife a hug, noticing the dark circles around her eyes. She was still maintaining her work schedule, then taking up her visiting duties. Prez was doing the bulk of it, with no formal job to hold down but Nessa regarded it as the last duty she would be performing for Edna and wouldn't let something like personal discomfort get in the way of her executing that duty.

She would've made a great biker brother. Prez thought as they both sat down. Duty and self-sacrifice being the very ethos that the Club was founded upon. Nessa wiped her brow with the back of her hand,

"Flipping heck, it's hot in here isn't it?"

"Always is kiddo. I think they've got the thermostat on max!" Prez smiled back. It never failed to amaze them how hot the hospital was. A perfect breeding ground for airborne viruses. Upon their first stay with Edna Prez had tried to open the window, only to find that it wasn't designed to open as the entire hospital was fitted with air conditioning, another certain way to spread disease! Nessa decided to change the subject,

"You got the boys sorted for the Egg Run?"

"Yeah, pretty much. I told 'em I may not be able to make it, that I might be on duty here." Prez shrugged. The Egg Run was later this year, following St Georges Day. Prez had made it clear at the previous Unkindness that no one knew how long his Mum would continue to fight for her life. Even the doctors and nurses had been surprised that she was still rasping along.

The two of them sat down on the uncomfortable chairs, their gazes lingering on Edna lying in the bed. She was facing them with her eyes shut. Prez decided to make some small talk,

"Yeah, they'll be plenty of us at this year's Run. I thought we'd outdone ourselves last year with that turnout, but this one'll be even better. We've got more members to ride out, what with Tommo, ATV and Stevil patching over and I'm sure that the impetus that last year's Run created will carry on to this one."

"I see in the local paper that it's already been mentioned. I should've brought it in, but I've left it at home........" Nessa purred. Prez put his arm around her shoulders,

"Hey, no worries, you must be knackered with coming here and working. Why don't you go home? I'll wait here until Bear anc-" suddenly Prez realised that the rasping had stopped. Both of them looked over at Edna who produced a hideous rattle from her throat and her eyes popped open, unseeing yet staring. Prez leant forward and Nessa stood up. Then the eyes shut and there was silence. The seconds ticked past like molasses pouring from a jar, each tick of the clock on the wall taking an eternity. Prez and Nessa looked blankly at each other. Nessa spoke, her voice trembling,

"Is she......................?"

S.O.S.

Prez stood and gently moved his wife from the doorway. He stepped out of the room and called to a nurse who was talking to colleagues. Moments later two other nurses were bending over Edna's prone form, then one turned to face the couple.

"Your mother has passed away. You can stay here as long as you like." With that, the nurses filed out. Prez looked at Nessa. There was no huge outpouring of grief, they had already done that, when they had lost the person that was Edna over the preceding few years. Now there was just a feeling of numbness. Prez hugged his wife and whispered in her ear.

"We'd better tell Julie and Bear."

Nessa nodded back, a tear now trickling down her cheek,

"I'll do it, I've got my mobile. You wait here." She stepped outside the room to get better reception on her 'phone. Prez looked at the body of his mother, appearing to be in a deep silent sleep.

So, it ends with a whimper. All those years of life, sacrifice, helping others. All those petty arguments over motorbikes and the length of my hair and my being in a band. All that friction with Julie over God knows what. All the work on her garden, all that caring *for Dad when he was ill for many years. All those memories and that wealth of knowledge accumulated through life. All gone. Gone for good.*

Prez put his hand over his mouth as he felt his lip quiver. His stomach churned with anxiety, although in truth there was nothing to be anxious about now. He had always put women he respected upon pedestals. Nessa and his Mother, being the two women, he respected most in the World. Now, one had gone, although in reality he knew she had gone long ago. It was still a bitter pill to swallow, seeing the person who brought you in to the World, leave without you. He suddenly felt alone, abandoned. The last moments, the hideous death rattle, the staring eyes would haunt him for the rest of his own days. It was truly the worst thing he had ever witnessed; indeed, it was the first time he had seen a human being die in front of him. He felt an empty, impotent stillness saturate his being, unlike anything he had ever experienced. When Edna had been diagnosed with her illness he had felt distraught, but at least initially he fought the situation. Now there was nothing to fight, nothing to do at all. Nothing except to accept the unacceptable, it was over, finally and irrevocably, over. He didn't do acceptance, Prez was a fighter, he did not accept situations, he fought or manipulated them to ensure positive outcomes for folk. He didn't like losing. But of course, he always knew that this had been a fight where he was always going to lose. It was the f ght that, inevitably, everyone was going to lose. It didn't make Prez feel any better. He didn't like change, although change is as much a part of ife as life itself, as is death. That didn't mean that Prez had to like it.

The following weeks were a blur for Prez. If he had needed time to grieve, which fortunately, he didn't, he would not have had any. There was too much to do. His Power of Attorney, which had caused him so much angst when he had taken Edna to the solicitors to obtain, everyone knowing they were sharing the dirty little secret of the "being of sound mind" part of the machinations, was now useless. As Executor of the Will, Prez was left to collate information, ensuring that there were enough copies of Edna's death certificate to satiate the apparently insatiable organisations he had to deal with. From banks and building societies to the council and the funeral directors, everyone needed proof of his mother's passing before allowing him the opportunity to complete proceedings with them.

Then there had been the funeral service itself. Conducted by the vicar from Barnston Church and held at Landican Crematorium, all as requested by Edna. Prez scanned the pews as a handful of people took their seats.

What a pathetic turnout. All the folk that Mum had helped by acting as a key holder to their properties or looking after pets whilst people went away on holiday. The people she'd helped and befriended in the Post Office where she had worked for many years, before retiring, where were they? Most of all and to his undying shame and winning my eternal disgust, Mr Dory, whom Mum had so admired as an upstanding member of the community, couldn't even be bothered to show his face. I had asked the Club to stay away, however BS was there, like myself adorned suitably in a black suit and tie for the occasion. Indeed, it was he at the culmination of proceedings who was left to shed a tear, whilst I kept a stony-faced resolve. Oddly, I recalled the scene from the film "Conan The Barbarian", where Conan doesn't cry over the funeral pyre of his lover, yet his friend does, saying that "Conan won't cry as he is a Cimmerian, so I cry for him". To the credit of the Woodland Nursing Home, they sent along a little girl I recognised from their staff, whom I thanked and invited back for the buffet. She gracefully declined. One pleasing aspect of the whole scenario was Eddie missing it due to his studies. I would not want to put anyone in a position where they have to attend a funeral. He was fortunately out of the country and whilst it may have given him some closure, the scars that it may have opened up would never heal. He was best remembering his Grandma the way she was.

The service had passed in a flash and Prez was left to contemplate on things.

How on earth do people who have suffered a sudden and shocking passing of a close relative deal with all this stuff? I remember when my father passed away and I took Mum to see him at the funeral directors. She touched the side of his face as he lay in the coffin. I couldn't believe it was him. He was made up to look like some kind of ventriloquist's doll. It was hideous. Indeed, it was the main reason that I decided to have a closed coffin for Mum. I couldn't bear to see a funeral directors approximation of what she had looked like in life. A grotesque interpretation of her real appearance. I've seen enough of the way she physically deteriorated before my very eyes over the past few years, those are memories that will never leave me, I figured I didn't need another set of scars looking at a stranger in a shroud. My memory was already working on blocking out all the positive things about Mum, resulting in me finding myself only

S.O.S.

dwelling on the ordeal of the most recent years of her life. The future was another place now, a place that my Mum wouldn't inhabit. I talked to people at the funeral, at the buffet, I comforted Nessa, yet it I felt nothing. I feel that this should signify the end of a chapter of my life. If only I could treat it like a book and merely turn the page to the next adventure. It just is not that easy. I do not choose to carry this baggage around with me, the memories and horror of the last few years. The experiences are seared in to my consciousness. Mostly I keep them buried and compartmentalised at the back of my mind. Yet sometimes the latch slips and the memories flood back. Most disturbing of all, is the fact that I cannot ever remember my Mum saying, "I love you."

Robert C. Holmes

Epilogue

Prez relaxed in his chair. He had just finished reading through the final draft of his novel "S.O.S.". Sitting in the study facing his computer screen, he reflected on things past and present as another Christmas approached.

All the Christmas shopping done for another year and it's only November! I always like to get it all sorted before the great unwashed hit the shops!

So that was the year that was. Eddie will be starting his final year at university next year. He's grown in to a fine upstanding young man and I am proud of him. Nessa has changed her job and is now working at Sainsbury's. She'd had a bellyful of being treated as a doormat by her previous employer and had decided that it was all too much. I think she only stayed until Mum had passed, as she was dealing with enough aggravation with all that, never mind looking for a new job! In the end she just wanted something part time to keep the pennies rolling in to keep paying for her hectic social life! We all enjoyed a cracking holiday in Copenhagen, the highlight of which for me was me being mistaken for a local! It must have been the long-plaited hair and all round "Norseness" of my appearance! I even managed to sell Mum's house. Although with an estate agent, it was a couple the agent actually asked me to show around the property myself who bought it! The agent still had the cheek to demand payment for their services though!

The Club is looking to the future, although with an ageing membership, I don't know what the future holds. Financially things are looking better, as an increased membership has helped. Our new charity Runs raised our profile as "the good guys" and we're in a good place. Whilst the Unholy Trinity are together, the S.O.S. will carry on.

I met up with Angel Dubois and she has given me a number of names of literary agents she knows well, who may be interested in the work that I've done. It is really a matter of me selling it now. Who out there will be interested in an autobiography of a biker? Certainly, anyone looking for sex, drugs and rock and roll would be disappointed. If there's anyone out there looking for a story of real life, led by real people with real problems, they may just find what they are after though. The very title of the tome "S.O.S." came to me whilst on one of the many countryside walks Nessa and I enjoy. She had asked me what the novel was about and as we walked thought the dappled sunlight of a November afternoon, I explained it was about people's strength of spirit (S.O.S., how apt!) in overcoming adversity. Guidance from a higher place? Or merely inspired imagining? I am not a religious person, but I am a spiritual one.

At the end of it all, writing this novel has been about a catharsis, a way of enabling me to release the inner angst that has burned *in my soul over the important issues in my life. A way of communicating the way I have coped with the hand that I've been dealt thanks to the love and loyalty of those around me. Books are a lot like tattoos. They capture who you **are** for that moment, frozen in time, yet they capture who you **were** forever.*

If life has taught me anything, it is that it's what you leave behind you that's important. I intend to ensure that the people I care for know what I feel is important. I want them to remember that I told them those three words that mean so much to me, and to never be in any doubt of my sincerity when I say, "I love you."

S.O.S.

𝔄𝔠𝔨𝔫𝔬𝔴𝔩𝔢𝔡𝔤𝔢𝔪𝔢𝔫𝔱𝔰

I wish to thank my wife Debbie for her unstinting support and faith in my ability. My son Charlie for his support (especially his IT skills) and Star the cat for her undivided attention! Obviously many thanks to all members of the S.O.S, past and present. Most notably BS and Oz, I couldn't have done it without you. Thanks also to the following; Mum and Dad (if they were still here, maybe, just maybe, they'd think I've done something right and they can finally be proud of me!), Mike "drop me in here" Swaby, Jeff "barf at the moon" Wynne, Brenda and Paul Carden, not forgetting the ever loyal Scott, Paul and Red Majors.

I would like to thank the following for the positive impact they have made upon my life. Whether they are from the fields of literature, cinema, theatre, philosophy, or simply folk I met along the way, they made me the man I am today:

Lemmy, Phil Campbell, Eddie Clarke, Mikkey Dee, Phil Taylor, Wurzel, Joe Abercrombie (thanks for the good luck wishes Joe!), Sly Stallone, Arnold Schwarzennegger, Kurt Russell, Kirk Douglas, Robert E. Howard, Paul Stanley, Rachel "Spencie" Baldock, Basher Cross, Uncle Wolf, Erik Bloodaxe, Jane Fonda, Alan Burridge, Adam Svenson, Tommy "Nurnburg" Brunt, Bazzer, Jean Hewitt, Paul Metcalf, Troy Tempest, Ron Perlman,

Michael Moorcock, Gregg Gregson, Caroline Munro, Bon Scott, Phil "Spartacus" Jennion, Hunter S. Thompson, The Ched, Amy Adams, Alice Cooper, George Best, Anna Chisholm, Sean Long, Jim Fowles, Sonny Barger, Barry Sheene, Mel Gibson, Bruce Wayne, The Mad Mullah, Tony Sandwell, Peter Parker, Jim Dandy, Mandy Campbell, David Lee Roth, Jack Daniels, Harley- Davidson, Karl Ove Knausgaard, B.C. Rich, Darren "pipe and slippers" McGrath, Hanoi Jane, St. Helens RLFC.

Thanks also to you the reader for investing your time in my world.

Apologies to anyone I've forgotten, the omission is my fault not yours.

About The Author

Robert C. Holmes lives on The Wirral with his wife and son. He is a writer, biker, musician, walker, cat lover and tortoise wrangler. He is passionate about Norse culture and mythology, holds a BA (Hons) degree in Humanities with Classical Studies and has visited Denmark, Norway and Germany on numerous occasions. He enjoys long walks with his wife, cinema, theatre, music gigs, reading, riding his Harley Davidson and supporting St Helens RLFC.

Printed in Great Britain
by Amazon